Tailing Trouble

Also available by Laura Scott

Tailing Trouble

A FURRY FRIENDS MYSTERY

Laura Scott

CROOKED
LANE

NEW YORK

Copyright © 2022 by Laura Iding

Published in the United States by Crooked Lane Books, an imprint of The Quick Brown Fox & Company LLC.

Crooked Lane Books and its logo are trademarks of The Quick Brown Fox & Company LLC.

Library of Congress Catalog-in-Publication data available upon request.

ISBN (hardcover): 978-1-64385-834-0
ISBN (ebook): 978-1-64385-835-7

Cover design by David Malan

Printed in the United States.

www.crookedlanebooks.com

Crooked Lane Books
34 West 27th St., 10th Floor
New York, NY 10001

First Edition: January 2022

10 9 8 7 6 5 4 3 2 1

This book is dedicated to my amazing siblings, Joan LeRose, Michele Glynn and Michael Wanke. I hope this series honors the memories of our grandparents!

Chapter One

Veterinary doctor Ally Winter held Roxy's leash firmly as she knocked at the door of the Legacy House. The Lannon stone ranch had been transformed into an assisted-living residence, and her grandfather had been living there for the past five months after breaking his hip and requiring surgery back in April. The house was located on Legacy Drive in Willow Bluff, Wisconsin, a small town on the shore of Lake Michigan.

"Good morning, Ally." Harriet Lehman, a rectangle-shaped woman who liked to wear flowery dresses over sturdy support hose and boxy black shoes, greeted her with a wide smile, which dimmed when she saw Roxy the boxer at Ally's side. "Oh, you brought the dog. Oscar is just finishing breakfast." She hesitated, then reluctantly asked, "Would you like to come in?"

"Thanks, Harriet, we won't stay long." Harriet was one of the Willow Bluff widows, or WBWs, as Gramps liked to call them. Harriet and her sister Tillie shared the large master suite, while Lydia and Gramps each had their own room.

The Legacy House was owned by Beatrice Potter, who made sure the place was well stocked with food for Harriet to cook and managed the cleaning and utility payments. All the widows and

1

Gramps had to do was pay their monthly stipend and find a way to get along.

The latter was often easier said than done.

"Hey, Ally." Her grandfather greeted her from his spot at the kitchen table with a wide smile. He was tall, about six feet in his prime but having lost a few inches along the way, with a lean frame. Gramps normally wore khaki slacks, either tan, gray, or black, and a button-down short-sleeved shirt with a white T-shirt underneath. In the winter he'd switch to long-sleeved flannel shirts, but never once had Ally seen him in jeans. Today he wore a short-sleeved shirt, as summer temperatures had lingered into the first week of September.

"Hi, Gramps." Ally gave him a quick kiss on his temple. Roxy greeted him with a lick and a snuggle.

"Would you like some breakfast?" He grinned. "I'm sure Harriet has extra to spare."

"I do," Harriet said with a nod, her tight gray curls barely moving with the gesture.

"No, that's okay. I already ate." Ally did her best to resist temptation, even though she had eaten her measly bowl of oatmeal two hours ago already, as Roxy was an early riser. Still, she'd learned to minimize how much of Harriet's cooking she sampled. Her jeans fit at the moment, but she knew just how easily that could change after a few days of eating at the Legacy House. She rested her hand on Roxy's head. "Ready to go?"

"Yep." Gramps swiped his mouth with a napkin. "Thanks again, Harriet."

The widow beamed. "You're welcome, Oscar."

Ally knew each of the three WBWs was doing her best to snag her grandfather as a potential husband. Harriet figured the way to

Gramps's heart was through his stomach, which might be the best path, considering his voracious sweet tooth. But Lydia was constantly knitting him things, while Tillie kept him entertained playing cribbage and poker.

Gramps insisted their efforts were for naught, as he'd always love his wife, Amelia, despite her passing two years ago. Gramps and Granny had been married fifty-five years, and Gramps claimed there was no replacing her. Ally knew Gramps was lonely without Amelia, and she had moved back to Willow Bluff to be there for him.

Both Tillie and Lydia, along with Gramps, had taken to volunteering as receptionists at her Furry Friends veterinary clinic three days a week. She appreciated their help, since she wasn't making quite enough money to hire a veterinary technician, much less a receptionist.

"Are you finished cleaning already?" Tillie asked in a loud, sarcastic tone. Ally glanced over. The voices were coming from the hallway, where the three bedrooms were located.

"Yes, I am." The defiant response came from a youthful voice. "The place is clean, and don't you dare tell my mother or Beatrice otherwise."

Before Ally could ask what was going on, a young woman with bright-purple hair sticking out of her head at odd angles, a lip ring, and an eyebrow piercing emerged from the living room carrying a bucket of cleaning supplies. Pricilla Green was twenty-one but acted younger, or maybe it was the permanent scowl etched on her face that made her look like a petulant child.

"Hey, Pricilla, how are you?" Ally asked with a smile.

"What do you care?" Pricilla wore a cropped blue-and-white-striped top that revealed her belly button ring, paired with bright-green skintight short shorts and three-inch red-and-white polka-dotted heels. Wow. Talk about interesting cleaning attire. The girl was lucky she hadn't broken her neck cleaning the bathrooms in those shoes.

Then again, maybe she hadn't bothered cleaning the bathroom.

"I'm telling your mother you were only here for two hours instead of three," Tillie called after Pricilla's retreating form.

"Go ahead! I hate this job." Pricilla brushed past Ally, the front door banging shut behind her.

Ally craned her neck to watch as Pricilla tossed the cleaning bucket in the back seat of a beat-up, rusty brown Dodge and climbed in. Within seconds, the girl had punched the accelerator and spun away.

"She's something," Ally said.

"Yeah, like useless," Tillie snapped. "I think her mother and Beatrice should be told what a loser that girl is."

Like Pricilla's mother couldn't figure that out for herself? Ally had to assume that Pricilla's mother, Hilda Green, who happened to be the Willow Bluff city executive, had asked Beatrice to give her daughter the cleaning job in the first place, but whatever. Ally was staying out of it. "Time for us to go, Gramps. I have a grooming appointment at ten." She frowned, then added, "The one for which you didn't write down the name of the owner or the dog."

"I know, I know. Sorry about that." He reached for his cane, and Ally put a hand beneath his arm to help him stand.

"Don't forget your library book, Oscar," Lydia called from the living room.

Wednesday was Gramps's day to help at the clinic. They'd gotten into the routine of stopping at the library over the lunch hour so her grandfather could get the latest true-crime book.

Tailing Trouble

Ever since he'd helped solve the murder mystery that had rocked Willow Bluff a few months ago, he'd become even more obsessed with true crime, religiously watching shows like *Dateline* and *48 Hours*.

Ally wished he'd find a different hobby, but so far he'd resisted every suggestion she'd thrown at him.

"Hold Roxy's leash for a minute," Ally said. She walked into the living room to grab the library book from the end table next to Lydia. The woman was knitting what looked to be another sweater for Gramps in yet another shade of blue to match his eyes. Eyes Ally had inherited from him. "Looks great, Lydia."

"Thank you, dear." She smiled sweetly. "This one is for you."

Ally tried not to look horrified. "Oh, Lydia, you don't have to do that."

"Tsk, tsk. It's my pleasure, dear. Anything for Oscar's granddaughter."

"Well, thanks." Ally summoned a smile, then quickly returned to the kitchen. That was a new one, although she'd always sensed that the widows were exceptionally nice to her in hopes of swaying her grandfather's attention in their favor.

What was she going to do with a knitted sweater?

Wear it? The very thought made her feel itchy.

Ally tucked Gramps's book under her arm and took Roxy's leash. Gramps made his way outside to her ancient Honda Civic hatchback. When she had him safely tucked into the passenger seat, she placed Roxy in the crated area, then slid in behind the wheel.

"What else is on the Furry Friends schedule for the day?" Gramps asked.

"Remember Domino? The black standard poodle I groomed a few months ago? His owner is dropping him off later this afternoon to be boarded through the weekend."

"Good for you."

"Yeah." Ally flashed him a sidelong glance. "The tough part will be keeping him and Roxy separated. They get a little out of control when playing together." And she had a cracked window in the clinic to prove it. "But I'm happy to have him. Business has been lagging the past few weeks, so having a boarder for a few days will be a lifesaver."

"Don't worry, business will pick up again," Gramps assured her.

"I know." At least she hoped so. Relocating to Willow Bluff from Madison had started out rocky. In Madison, she'd had a thriving business until her former veterinary partner and fiancé, Tim Mathai, embezzled from the Mathai-Winter Veterinary Clinic they'd jointly owned. She hadn't realized what Tim had done until it was too late. He'd taken all the money out of their joint business account and fled the country with Trina, the young, blonde, and buxom veterinary assistant he'd been sleeping with on the side, leaving Ally with a building that was mortgaged to the hilt and a pile of prewedding debt. She'd managed to salvage just enough money from her personal home to buy the new veterinary business here in Willow Bluff, the town she'd grown up in.

At first, the citizens of Willow Bluff had lamented the retirement of Greg Hanson, the former vet. And Ally knew part of the problem had been that she'd returned home under scandalous circumstances. But over time, the townsfolk's memories of Ally as a high school Calamity Jane had faded and her business had picked up.

To be honest, even though she wasn't making a lot of money over and above her living expenses, Ally preferred running the business herself, accounting for every nickel, dime, and penny she earned. Ally had learned to groom dogs while working summers in college, which meant she could offer grooming, dog walking, and boarding services in addition to being a veterinarian.

Her motto remained *No job too small!*

Ally pulled into the driveway in the rear of the clinic and parked. She helped Gramps stand and let Roxy out the back of the Civic. After allowing the dog a quick bathroom break, she unlocked the clinic and held the door open for Gramps.

Gramps thumped his cane as he entered the building, crossing over to take his position in the chair behind the counter.

Glancing at her watch, Ally estimated that she had about twenty minutes before her grooming appointment was scheduled to arrive. She put Roxy up in the apartment upstairs, then returned to the main lobby, pulling on her lab coat. "Can I get you anything, Gramps? Water? Coffee?"

"Nah. That'll just make me have to pee more than I do already." He sounded cranky, and she knew he hated the physical limitations that plagued him. "By the way, did you hear about the robbery last weekend?"

Robbery? Oh no. She wasn't going down this crime-solving path with him. Not again.

"Stop." She lifted a hand. "I don't want to hear about it, Gramps. I'm sure the Willow Bluff Police have everything under control."

He let out a snort. "Hardly. That detective of yours didn't even know that those security video cameras had been tampered with, enabling the robbers to steal stuff over the course of several days. What kind of police work is that, I ask you? Why hasn't your detective figured out that the jokers robbing the joint had insider information?"

Ally strove for patience. Just because she and Detective Noah Jorgenson had been on exactly one date—a double date with two old high school friends almost three months ago—didn't mean they were a couple. As her grandfather knew very well.

And considering that Gramps couldn't even use his cell phone properly and was always screaming into her ear, she felt certain he wouldn't know the first thing about robbers tampering with video feeds.

He didn't know a computer chip from a potato chip.

"Gramps, you know from past experience Noah isn't going to share information about an ongoing investigation. We need to stay out of it."

"Bah." Gramps waved a hand. "He should share information with us, since it's clear he needs help. Take that girlie Pricilla Green. Did you notice how she was dressed? If that girl isn't an inside source leaking information to crooks, I'll eat my cribbage board."

Ally tried not to roll her eyes. "Pricilla doesn't work at the store, Gramps. I've seen her coming out of the café. I'm sure she isn't an inside source for a robbery ring." At least, she didn't think so. It didn't seem likely that the young woman was either savvy enough to create a fake video feed or smart enough to know which information to give out to crooks. Ally patted his arm. "The purple hair, facial piercings, and wild clothes are just her way of embarrassing her mother."

"It's working. Hilda Green revels in her position as the city executive and despises the way her daughter looks. According to the rumor mill, she has no use for Pricilla's boyfriend, Jake Hammond, either." Gramps shrugged. "I still think they're involved in the robbery ring. Who wears three-inch heels to clean a house?"

"I don't know, maybe she had a hot date with Jake and didn't want to take time to change." It was a lame excuse, considering it had been too early in the morning for a hot date, but she wanted to distract Gramps. Especially since she didn't see how wearing three-inch red-and-white polka-dotted heels was an indication of criminal activity. "Don't even think about trying to investigate the robbery."

"Who, me?" As usual, Gramps tried and failed to look innocent.

She narrowed her gaze. "Yes, you. Don't forget what happened last time. Noah was close to throwing both of us in jail for interfering in his murder investigation."

"He was bluffing." Gramps sounded certain, but she wasn't convinced.

The veterinary clinic door opened. Ally turned, expecting to see her grooming appointment, but instead a frazzled-looking woman stood there, holding the leash of a pretty yellow Lab.

"I need to talk to Dr. Hanson right away! It's an emergency!"

It had been a while since anyone had mentioned Greg Hanson. Ally stepped forward with a smile. "I'm Dr. Ally Winter. Why don't you tell me what's going on?"

"Where's Dr. Hanson?"

She stifled a sigh. "St. Pete's Beach, Florida. I'm Dr. Winter. How can I help you?"

"But . . . I've always met with Dr. Hanson." The woman looked to be in her late fifties, had obviously dyed red hair, and was sniffling as if she was about to cry. "Puddles knows Dr. Hanson. He doesn't know you."

Ally looked down at the yellow Lab, who limply wagged his tail in greeting, clearly not looking perky. "What happened to Puddles?"

"He ate a bunch of chocolate."

Not good. "Come into room number one so I can examine him."

"Okay," the woman agreed tearfully. She took a few steps forward, glancing around the empty clinic with a frown. "Are you sure Dr. Hanson isn't able to help?"

From St. Pete's Beach? Seriously? "Yes, I'm sure." She turned toward Gramps. "Keep an eye out for my mystery grooming appointment."

"Will do."

"Let's get Puddles up on the table, shall we?" Ally did her best to exude confidence. She took a moment to let the dog sniff her before quickly scooping him up and onto the table. "Do you have any idea how much chocolate Puddles ate?"

"Lots," the woman answered.

It was all Ally could do not to roll her eyes. "Can you be more specific? Chocolate is toxic, and the amount of chocolate Puddles ingested will determine how I treat him."

The woman blushed. "He jumped up on the table when I wasn't looking and ate two entire bags of semisweet chocolate chips."

"I see." Semisweet chocolate had a lot of theobromine, which was very poisonous to dogs. And two bags was enough to require a dose of activated charcoal given through a tube into the stomach, much like how people were treated for drug overdoses. Messy, yes, but highly successful.

"Let's take a listen, shall we?" Ally used her stethoscope to listen to Puddles's heart. It was beating faster than normal, an indication that the chocolate and theobromine were already being absorbed into his bloodstream. She removed the stethoscope from her ears. "Okay, I'm going to need to give Puddles something to counteract the poison in his system. I need you to hold him for a moment so I can give him something to help him relax."

"Oh dear, poor Puddles." The redhead wrapped her arms around the yellow Lab's neck and buried her face against his fur. "I love you. You're going to be okay."

Ally took advantage of the moment, using a hypodermic to inject a mild sedative into the animal's hindquarters. Puddles yelped but quieted quickly.

"Hey, I wasn't ready." The woman lifted her head and glared at Ally. "Dr. Hanson would never have done that until we were both ready."

Ally could feel her smile slipping away. "I'm sorry, but I've always found that creating a distraction works beautifully. Look, Puddles is already beginning to relax."

The redhead frowned, but there was no denying that Puddles was calmer, his eyes closing with the need to sleep.

"I'll take over from here. Why don't you wait outside, Ms. . . . ?" Ally paused, waiting for the woman to provide her name.

"Okay." Without a word, the woman left the exam room.

Ally carried the Lab into the back room, placing him in the deep sink. He was awake but definitely mellow enough that she could quickly pull the necessary supplies together. From there, it didn't take her long to place the gastric tube into the animal's stomach. After giving a full dose of activated charcoal, she waited.

The results were good, if messy. Puddles barfed up some of the charcoal. She cleaned him up, knowing more charcoal would come out through his back end.

When he seemed stable enough to be left in a crate, she washed up and went out to the main lobby.

"How is Puddles?" the woman asked.

"Doing fine so far, but I'd like to watch him for a couple of hours."

The redhead frowned. "Is that really necessary?"

"I wouldn't keep him if I didn't think it was," Ally said gently.

"Okay, I'll come back in two hours." The woman jumped up and left before Ally could say anything more.

Ally crossed over to the counter. "Any sign of my grooming appointment, Gramps?"

Her grandfather grimaced. "That lady called and said she'd have to reschedule for tomorrow. She said her name, something with an M, but I didn't catch it all."

Again with no name? Gramps still had some things to learn about being a receptionist, but now wasn't the time to remind him. Especially since he was volunteering his time to help her out. "Okay, that's fine." She went around to pull up her client list on the computer. "Here's Puddles. Looks like the redhead is Valerie Wagner."

"Always great to have a paying customer," Gramps said cheerfully.

"Yes." Even one who still missed the old vet. Ally made a note about the visit next to Puddles's name in the computer, printed out the invoice, and then headed back to check on the Lab.

Black charcoal was definitely coming out the back end, and she tried to strip off her white lab coat before Puddles could—well—make a black puddle on it. She hauled him back over to the large sink to minimize the mess.

After almost two hours, Puddles looked much better. She cleaned him up again and listened to his heart, nodding with approval.

His pulse was within the normal range.

"You're a good boy, yes you are."

Ally heard the clinic door open and close. She lifted Puddles from the sink and set him on the floor. After drying him off with a towel, she stood back as he shook the remaining water from his coat. He walked slowly but steadily, as if sensing his owner was nearby.

Ally smiled as she brought the Lab into the main lobby. "Puddles is ready for you now."

"He is?" Valerie Wagner hurried over, then stopped with a frown. "What on earth is that awful stench?"

Ally did her best to remain professional. "The best way to get rid of the poison is to use activated charcoal. It's messy and smelly but works like a charm. Puddles may have loose dark stools for a while, but he'll be fine."

"Thank you," Valerie said begrudgingly.

"I have the invoice ready for you." Ally pushed the paperwork toward her.

"Oh, I'm sorry, I don't have any money with me."

Who came to the vet without money? Ally wasn't falling for that one. "Okay, but I'll need a credit card if you don't have cash."

"Oh, I cut those up years ago." Valerie waved a hand. "I'll be back with the cash, I promise." The redhead and Puddles disappeared outside.

Ally sighed, wondering if she'd ever see Valerie, Puddles, or the promised cash again.

Chapter Two

"Are you going to let her get away with that?" Gramps asked indignantly.

"What am I supposed to do, chase her down Main Street? It'll be fine." She hoped. "I'm sure she'll pay eventually."

"You gotta be firm with these people, Ally." Gramps wagged his finger at her. "You can't give away your services for free."

"I know." It was her own fault for not getting the payment before taking Puddles into the exam room. But time had been of the essence, and she hadn't wanted to delay caring for the poor Lab. And, other than the occasional snafu of a credit card being declined, no one had ducked out of paying before. "So my mystery grooming appointment has been postponed until tomorrow?"

"Yep." Gramps looked chagrined. "Sorry I didn't catch her full name. Maggie? Martha? Molly? Something with an M. I'll do better next time."

"No worries." Ally suspected Gramps was becoming hard of hearing; maybe that was why he yelled into his cell phone. She glanced at her watch. "It's lunchtime. You ready to head over to the library?"

"Sure." Gramps looked excited at the prospect of getting a new book. "Let's bring Roxy."

"Sounds good." Ally quickly went up the stairs to the small apartment over the clinic she called home. Roxy greeted her like a long-lost friend. Ally bent down to smooth her hands over Roxy's golden-brown fur. "Let's go, Rox."

Willow Bluff wasn't a large town—about four thousand people according to the last census. Furry Friends Veterinary Clinic was located on the south side of Main Street, and the municipal building, which housed the library, city hall, and the police station, was on the north end.

"Are you okay to walk that far?" Ally asked as Gramps leaned on his cane.

"Stop asking me that," he groused. "I'll tell you when I'm not okay to walk to the library."

"Just checking."

Her grandfather was a Vietnam vet and preferred to think of himself as the soldier he'd once been, refusing to give in to any sign of weakness.

She shortened her steps to match her grandfather's, enjoying the unusually warm weather. Fall was her favorite season, although the leaves on the trees had only just started to change color.

"What we need is more information on the robbery," Gramps mused.

"No, Gramps, we don't." Ally didn't even want to think about Gramps involving himself in another of Noah's investigations. Noah, her former high school crush and tormentor—who'd dubbed her Hot Pants after she accidently started a fire in the chemistry lab and *then* sat on a nest of fire ants, which sent her screaming and yanking off her shorts as she jumped into Lake Michigan—had developed an eye twitch and nearly lost his temper several times when Gramps interfered in his last investigation. Ally had no doubt that if Gramps continued butting in, Noah would make good on his promise to arrest him.

As they approached the municipal building, she said, "I heard there was a croquet league starting up for next summer. Care to be my partner?"

"Croquet is for old people."

Ally decided not to point out that her grandfather was seventy-eight, which probably qualified as old enough to play croquet. And there were younger people playing too. She pulled open the door to the library, holding it for Gramps.

"Hello, Oscar." Rosie Malone, the Willow Bluff librarian, greeted him with a smile. "I have a new book for you."

"Great!" Gramps grinned. "I can't wait."

"Ally, you know dogs aren't allowed in here," Rosie chided.

Rosie had been telling her that for several weeks, and each time Ally had ignored her. "We won't be long." She placed Gramps's library book on the counter.

"Have you heard about the big-box store robbery?" Gramps asked Rosie.

"Yes, at Electronics and More, right? It's terrible, isn't it?" Rosie took Gramps's library card and checked out his new book. "I can't imagine who would do such a thing."

"Hear anything through the grapevine?" Gramps pressed. Ally shifted her weight from one foot to the other, trying not to show her impatience.

"No," Rosie admitted. "But apparently the mayor and city executive are very upset about it."

"Why is that?" Ally asked, curious in spite of herself. She hadn't heard that either the mayor or the city executive had been very upset back in June when two people were murdered.

Rosie leaned forward and dropped her voice to a loud whisper. "They're concerned about a drug connection."

"Drugs, huh?" Gramps mused.

Rosie nodded. "I guess drug users tend to steal stuff to support their drug habit. And that's not going over well with the city leadership. They don't want Willow Bluff to be tainted by druggies."

"Interesting theory." Gramps reached for his book. "Thanks again, Rosie."

"You're welcome, Oscar."

Ally took the book from Gramps and tucked it under her arm. As they walked outside, she gestured to the Lakeview Café. "Ready for lunch?"

Gramps nodded, his gaze thoughtful. Ally knew he was already imagining suspects in the robbery case who might be addicted to drugs. It was all she could do not to scream in frustration.

They were seated at a table near the edge of the patio, in deference to Roxy being with them. The dog stretched out on the concrete, seemingly content.

"Iced tea, please," Ally said, when their server came to take their order.

"I'll have lemonade." Gramps waited until the server was out of earshot to lean forward. "I bet Pricilla Green is on drugs."

"Why, because of the way she looks?" Ally threw up her hands. "Come on, Gramps. You can't judge a person by their outward appearance. Would a cop on *Dateline* do that?"

"Maybe not, but you have to admit, her showing up to clean the Legacy House in that getup is weird."

There was no arguing that Pricilla's attire was strange. "I agree. But that doesn't make her a crook or a drug addict. She didn't look like she was high or on something."

"Could be that she knows someone who is," Gramps pointed out. "Like that boyfriend of hers, the one Hilda doesn't like."

"You're grasping at straws, Gramps."

They lunched at the café so often that Ally had the menu memorized. When their server returned with their drinks, they ordered their meals. Ally stayed with the Cobb salad, while Gramps went for his usual cheeseburger.

"Hey." Gramps gestured to a table that was catty-corner from them. "Isn't that Valerie Wagner? The woman who stiffed you for Puddles's care?"

Ally twisted in her seat, her gaze narrowing as she recognized Puddles's owner, dyed red hair glinting brassily in the sun. Without hesitation, she threw her napkin on the table and stood. "Watch Roxy," she told Gramps before stalking over.

"Hi, Ms. Wagner." Ally greeted the redhead with a broad smile. "How is Puddles doing? Better, I hope."

"Oh, um, Puddles is doing fine, thanks." Valerie looked flustered at Ally's showing up so unexpectedly.

"I hope you can make time to pay the bill later this afternoon," Ally said before turning to Valerie's companion. "Did you hear what happened? Poor Puddles ate two bags of semisweet chocolate, and I had to give him charcoal to counteract the poison in his system."

"Oh my, how awful," Valerie's companion said.

Valerie flushed beet red, clearly annoyed to be caught off guard by Ally's comments. "I was planning to come right after lunch." She riffled through her purse and pulled out some cash, which Ally felt certain she'd possessed earlier in the day. "Here you go. Thanks again."

Ally refused to feel guilty as she pocketed the fee. "Thanks. I'm just so glad Puddles is feeling better. Take care." She offered a tiny finger wave as she returned to her seat.

"Good job," Gramps praised, holding on to Roxy's leash. "I'm proud of you."

"Thanks." Ally was proud of herself too. She hated conflict, and if she hadn't needed the money, she wouldn't have done something so bold as to confront Valerie in a public place.

But she needed her business to survive and thrive. And she deserved to be paid for services she'd provided.

Gramps was right. She needed to stand up for herself. She couldn't let people walk all over her. Maybe word would spread around town that she wasn't a pushover when it came to expecting payment for services.

When their food came, Ally noticed Gramps scrutinizing their server. She groaned inwardly, knowing exactly what he was going to say before the words popped out of his mouth.

"Did you notice she's wearing long sleeves on this hot day?" Gramps asked as he picked up his burger. "Very suspicious, if you ask me."

Ally hadn't asked, so she ignored him. She took a bite of her salad. "This is good. How's your cheeseburger?"

"We need her name," Gramps continued, as if she hadn't spoken. "Don't most servers greet you by telling you their name?"

"She did tell us her name. It's Darla. She's a perfectly nice young woman. She brought her cat Jessy in to the clinic just two weeks ago." Ally reined in her temper with an effort. "And you have absolutely no reason to suspect every person we see as being involved in the Electronics and More store robbery and/or on drugs."

"Pays to keep an open mind." Gramps tapped his temple.

Really? Ally swallowed a sarcastic reply. They finished their meal and returned to the clinic.

When they arrived, Ally made a quick note on Valerie Wagner's invoice that she'd paid in cash, then tucked the money into her petty cash drawer. From there, she cleaned the exam room and the large tub.

The rest of the afternoon passed slowly, with no calls coming in. At four o'clock sharp, Kayla Benton arrived with Domino. Ally had purposefully tucked Roxy upstairs to prevent doggy mayhem.

"Thanks for boarding him," Kayla said in a harried tone. "My parents are watching the twins while Mark and I have a long weekend together. Easier for them if they don't have to deal with the dog too."

"Of course. It's not a problem." Ally smiled and took Domino's leash. She felt a kinship with the animal, as her hair was dark, naturally curly, and out of control, much like the poodle's. "Have fun."

"Trust me, we plan to." Kayla bent to give Domino one last rub. "See you later."

Domino whined for a few minutes after Kayla left. Then he sniffed Ally and the area around the clinic, no doubt looking for Roxy. The two had played together once when Ally thought it might be good for the animals to socialize.

It hadn't gone well. Roxy had grabbed the scarf she'd tied around Domino's neck and tried tossing him around like a rag doll. Domino had fought back with surprising strength. It had been difficult for her to pry them apart.

"Come on, Gramps. I'll crate Domino and take you home."

Gramps didn't argue, and soon they were back at the Legacy House.

"Ally, won't you stay for dinner?" Harriet asked, beaming when Ally showed up without a dog at her side. "I'm making one of my mother's special recipes."

Ally's mouth watered at the enticing scent wafting from the kitchen. Harriet was an amazing cook and had more German recipes than Ally had veterinary patients. "What is it this time?"

"German dumplings."

Tempting, very tempting. Remembering her boarder, she declined. "I'm sorry, Harriet. As much as I'd love to stay, I have two dogs that need to be walked tonight."

"Maybe next time," Harriet said, although she looked keenly disappointed.

"Stop back later, Ally, and bring one of the dogs with you," Gramps said, giving her a sly wink. "Harriet made pumpkin pie for dessert."

No dessert! a tiny voice in the back of her mind shouted, but Ally's resistance melted. Pumpkin pie was one of her favorites. "Okay, I'll see you later, then."

The return trip to the clinic didn't take long. Ally ate a quick microwaved Lean Cuisine meal, then decided to take Roxy out first. Domino would be stuck in his crate all night, so she'd save him for last and do her best to wear him out.

When it was Domino's turn for a walk, he was überexcited to be out of the crate. Domino was tall as her hip, and when he stood on his hind legs, with his front paws over her shoulders, he was taller than she was by several inches.

Kayla hadn't spent much time training him to sit, stay, or come, likely too busy caring for twins, but that was okay. Ally let him set the pace as they walked down toward the Legacy House.

Twice Domino caught sight of a squirrel, lunging toward it with enough force to yank her off her feet.

"No, Domino. Heel!"

He glanced back at her, his black curls almost obscuring his vision, then turned back to where he'd seen the squirrel, straining against the leash.

"This way." She tugged, drawing him back on course. Just beyond the Legacy House was the lakefront, the clear rippling water of Lake Michigan looking serene and peaceful. The only concern about strolling there was that there had been a coyote attack on a small schnauzer belonging to her high school friend, Erica Kirby, a few months ago.

Ally felt confident Domino could hold his own against a coyote. Smart coyotes went after much smaller prey. But first she'd swing by the Legacy House for dessert.

She found Gramps sitting outside on the patio overlooking the lakeshore.

"Just in time," he said by way of greeting. "Harriet is sending Lydia out with two slices of pumpkin pie."

"Great. Sit, Domino." Ally pushed hard against his hindquarters. "Sit!"

"That dog needs training," Gramps observed. "Roxy behaves much better."

"I know." Ally looked up as Lydia came outside with two generous slices of pie topped with whipped cream.

"Here you go," Lydia said.

Ally smiled. "Thanks, Lydia." Domino surged against the leash at who knew what, nearly toppling Ally off her chair. "Sit!"

Domino stood for a long moment before relaxing and dropping to his haunches beside her.

"Yum, this is great," Gramps said, making quick work of his pie.

Ally took a bite and nearly moaned in pleasure. "It's fantastic. Did she make this from scratch?"

"She did." Gramps's smile faded. "But Amelia's cooking was much better."

"It's very sweet the way you stay loyal to Granny."

"My one true love," Gramps agreed.

Ally steered the conversation to important matters. "Gramps, you have to promise me to behave tomorrow. Don't make me worry about you getting a ride into town in an attempt to work the case."

"Scout's honor," he assured her.

She frowned. "You were never a Boy Scout."

"Vet's honor." Gramps cackled at his own joke. "Get it? I'm a vet, you're a vet."

"I get it." Domino suddenly lunged toward a chipmunk, pulling hard against the leash. "No, Domino! Sit! Heel!"

Domino ignored her, straining against the leash, his gaze zeroed in on the offending animal.

"I'm telling ya, start a training class and force the Bentons to enroll that dog."

"Domino!" She yanked the leash, but the dog was stronger than he looked. She yanked again, harder, and Domino finally gave up on the chipmunk and returned to Ally's side. "You might be right about offering training classes," she said wearily. "I can't imagine how Kayla handles this dog along with her young twins."

Gramps lifted a brow. "That's why they're boarding him with you, right?"

"Right." Ally's jeans pinched at her waistline, so she stood to relieve the pressure. "Listen, I should get going. I'm going to take

Domino down to the lakefront for a bit before crating him for the night. Can I help you inside?"

"Bah, I can do it." Gramps reluctantly accepted her help in standing and taking the single step up and into the house. "I think my hip is worse instead of better."

Ally frowned. "Maybe you need more therapy. I'll call your doctor in the morning."

"Therapy, schmerapy," Gramps groused. "Why can't the doc just admit they screwed up the surgery?"

Gramps was convinced they'd done more harm than good in doing the operation but didn't seem to remember how much pain he had been in prior to having the procedure. "I know you're frustrated with your limitations, Gramps. Try not to take your anger out on the widows, okay?"

"Yeah, yeah."

She leaned over and gave him a hug and a kiss. "Love you, Gramps."

"Back at ya, Ally."

Turning away, she tried to keep a firm grip on Domino's leash. As if sensing that they were going on another walk, Domino lunged forward.

"No! Domino!" Ally tried to dig in her heels, but the dog strained toward the lake. "Okay, fine." What was the point in fighting him?

Domino trotted faster, his nose twitching as he picked up a variety of interesting scents. The faster she walked, the less Domino tugged on the leash, and soon they had a nice pace going.

They cruised toward Lakefront Park, the area along the shore owned by Willow Bluff. The city refused to issue any zoning permits to build there, much to the chagrin of the rich and famous who longed to own a piece of the lakeshore for their very own. There were large sand dunes off to the right, with several weeping willow trees rustling in the light breeze.

Woof! Woof! Domino barked loudly and took off running. Caught off guard, Ally lost her footing, her heel slipping in the sand. Somehow she lost her grip on the leash.

Domino sprinted off.

"No! Domino!" She scrambled to her feet. "Come back here!"

There was only the barest sliver of moon in the night sky. She squinted through the darkness, squelching a flash of panic. What if she lost him? "Domino! Here, boy!"

The animal's black coat was impossible to see in the dark. She pulled out her cell phone and turned on the flashlight app, then quickened her pace, trying to follow him. "Domino, come back here! Domino!"

There! She caught a glimpse of the dog's silhouette as he darted beneath a weeping willow. Fearing coyotes, she broke into a run. "Domino!" She hoped the trailing leash would slow him down.

She couldn't, wouldn't, lose her boarder.

"Domino!" She yelled his name as loudly as she could. "Come back here this minute!"

Nothing. Ally crept forward, trying to peer beneath the long, sweeping branches of the willow. Had he escaped out the other side?

"Domino!" Her chest tightened with panic, and it was hard to breathe. She had to find him; she just had to. Ally pushed the branches out of the way.

The beam of her flashlight caught the whites of Domino's eyes. His dark shape hesitated for a moment as if he was poised to run.

"Good boy!" She eased toward him, hoping to catch him before he ran off again. "Here, Domino."

For once he listened, wheeling around and coming to her side. He dropped something from his mouth that landed at her feet. She grabbed his collar, felt for the leash, and let out a sigh of relief, knowing she had him.

"You were naughty to run off like that," she scolded. Domino's mouth was open, revealing his white teeth. "What did you bring me?"

Bracing herself for a dead animal of some sort, she shined the beam of her phone's flashlight down at the ground. Domino had brought her a red-and-white polka-dotted high-heeled shoe.

She stared at it in horror. The shoe looked exactly like the one Pricilla had been wearing earlier in the day.

Dropping down on her haunches, she looked closer at the shoe. Was it possible that Pricilla Green had left it in the woods after a tryst with her boyfriend, Jake? It wasn't difficult to imagine that more than one teenage fling had taken place at the lakefront. Not by her, as she'd been a science geek—but others had surely taken advantage of the place.

Wait a minute. What had caught Domino's attention under the weeping willow in the first place?

Ally tightened her grip on Domino's leash, then stepped forward, going deeper beneath the branches. She held up her phone flashlight to see better.

The beam of light picked up the sheen of white skin. A slender arm, thrown out as if reaching for help.

No! Not again!

Feeling sick to her stomach, Ally forced herself to move closer. The pale arm belonged to Pricilla Green, and the young woman was dressed in the same outrageous getup she'd worn to clean in, with the addition of a paisley scarf wound tightly around her neck. The girl's eyes were open and staring off into the distance without focus.

Ally knew before checking for a pulse that Pricilla Green was dead.

Chapter Three

Ally pulled Domino away from the young woman and fumbled for her phone. Unfortunately, it wasn't the first body she'd stumbled across, but she really hoped it would be the last.

"Willow Bluff Police," the dispatcher answered. "What's the nature of your emergency?"

"I found a dead body." Ally's voice hitched a bit. "I—uh, well, actually Domino found her beneath a weeping willow at Lakefront Park. Her name is Pricilla Green, and I'm fairly certain she's been murdered."

"Please stay on the line while I send an officer and a detective to your location."

"Okay." Ally glanced around, acutely aware of how alone she was on this stretch of the lakefront. Surely the killer was long gone, but she was glad she had Domino with her. She winced, imagining Noah Jorgenson's reaction to finding her here. What were the odds of her discovering two dead bodies in the past three months?

About the same as getting struck by lightning twice in one lifetime.

She tried to convince herself that the only reason this kept happening to her was because of her career. She'd been performing dog-walking services when she'd stumbled across the first body back in June, and now her boarding services had brought her to this one.

Not her fault, right? She wasn't some dead-body magnet, was she? No, of course not.

Domino was pulling against the leash, his nose quivering again. This time she dug in her heels and yelled, "*No!*"

Domino looked at her over his shoulder, then stopped resisting. Was it possible he might actually start listening to her?

She wouldn't bank on it.

Staring at Domino didn't help erase the image of Pricilla lying beneath the weeping willow. Ally couldn't believe the young woman who'd been so snarky earlier this morning was now dead.

Poor Hilda Green. As much as Pricilla's attention-seeking behavior drove her mother crazy, this news would be devastating to her.

Ally glanced up when flashing red and blue lights cut through the darkness. Despite the mild weather, she shivered when she thought about how long Pricilla might have been left here if Ally hadn't decided to bring Domino down to the lakefront for a long walk.

And if Domino hadn't dropped the red-and-white polka-dotted high-heeled shoe at Ally's feet.

A dark SUV pulled up beside the squad, and the tall, familiar figure of Noah Jorgenson slid out from behind the wheel. Noah was fit and lean, with broad shoulders and a chiseled jaw. He wore his dark hair short and had bright-green eyes that she couldn't see clearly now in the darkness. As he and one of the police officers approached, she saw the expression on Noah's face turn incredulous.

"Ally?"

At least he hadn't called her Hot Pants. She forced a smile. "Hey, Noah. Long time no see."

He swept his gaze over the area. "You're here alone? Where's your grandfather?"

"He's at the Legacy House, and I'm not alone, I have Domino." She tugged hard on the poodle's leash. Domino apparently loved people and was doing his best to jump all over Noah and the officer, someone she didn't recognize who came to stand a few feet from her.

Like she was afflicted with some communicable disease.

"I—uh, she's under there." Ally gestured toward the weeping willow. "Domino found her and brought one of her shoes out for me."

Noah stared at her for a long moment. He glanced at the red-and-white polka-dotted high-heeled shoe, then moved toward the weeping willow. The officer joined him, using his large flashlight to illuminate the area. Noah moved the long willow branches out of the way and ducked beneath them.

Noah returned a few minutes later, pulling a small notebook from his pocket. "I need you to start at the beginning."

"There's no big story here," Ally protested. "I brought Domino out for a walk. He got away from me, and it took me a while to find him in the darkness. When I caught him, he dropped Pricilla's shoe at my feet. At first I thought she might have simply lost it here, but when I went farther beneath the willow, I saw her outstretched arm and the rest of her body. I knew before feeling for a pulse she was dead."

"How did you know that?" Noah asked.

"The scarf around her neck." Ally shrugged. "It was the only item of clothing that was different from when I saw her earlier this morning. I figure she was strangled with the scarf."

"When and where did you see her?" Noah demanded.

"At the Legacy House, around nine o'clock this morning. Her mother, Hilda Green, made some deal with Beatrice to pay Pricilla a modest sum to clean the place."

If anything, Noah now looked more perplexed. "Are you telling me the victim wore that outfit to clean the Legacy House?"

"Yep. Even the shoes."

He muttered something under his breath, and it made her smile to realize Noah sounded much like her grandfather at that moment. In some ways, the two men were very similar. Not that either of them would appreciate the comparison. Noah made a few more notes in the little book.

"Okay, do you know anything else about her?" Noah finally asked. "Like why she's under the weeping willow tree?"

"No clue, although when I found the shoe, I assumed she lost it during, ah—" She stumbled over the words, glad the darkness would hide her blush. "You know, a liaison with her boyfriend."

"What boyfriend?" Noah demanded.

"I've never been introduced to him, but I've seen him around town. His name is Jake Hammond. Rumor has it Pricilla's mother doesn't like him because he dresses just as outrageously as Pricilla did." Ally glanced back at the weeping willow. "Hilda's going to be devastated by this."

"Yeah." Noah made a note of the boyfriend's name. "Anything else you know about the victim?"

Ally thought about Gramps's wild theories of Pricilla being involved in drugs or the robbery ring but shook her head. "Nope. I've seen her cleaning the Legacy House, and I think she works in the kitchen at the Lakeview Café, but that's about it."

Again, Noah stared at her for a long moment. She tried to ignore him as she fought to keep Domino under control.

"Is that all?" she finally asked. "Because I have to get Domino back home."

"Yeah, that's all." Noah tucked his notebook back into his pocket. "I know where to find you if I need more information."

She turned and pulled Domino away from the scene of the crime. She'd taken only a couple of steps before Noah called out, "Ally?"

She turned to face him. "Yes?"

"I'll give you and Domino a ride." He glanced at the officer who stood beside him. "Timmons, can you handle securing the scene for a few minutes? I won't be gone long."

"I don't need a ride—" she began, but was cut off.

"Sure, Detective." Timmons rested his hand on his weapon. "Not a problem."

"This way." Noah directed her and Domino to his SUV. "Put the dog in the back."

"You . . . don't think the killer is out here somewhere, do you?" Ally glanced around with apprehension. It was the only reason she could think of for Noah to offer her a ride. "I mean, I assumed he or she would be long gone by now."

"Humor me," Noah said, opening the passenger side door for her. After she urged Domino into the back, she slid into the SUV and was surrounded by the woodsy aroma of Noah's aftershave. He'd never called or come by after their one and only date, so she tried to ignore her visceral reaction to the scent.

But it wasn't easy.

Noah slid into the driver's seat and pulled away from Lakefront Park. "You have two dogs now?"

"No, just Roxy. Domino is a boarder I have through the weekend."

"Ah, I remember now. He belongs to Kayla and Mark Benton, who have twin girls, Bridgit and Brooke."

"Yes, that's right." Ally wondered if Noah felt as awkward about this conversation as she did. Had he really offered her a ride because he was worried about the murderer still hanging around? "I guess they're enjoying a much-needed getaway."

"I'm sure." Noah hesitated, then said, "I'm sorry I haven't been in touch for a while. My mother was in the hospital with some heart issues that eventually required surgery. Between that and stumbling across a couple of local robberies, I haven't made much time for my friends."

They were friends? She supposed that was a step up from mere acquaintances. "I'm sorry to hear about your mom. Hope she's doing okay."

"She's fine now that she had a stent put in one of her coronary arteries."

"Scary." Ally was glad her parents were both doing well, even if she didn't see them much. They were both professors at a local private university and had recently returned from a long summer vacation just in time to go back to work.

"Yeah, tell me about it." Noah's tone sounded serious.

"Any leads on the robberies?" The question popped out before she could pull it back. It was almost as if Gramps were seated beside her, whispering the questions he wanted answered in her ear.

"What do you know about it?" Noah demanded.

"Nothing other than what I've heard from Gramps."

Noah let out a heavy sigh. "Keep your grandfather out of this, Ally."

"Of the robberies? Or the murder?"

"Both." His voice was sharp. "I don't need Oscar's help."

Far be it from her to point out that he'd been singing a different tune after they'd captured the perp who'd murdered sleezy attorney Marty Shawlin.

"Did you hear me?" Noah pressed.

"Loud and clear." She didn't bother to assure him that Gramps would stay out of it, because knowing her grandfather, he'd be knee-deep in theories come morning.

And she'd already tried to tell Gramps to stay out of the criminal investigation related to the robberies but failed to convince him. Now that Pricilla had been murdered, getting Gramps to stay out of it would be like telling the sun not to shine or the lake water not to lap at the shoreline.

Utterly impossible.

*   *   *

The following morning, Ally woke to Roxy's nose in her face. For some crazy reason the boxer liked to get up at six in the morning, despite the fact that Ally was not a morning person.

She quickly took care of Roxy, then hurried down to take Domino out. Having two dogs that couldn't be taken outside together was twice as much work, and she made a mental note to try another socialization experiment later in the morning.

This time, she'd be better prepared.

Typically Ally didn't have any help on Thursdays, but she wasn't the least bit surprised when her cell phone rang.

Recognizing the number, she held the phone at least twelve inches from her ear, knowing it wouldn't help much. Gramps always felt as if he needed to shout when using his cell phone.

"Hi, Gramps."

"ALLY! PRICILLA IS DEAD!"

"I know, Gramps."

"I HEARD YOU FOUND HER BODY?"

She inwardly groaned and glanced at her watch. It was eight thirty, plenty of time to get out to the Legacy House and back before her rescheduled grooming appointment arrived. "Yes. Listen, Gramps, why don't I pick you up and bring you to the clinic? We can talk more about this later."

"I'LL BE READY!" he shouted.

Ally disconnected the call. Volunteering at the clinic two days in a row usually wore Gramps out, but since he'd obviously heard about the murder, she knew it was better to have him here, where she could keep an eye on him.

There was no telling what Gramps would do if left to his own devices. She'd watched him in action more than once, turning his charm on and off like a light switch, somehow getting women of all ages to open up and tell him whatever he wanted to know.

Ally decided to bring Roxy along on the drive to the Legacy House, although leaving Domino behind in his crate wasn't easy. She ignored a stab of guilt.

She pulled in and freed Roxy from the back. As she walked toward the house, her heart jumped into her throat. The front door stood ajar. She quickly entered the ranch-style home. "Gramps? Harriet? Lydia? Tillie?"

"In here," Gramps called.

Ally entered the living room. Tillie was sitting on the sofa, but the other widows and Gramps were crowded around her, clearly concerned.

"What happened? Should I call 911?" Ally knelt beside the sofa as Roxy greeted Gramps with enthusiasm.

"I'm fine," Tillie groused. "Lost my balance and hit my elbow on the doorjamb. For a few minutes there, my fingers went numb."

Numb fingers weren't a good sign. Ally only knew enough about human medical practice to be dangerous. "You need to call your doctor to have your arm looked at."

"It's better now, see?" Tillie waggled her fingers. "Not numb anymore."

"Can you straighten it?" Ally noticed that although Tillie was talking tough, her face was pale beneath her straight white hair and her arm was bent up against her chest.

"Hurts to do that," Tillie admitted.

On days like this, Ally felt as if she had four grandparents instead of one. "Call your doctor. You should get an X-ray in case your arm is broken. And I can give you a ride to the hospital if needed."

"Tillie, do as Ally says," Harriet said, her expression full of concern. Tillie and Harriet were sisters and argued like mad, but in times of trouble, they stuck together like glue.

"Fine. Call for me, would you, Harriet?"

Ally waited as Harriet went into the kitchen to use the house phone. It didn't take long, which was a minor miracle, since anytime she needed to call the doctor's office, she was put on an interminable hold.

"The nurse agreed with Ally that you need to have the arm X-rayed. She suggested the fastest way to do that is to go to the ER. I'll come with you."

Ally nodded. "Okay, I'll take Harriet and Tillie to the ER, but then I have to get to the clinic for an appointment. Gramps, you want to stay here with Lydia?"

"I'm coming with you," Gramps said firmly.

"What about you, Lydia?" Ally was trying to think of a way to fit all of them in her small car. If the Honda ever died, she'd have to consider buying a minivan.

"I'll be fine here for a while," Lydia assured them. "It's just for a few hours, and there's plenty of food in the fridge."

"Okay, let's go." Ally hoped she had enough time to get the elderly sisters to the ER and back to the clinic before her grooming appointment arrived.

Ally tucked Tillie in the front seat, which meant Gramps and Harriet had to sit in the back near Roxy. Harriet didn't like dogs, but of course that didn't faze Roxy. The boxer loved everyone and likely associated Harriet with the food scraps Gramps often sneaked under the table for her. Roxy pressed her nose against her crate near Harriet's head, as if trying to get a good whiff of whatever was on the menu for dinner. Harriet batted Roxy away.

"I'm sure it's not broken," Tillie said for the third time. Because she protested so much, Ally felt certain the bone was in fact fractured.

"Since you don't have X-ray vision, I'd prefer to wait to see what the doctor thinks," Harriet said with a huff of impatience.

Ally pulled up in front of the ER of the Willow Bluff Community Hospital. She helped Tillie out, and Harriet quickly joined them. Ally escorted them inside, then hesitated, feeling guilty leaving Harriet and Tillie to navigate the medical system by themselves. "Are you sure you'll be okay?"

"We'll be fine, dear," Tillie said.

Ally wasn't convinced. "I'll come back to check in on you as soon as my grooming appointment is finished."

"No rush," Harriet said in a no-nonsense tone. "The wait times here are ridiculous."

"Call if you need me sooner," Ally insisted.

"We will." Harriet took Tillie over to the front desk. "My sister broke her arm," she announced loudly.

Hoping they'd be all right, Ally hurried back out to the car. She was surprised to find that Gramps had moved into the front passenger seat.

"Now that they're gone, tell me everything," he demanded.

Ally felt a stress headache coming on. First Tillie's injury, and now Gramps's thirst for all the grisly details of Pricilla's murder. "There's not much to tell." She quickly filled him in on the sequence of events.

"Did that detective of yours think her murder is related to the robberies?" Gramps asked.

"He didn't say." She held up a hand. "And I didn't ask. He's already told us to stay out of it."

"Bah. He's being shortsighted to think he doesn't need our help." Gramps looked disgruntled. "No way would he have solved those last murders without us."

"Mostly Roxy," Ally reminded him. "And Domino wasn't a witness to the murder this time."

"Domino is also not very well trained." Gramps's expression was thoughtful as she pulled into the parking lot. "That just means we'll need to do more legwork on this one in order to figure out who killed that girl."

They were doing no such thing, but Ally wisely kept her mouth shut. She helped Gramps from the car, then released Roxy from the back hatch. After a quick bathroom break, she took Roxy upstairs and followed Gramps inside.

Domino began to bark as they entered the clinic. "Gramps, keep an eye out for my grooming appointment. I need to take Domino out for a minute."

"Oh yeah, that lady. Starts with an M, right?" Gramps asked.

"Right." It was all she could do not to snap at him. She loved her grandfather very much, but some days he pushed her patience to the absolute limit.

She took Domino outside and struggled to keep him from dragging her down Main Street. The dog really needed obedience lessons in a big way. When she saw a slender woman walking toward the clinic with a tuft of brown fur in her arms, she instinctively knew it was her grooming appointment. Oh yeah, and the dog's name was Molly.

"Domino! This way!" She muscled the dog around to the back of the building so she could get him in the kennel. But she must not have closed the door to her apartment all the way, because Roxy bounded down toward them.

Domino jumped up, plowing Ally over in his haste to get to Roxy.

"No, Domino! Down, Roxy!" The dogs were only trying to play, but she was squashed between them like melted cheese in a grilled sandwich.

Teeth nipped at her knit top, and it took far longer than it should have for Ally to get Roxy and Domino separated. Roxy finally sat on command, tongue lolling off to the side as her sides heaved from exertion.

"Stay, Roxy." Ally gave her a stern look. Then she eased Domino through the back door of the clinic and wrestled him into his crate, where he began to bark like a mad dog.

Ally brought Roxy over and placed her in the crate next to Domino's. Instantly Domino stopped barking, pressing his nose against Roxy's.

If she didn't know better, she'd have thought they were in love.

As long as they were quiet, she didn't care if they exchanged doggy kisses all morning. Ally ran a hand through her wildly curly hair and tried to straighten her clothing, which was now wet with dog slobber. She went out to the clinic lobby, but Molly's owner was nowhere to be found.

"Didn't my grooming appointment show?" Ally asked, perplexed. For the life of her, she couldn't remember the woman's name. "I thought I saw her and Molly outside."

Gramps nodded slowly. "She came but left when she heard you and the dogs. Said something about finding another groomer that knew how to control animals."

Great. That's just peachy. Her only appointment of the day had left and wouldn't be back.

"Oh, and Tillie does have a broken arm. We'll need to swing by and pick them up within the hour to take them back to the Legacy House."

Murder, a broken arm, and no clients on the schedule.

Could this day get any worse?

Chapter Four

"I have a theory," Gramps said as they drove to the hospital to pick up Tillie and Harriet. This time she'd left both dogs at the clinic. She wasn't happy with either one of them at the moment.

"Gramps . . ." She sighed. "Noah told us to stay out of it."

"I think Pricilla and Jake were both involved in the box store robberies," Gramps went on, as if she hadn't spoken. "Pricilla was afraid of her mom, the county exec, discovering what was going on, so she wanted out. Jake wasn't having it, and when Pricilla threatened to go to the police, he killed her."

Ally glanced at him. "Pricilla didn't work at Electronics and More, remember? And I thought you believed the robberies were drug related."

"Jake could be mixed up in drugs," Gramps agreed. "And maybe Pricilla didn't like that either. They argued about the drugs and the robberies, so he killed her."

"Out on the lakefront, under the weeping willow tree?" That didn't seem likely.

"Maybe he dumped her body there, hoping the coyotes would get to it before she was found." Gramps had an answer for everything.

The idea of coyotes eating Pricilla made Ally's stomach churn. She shivered. "Thanks for that grisly image, Gramps. You need to stop reading those awful books."

"Hey, I'm just thinking like a cop," Gramps protested.

Ally shook her head. Gramps had never been a cop, and she wasn't sure why he'd chosen to pretend to be one now. She pulled into the emergency department parking lot, threw the gearshift into park, and glanced at Gramps. "Stay here. I'll be back shortly with Harriet and Tillie."

"Okay." Gramps didn't protest, which surprised her. Maybe his hip was bothering him more than she'd realized, and she made a mental note to follow up with his surgeon.

Ally strode inside and glanced around the waiting room. She frowned when her gaze landed on the familiar face of Martha Cromlin, Willow Bluff's esteemed mayor.

Swallowing her curiosity about what the mayor was doing there, Ally approached the front desk. "I'm here to take Tillie Carbine home?"

The clerk tapped her computer keyboard. "Ah yes. She'll be out soon."

"Thanks." Ally turned back to the waiting room in time to see a woman in a wheelchair being pushed over toward Martha Cromlin.

It took her only a moment to recognize Hilda Green, Pricilla's mother. Hilda looked rough, as if she'd spent the night in the ER crying hysterically. And maybe she had; after all, it couldn't be easy losing a daughter. Her current appearance was in sharp contrast to her usual way of presenting herself: perfect hair, nice clothes, and heels.

Ally didn't try to eavesdrop but overheard their brief conversation anyway.

"Are you sure your heart checked out okay?" Martha asked. "When you screamed and passed out, I thought you'd had the big one."

"They said I'll be fine." Hilda waved a limp hand. Then her face crumpled. "My baby . . ." Her voice trailed off as she buried her face in her hands.

Ally felt terrible for Hilda and wanted to offer her condolences but wasn't sure if the woman knew that Ally—well more accurately Domino—had found her daughter's body. If so, Hilda might not want to see Ally at all.

And she couldn't blame her for not wanting a gruesome reminder of what had happened to Pricilla.

Ally had found it difficult to erase the image of Pricilla from her mind.

"Oh, there's Ally," Harriet said loudly.

Ally turned to see Harriet and Tillie slowly making their way toward her. Tillie's casted arm was in a shoulder sling, and brackets of pain were deeply etched at the corners of the widow's mouth.

"Oh, Tillie. Are you okay?" Ally gave the little woman a gentle hug. "Let's get you home."

"You! It's your fault!" A sharp screech had Ally turning toward Hilda Green. The woman's wild eyes were full of hate. "You did this! You did this!"

"Me?" The accusation was ridiculous. Ally glanced around nervously at the group of patients and visitors sitting in the waiting room. "I didn't hurt your daughter."

"Hilda, stop it. This isn't Dr. Winter's fault," Martha Cromlin said firmly. "You're distraught. Come now, I'll take you home."

43

Once again Hilda abruptly covered her face in her hands, which made Ally slightly suspicious. As if the woman was hiding something from Ally's keen gaze.

Wait a minute, was she letting Gramps's penchant for crime mess with her head? Hilda had appeared really distraught about losing her daughter. Or had she put on this performance to cover up a terrible secret? After all, the town gossip had indicated that Hilda Green was extremely frustrated with her daughter. Even so, it was difficult to imagine the woman killing her own flesh and blood.

As Ally helped the elderly sisters to her car, she was secretly glad Gramps hadn't witnessed Hilda's bizarre accusation. He'd have been all over the idea of Hilda being guilty of some crime.

Or of knowing more than she'd let on.

"Thanks, Ally," Tillie murmured as she awkwardly slid into the back seat. "I appreciate the ride."

"No problem, Tillie." Ally waited for Harriet to get situated beside her sister, then slid behind the wheel.

"Why did Hilda accuse you of hurting her daughter?" Tillie asked as Ally headed back to the Legacy House. "Did she know you found Pricilla's body?"

"What happened?" Ally stifled a groan as Gramps twisted in his seat to look at Tillie. "That goofy woman blamed Ally for her daughter's murder?"

"She did," Tillie said with a nod. "In front of the whole waiting room."

"Why on earth would that daft woman say something like that?" Gramps demanded irritably.

"She's upset," Ally said soothingly. "I'm sure she didn't mean it. I think she was in the hospital all night, ever since learning of her daughter's murder."

"Why would she be in the hospital for that?" Gramps asked with a scowl. "Doesn't make any sense."

"I think she must have had chest pains or something." Ally glanced at her grandfather. "But she came out saying her heart was fine, so I'm sure it was just stress related to her devastating loss."

"Devastating loss," Gramps muttered with a snort. "More likely relief from not having to worry about the girl parading around town in her outrageous outfits."

"Gramps," Ally said in a warning tone. "Mothers aren't relieved to lose their daughters. Even if they can be a bit trying."

"Okay, okay." Gramps waved a hand. "But it's still strange that she'd blame you."

Ally secretly agreed, although she did her best to shrug it off. She pulled into the small parking area in front of the Legacy House. "Let me get Tillie inside first, okay?"

"Bah. I can get out on my own." Gramps stubbornly did just that.

Ally felt a little frazzled by the time she'd managed to get Tillie, Harriet, and Gramps safely inside. Lydia joined them in the kitchen, seemingly fine after being left alone. Tillie dropped into a chair at the table, cradling her arm.

"Did the doctor give you pain medication?" Ally asked, sitting beside Tillie.

"I don't like narcotics," Tillie said staunchly. "He said alternating Tylenol and ibuprofen would work just as well."

"I'm hungry," Gramps announced. "Maybe we should order takeout, since Harriet hasn't been here all morning."

"No, no, I can throw something together for lunch." Harriet took it personally if she couldn't feed them. She hustled over to the fridge. "Just give me some time. I think I have some frozen butternut squash soup, and I can easily make grilled cheese sandwiches to go with it."

"Yum," Ally said, aware of her own stomach rumbling. "Are you sure it's no trouble?"

Harriet didn't answer, already pulling a container of soup from the freezer and filling the sink with hot water. The woman was clearly on a mission, and since there wasn't a restaurant in Willow Bluff that could compete with Harriet's cooking, Ally gave up trying to stop her. Instead, she went to find the over-the-counter medications for Tillie.

"Take these," Ally said, handing the widow several ibuprofen.

"Thanks, dear." Tillie downed the meds with a glass of water Gramps brought to the table.

A knock at the door had everyone turning in surprise. Guests didn't often come to the Legacy House, except for Ally, who was treated like family.

Ally crossed over to answer the door. When she saw Noah standing there, her heart did a funny flip in her chest. Then she took note of his frown. "What's wrong?"

"Do you have a minute to talk?" Noah asked. He looked over her shoulder at the curious faces of the widows behind her. "Alone?"

"Sure." She glanced guiltily at Gramps, then stepped outside to join Noah. He took several steps away from the house. "What's going on?"

"I need to ask you about the incident at the Legacy House yesterday morning," Noah said.

She stared at him blankly. "What incident?"

"Involves one of the widows shouting at Pricilla."

She scoffed. "That's hardly an incident, Noah. Pricilla is supposed to clean the Legacy House once a week for three hours. That's what Beatrice Potter, the owner, pays her for. Yesterday she claimed she was finished after two hours. Tillie confronted her about it, and Pricilla stalked off."

"You weren't involved as well?" Noah pressed.

Ally planted her hands on her hips. "No, why would I be?" Then it dawned on her. "Is this why Hilda Green blames me for her daughter's death? Come on, Noah, don't be ridiculous."

"I'm just covering all bases," he said, although she could tell he wasn't happy to be talking to her about this so-called incident at all. Noah was smart; he'd never see a simple disagreement as motive for murder.

The previous sympathy she'd felt toward the grieving mother faded. Her eyes narrowed. "Let me guess, Hilda Green is the city executive, and she's best friends with the mayor, and the mayor hires the chief of police, who told you to consider me a suspect."

The flash of guilt in Noah's eyes confirmed her suspicions. "I don't consider you a suspect, Ally," Noah said firmly. "But you are right that the mayor is putting pressure on the chief to get this murder solved as soon as possible. And they insisted I follow up on the argument that took place here."

"Stupid," Ally muttered, shoving a wayward curl away from her face. "Okay, fine. You asked, I answered. Do you need anything else?"

"No, other than the usual," Noah said.

The usual? Her heart fluttered. "I . . . don't know what you mean."

"The usual," he repeated. "I need you and your wily grandfather to stay away from my case."

She rolled her eyes, angry at herself for thinking he'd meant something personal. "Good-bye, then." She turned and marched back into the house, doing her best to ignore Noah's keen gaze boring into her back.

* * *

Harriet's impromptu lunch was delicious, but Ally left quickly afterward, using the dogs as an excuse. Which was valid, since she had both Roxy and Domino to worry about.

"I'll come with you," Gramps said stubbornly.

Even though she knew what he really wanted was to talk about the case, she gave in. Mostly because sitting at home by herself wasn't much fun.

And being with Gramps was never boring.

"Okay, spill it," Gramps said once they were back in her Honda.

"It's nothing," Ally downplayed her brief conversation with Noah. "Just the city exec and the mayor putting pressure on Noah to solve this thing."

"Well, then, that detective of yours should let us help," Gramps declared. "We worked well together this past summer."

She slanted him an exasperated glance. "I don't think that's how Noah remembers it."

"Hrmph." Gramps waved his hand. "It was Hilda Green accusing you, wasn't it?"

"Yes." She blew out a breath. "But Noah knows she's off base. It'll be fine. Once she gets over the initial shock, I'm sure Hilda Green will realize she was wrong."

"Did you tell your detective Hilda Green might be covering up for her daughter?" He snapped his fingers. "Maybe Hilda knew Pricilla was doing drugs but didn't do enough to get her into rehab."

Pricilla's slender white outstretched arm flashed in her mind. "She wasn't using drugs, Gramps. There were no signs of needle marks in her arms and no other reason to believe drugs were involved. Just because Rosie mentioned the possibility doesn't make it true."

"Okay, then, if the robberies are connected to Pricilla's murder, we need to understand the motive. Why did the perps need money?" Gramps asked.

"Doesn't everyone want more money?" Ally countered. "It's not like there has to be a specific reason." She pulled into the parking space behind her clinic. "Enough talking about murder and mayhem. I'll help you inside, then I need to take care of the dogs."

She took Domino out first, wincing at Roxy's dark, reproachful look. She walked Domino down Main Street, or rather Domino walked her.

"Heel," she shouted, tugging at his leash. She should have taken him out back, as people were staring at her. It wasn't as if the ill-mannered dog belonged to her. But remembering how Molly's owner had walked out on her scheduled grooming appointment because Ally couldn't control the dogs made her doubly self-conscious.

"No, heel!" She shortened Domino's leash and used all her strength to keep him at her side. After a few minutes, he seemed to calm down, although his nose was constantly working, taking in all the interesting scents.

Ally's right arm was aching by the time she returned to the clinic. In comparison, Roxy was a dream, trotting alongside her, but she knew it wasn't fair to hold Domino to Roxy's standards. Domino was the product of his owner's being too busy with twins to give him the care and attention he deserved. She wasn't an expert at training, but Domino sure needed help. The poor dog didn't even seem to understand the basics.

"Ally? Some Patsy woman called about a puppy. She thinks he's hurt and is bringing him in," Gramps announced when she had both dogs back in their side-by-side kennels. They seemed better behaved when they were together, which helped her feel less guilty.

"Patsy's the dog, Gramps. Wendy Granger is the owner." At least he'd gotten one of the names right. "Thanks for letting me know."

Ally hurried to double-check the exam room, relaxing when she found it as clean as she'd left it. When Wendy Granger had discovered her Lab Patsy was pregnant with puppies who were half Great Dane, she'd nearly gone off the deep end. But Patsy had delivered the puppies just fine, and they were all in very good health. Despite Wendy's fears over the entire birthing process, which Ally had participated in, staying for several hours in the Granger house during the whelping, she had become quite enamored of the pups.

The bell to the clinic rang. "Dr. Winter? I think Bandit hurt himself very badly," Wendy said dramatically.

"Let's take a look, shall we? This way." Ally took Wendy and the Labradane puppy into the first exam room. "Tell me what happened."

"He was playing on the sofa, and he rolled right off!" Wendy's eyes were large with concern. "I heard him yelp, and he wouldn't put any weight on his left front paw." Tears sparked in the woman's eyes. "Do you think it's broken?"

"From a fall off a sofa? I don't think so, but let me examine him." Bandit was all black with perky ears that were a cross between a Lab's and a Great Dane's. Ally gingerly pressed on Bandit's wounded paw, but the dog didn't cry out in pain or try to nip her. In fact, he leaned down and ran his sandpaper tongue over the back of her hand.

"Poor Bandit," Wendy murmured. "First his new home fell through, and now this. How will he ever find a home with a broken leg?"

Ally glanced at her. "I didn't realize his new family backed out. What about the other pups?"

"They all have homes and will be ready to leave by the end of the week. Except for Bandit."

"Well, the good news is that his leg isn't broken," Ally assured her. "He'll probably baby the paw for the rest of the day, but he should be fine by morning."

"Really? So—he won't need surgery or anything?" Wendy asked, her gaze hopeful.

"Positive. He'll be just fine." Ally scratched the pup behind the ears. "He's so cute, I'm sure he'll find a home."

"You said you'd help me find them good homes, Dr. Winter," Wendy said with a hint of reproach in her eyes.

It was on the tip of Ally's tongue to remind Wendy that she wasn't the one who had made the poor decision not to get Patsy spayed; therefore, finding Bandit a home wasn't her responsibility. But the vet in her couldn't stand the idea of the puppy ending up at Jeri Smith's shelter.

"And I did find one of the pups a home," Ally countered. "Misty Allen is taking one, right? She lost her Lab a few weeks ago and sounded very excited about the puppy."

"Yes," Wendy agreed.

"And I still have my sign on the counter, announcing free Labradane puppies to anyone interested." Ally had tried to convince Ellen Cartwright to take one for her daughter, but despite how much ten-year-old Amanda loved animals, constantly bringing in strays for Ally to care for, her mother steadfastly refused to take a puppy or even a cat. No animals of any kind were allowed in that woman's house.

As a real estate agent, Ellen Cartwright believed all homes should look like a showcase at all times. Unfortunately, puppies tended to make a mess.

"Keep trying, will you?" Wendy asked, gathering Bandit into her arms. "I can't keep him, no matter how much I'd like to."

"I'll do my best," Ally said. She left the exam room with Wendy following.

"How much?" Wendy asked, pausing at the front desk.

Ally printed an invoice with only the very basic exam fee, feeling bad about charging Wendy at all, considering the pup was fine.

Thankfully, the woman didn't blink an eye. As Ally ran Wendy's credit card, the door of her clinic opened and Noah Jorgenson walked in.

"What's the puppy's name?" Gramps was asking, scratching the little guy behind his overly large ears.

"Bandit," Wendy said. "Do you know of anyone looking for a puppy?"

"Detective Jorgenson here might be interested," Gramps said, putting Noah on the spot. Gramps's blue eyes gleamed with amusement. "A dog named Bandit is perfect for a cop."

"Oh, I—uh," Noah stammered.

Ally couldn't help but grin. She'd tried to get Noah to adopt Roxy in June after the boxer's owner had been murdered, but getting Noah to take a puppy would be even better.

"See how cute he is?" Wendy thrust the puppy into Noah's arms. Flustered, he looked down at the animal. "Oh look, Detective, Bandit already loves you."

The dog squirmed and licked Noah's chin. Noah's eyes pleaded with Ally to help him out of the situation.

"I don't think Detective Jorgenson's schedule is conducive to having a dog, Wendy, but we'll keep looking. Bandit will find a home, you'll see."

Noah mouthed *thank you* as a dejected Wendy took the puppy from his arms.

"I'll hold you to that, Dr. Winter." Wendy picked up her credit card and receipt and stalked out of the clinic.

"You owe me one," Ally said to Noah.

Noah nodded slowly. "Dinner Saturday night?"

She was stunned speechless but managed to nod.

"Hey, I think you also owe us information on Pricilla's murder," Gramps protested. "Got any suspects?"

"Don't push it, Oscar. See you later, Ally." Noah turned and left, leaving Ally wondering what on earth she'd wear for their date—then, belatedly, why he'd come to the clinic in the first place.

Chapter Five

Later that evening, Ally walked Domino around town, working hard to keep him at her side in an effort to train the poodle. When she finished with Domino, it was Roxy's turn. Along the way, she called her friend Erica Kirby, whom she had known since high school.

"Hey, Ally." Erica spoke in a hushed voice. "Good timing. I just finished putting Tommy to bed."

Ally glanced at her watch, surprised to see it was already eight thirty. Walking two dogs was giving her twice as much exercise, which was a good thing, as she could use the extra activity.

"Is this a good time to chat, or do you want me to call you later?" Ally knew Erica juggled working part-time as a hairdresser at the Bluff Salon in town with caring for her two kids, Tommy, who was two, and LeAnn, who was five. Her husband, Jim Kirby, ran a construction company that he'd taken over from his dad. Jim was good friends with Noah, and they'd had a great double date a few months back.

At least she'd thought it had gone well. But when she hadn't heard from Noah after, she'd assumed he wasn't interested. Until yesterday when he'd told her about his mother's health issues.

"It's fine, although I'd love to get together for lunch sometime soon," Erica said. "We haven't gotten together in weeks."

"I know," Ally agreed. "Listen, I don't want to keep you too long, but I'm dying to tell you. Noah asked me out to dinner on Saturday night."

"He did?" Erica squealed with excitement, then quickly lowered her tone. "Oops, that might have woken Tommy. Wow, Ally, that's great news. Any idea where he's taking you?"

"No clue," Ally admitted. "I'm kinda nervous. I mean, when the four of us were together, there was plenty to talk about. If it's just the two of us . . ." Her voice trailed off.

"Stop it, you'll be fine," Erica chided. "Don't sell yourself short, Ally. You're a super-smart veterinarian, which is really impressive."

Ally didn't feel nearly as successful as Erica made her sound, but she appreciated her friend's effort. "Yeah, except Noah tends to see me at my worst." She distinctly remembered an incident where she had cat diarrhea all down the front of her white lab coat and staining her red shoes when Noah had unexpectedly shown up. The memory still made her cheeks burn. She shook it off with effort. "How about we have lunch Sunday? I'll fill you in on the deets."

"I'd love that," Erica said enthusiastically.

"Don't say anything to Jim," Ally cautioned. "I don't know how much he talks to Noah these days."

"I won't," Erica assured her. "I think they see each other after work once in a while, when they can make the time. Jim's company has been super busy."

"Noah's been busy with the Electronics and More store robbery too," Ally said. "Okay, lunch on Sunday."

"Can't wait. Bye, Ally."

Ally found herself grinning like a fool as Roxy did her business. She cleaned up after the animal and headed back to her apartment.

Sleep didn't come easily, her brain circling around and around between Pricilla's murder, Hilda's wild accusations, and her date with Noah.

The next morning, Roxy woke her at six sharp. Ally groaned and went through the same routine of taking Roxy and Domino outside in separate trips. By the time she'd showered and changed, her cell phone was ringing.

Recognizing Gramps's number, she grimaced and braced herself for more shouting. "Hey, Gramps."

"ALLY! WHAT TIME ARE YOU PICKING ME UP?"

Friday was usually Tillie's day to play receptionist, but that wasn't an option with the widow's newly broken arm. Normally she didn't mind company, but she'd already had Gramps here two days in a row. Three would be pushing it. Despite his determination to play amateur detective, she knew he tired easily. "Maybe another time, Gramps."

"TODAY!" he insisted. "I HAVE A PLAN."

Uh-oh. Gramps having a plan was not a bit reassuring. She sighed and rubbed her temple. She could refuse to go get him but feared Gramps would just wheedle a ride from someone else.

"I'll be there soon," she said, caving under the pressure.

"OKAY!"

Ally shoved her phone into her pocket. She took Roxy down to the clinic to put her in the crate next to Domino. The two dogs rubbed noses through the wires and tried to lick each other.

"If you behave," Ally said in a stern tone, "I might let you both out at the same time."

Domino whimpered, and Roxy let out a sharp bark. Deciding to take that as agreement, Ally headed out the back of her clinic to her car.

The WBWs were in the kitchen with Gramps when she arrived.

"Tillie, how are you holding up?" Ally asked.

The woman's smile was wan. "I didn't sleep well, but otherwise I'm fine, dear. Thanks for asking."

"Tonight I'll make you herbal tea to help you relax," Harriet said, bustling around the kitchen. She looked at Ally. "Are you hungry? I can pull out something for breakfast."

"No thanks, Harriet." Ally steeled her resolve to stay away from Harriet's cooking. "Ready to go, Gramps?"

"All set." He nodded and struggled to his feet. Ally handed him his cane, then put a hand beneath his arm for extra support.

"I called your doctor," Ally said as they headed outside. "He really thinks physical therapy will help."

"Bah." Gramps scowled. "Shows what he knows."

Ally suppressed a sigh. Once Gramps was situated in the passenger seat, she slid behind the wheel. "Okay," she said as she headed back to the clinic. "What's your plan?"

"I want you to take me to the big-box store where the robberies took place." Gramps grinned. "I think we should check out the scene of the crime ourselves."

At least he doesn't want to go to the weeping willow. Ally didn't want to go anywhere near the place where she'd found Pricilla's body. "I guess that would be okay." She glanced at the time. "We'll head over there now. I think they're open."

"Great, thanks. Have any clients coming in today?" Gramps asked.

Ally shook her head. "Not yet, but I'm sure things will get better." She could only hope.

The parking lot outside Electronics and More had more cars than she'd expected to see, since the place had just opened for the day. As she drove up and down aisles to find a spot close to the store so Gramps wouldn't have to walk too far, she hit the brake, bringing the Honda to an abrupt halt.

"What is it?" Then Gramps saw it. "That's Pricilla's car."

"Yes."

The rusty brown Dodge sat in a spot that was blocked off with orange cones. Yellow crime scene tape was draped around the vehicle.

"Do you think she was strangled in the car, then dumped at the lakefront?" Gramps asked, his nose pressed to the passenger side window.

"I don't know." Ally shuddered at the horrible image that popped into her mind.

"Why do you think her car is here?" Gramps asked. "You said Pricilla didn't work here at the store, right?"

"She didn't. I think she worked in the kitchen of the café, maybe as a dishwasher or something. I'm not sure why Hilda arranged for Pricilla to clean the Legacy House too."

Gramps frowned. "Yeah, it's interesting, since Pricilla hated cleaning, not to mention she wasn't very good at it."

He had a point. Ally released the brake and continued searching for a parking spot.

"This is fine," Gramps said, waving a hand. "I can walk."

"Okay." After parking and helping Gramps out, Ally shortened her steps to match his as they walked into the store.

There was a strange hush inside the place, maybe because of the ongoing criminal investigation, which had now gone from robbery to murder.

Was it possible Pricilla's death had something to do with the robberies? The car in the parking lot was a bit of a coincidence.

A fact Noah hadn't mentioned.

Three store employees, all wearing the same navy-blue uniform shirt, were huddled near the end of an aisle. Gramps headed toward them, leaving Ally little choice but to tag along.

She pretended to shop but stayed tuned in to their muted voices.

"Did you hear about Pricilla?" A guy with dark hair looked around as if keeping an eye out for their boss.

"Yeah, and Marlie didn't show up for work today," said a girl with long blonde hair, roughly Pricilla's age. "They were best friends, so I'm sure Marlie is taking the news hard."

"You ask me, Steve looks like he had a rough night," said a third girl, who had dark hair with a dyed blue streak along the left side of her face.

The girl with long blonde hair nodded. "Steve knew Pricilla, the way we all did, so maybe it's understandable he's been upset."

"I heard that detective is coming in again," the guy with dark hair said. "And management says we're supposed to 'cooperate'"—he used two fingers to make air quotes—"with the investigation."

"I don't like it," Blue Streak whined. "He made me feel like I was guilty of something when I didn't do anything."

Ally hid a smile. Noah did have that way about him.

"What are you doing here?"

Ally jumped and spun guiltily at the sound of Noah's voice. She hoped her pink cheeks weren't too noticeable. "Shopping. Why, is that a crime?"

"Ally," Noah said in a warning tone.

"Can shop wherever she wants," Gramps interjected firmly. The trio of employees scattered when they saw Noah wearing his badge on a chain around his neck.

Noah folded his arms across his chest. "How many times have I told you to stay out of my investigation?"

"Did you know one of the store employees didn't show up for work this morning?" Gramps asked, his blue eyes gleaming. "A woman named Marlie, who is apparently very close to Pricilla. Is she a suspect in your robbery case? And are the robberies connected to Pricilla's murder?"

Noah's scowl deepened, and Ally winced when she saw the muscle twitch was back at the corner of his left eye. "Where did you hear about the employee who didn't show up for work today?" Noah demanded.

"The other employees were talking about it." Gramps clearly enjoyed getting the scoop before Noah. Which only made Noah's eye twitch faster.

"Come on, Gramps." Ally tugged on her grandfather's arm. "We're heading over to check out the cameras, remember?"

"Cameras? Why not just use the one on your phone?" Noah asked.

Ally didn't have a quick comeback for that. Thankfully, Gramps did. "I don't have one of those fancy camera phones. I take pictures the old-fashioned way."

"Yes, please excuse us." Ally nudged Gramps gently.

Noah didn't say anything more as she and Gramps moved farther into the store. As soon as they were out of Noah's earshot, Gramps started up.

"We need to find out what Marlie's last name is," he said in a loud whisper.

"And how are we going to do that?" Ally asked.

"You can check your client listing. Maybe she has a pet."

"Can I help you?" A kid with spiky brown hair and red-rimmed, bloodshot eyes approached them. This was Steve, according to his name tag. Ally had to admit, he did look a bit rough. And there was something familiar about him, but she couldn't place where she'd seen him before. Maybe the café?

"I'm looking for a camera," Gramps said.

Steve gestured listlessly to the long table with cameras mounted along the top. "Go ahead. Let me know if you find something you like."

Ally frowned at his less-than-helpful attitude, but he turned away, heading through a door marked *Employees Only* before she could say anything more.

"He does look like he's had a rough night," Gramps whispered. "Maybe he was up late killing Pricilla?"

"Stop it, Gramps." Ally suppressed a sigh. "You can't accuse people of murder because they look as if they've been up late. And this is exactly why Noah told us to stay out of it."

"Bah. That detective of yours needs us. Look at how we helped him already."

Ally grimaced, knowing that Noah didn't want or need their help. He would certainly have found out about Marlie not showing up for work and Steve's alleged late night once he began interviewing the staff.

Unfortunately, Gramps wasn't going to stay out of Noah's murder investigation.

And she felt certain her Saturday night dinner date was on the brink of being canceled as a result of Gramps's ongoing interference.

* * *

After they returned to the clinic and Ally had taken both dogs out for a bathroom break, she did as Gramps suggested and began searching her client list for the names Marlie and Steve.

She didn't find any Marlies on the list, but there were two Steves: Steve Norris and Steve Shaker.

"Steve Norris has a mixed-breed dog named Clancy," Gramps said, peering at the computer screen. "And Steve Shaker has a cat named Tubbs."

"That's it." Ally snapped her fingers. "Steve Norris stopped in last week to buy some heartworm meds. I remember because he paid the exact amount down to the penny."

"Aha!" Gramps looked excited at the news.

Her phone rang, and she quickly scooped it up. "Furry Friends Veterinary Clinic, this is Dr. Winter."

"Dr. Winter? This is Beverly Flynn. I received a message that my cat is due for her immunizations?"

"Yes, that's correct." Ally did a little fist pump of excitement. "When would you like to bring, ah"—she searched her memory for the cat's name—"Tulip in?"

"I have time this morning," Beverly said. "If you have an opening."

"Let's see, does eleven o'clock work?" Ally knew her schedule was wide open, but it didn't hurt to make it sound busier than it was.

"That would be great. Thanks for squeezing me in. See you soon."

Ally hung up the phone and beamed at her grandfather. "I have a client!"

"Glad to hear it." Gramps grinned and patted her shoulder. "You're a fine vet, Ally, and soon you'll be so busy you'll need more help."

"That's sweet. Thanks, Gramps." She didn't necessarily agree, but there was no point in stressing over the situation. She was convinced that the former owner, Greg Hanson, had padded his books when he'd sold the practice to her. She'd already found two dogs on the list of clients who had actually passed away.

And she felt certain that the women who'd wanted to date him hadn't minded coming in for silly concerns just to get his attention.

"I need to clean the exam rooms." Ally could hear the dogs getting restless in their respective crates but didn't dare give them a trial outing until after she'd immunized Tulip. No more scaring off potential clients with poorly trained animals running amok.

She wiped down the exam rooms with disinfectant and then pulled the file to familiarize herself with the immunizations Tulip needed. Her medications were locked in a cabinet in the back portion of the clinic. Not that she kept many narcotics on hand, only what she needed for the occasional traumatic emergency. It was important to keep them secure.

By quarter to eleven, she was dressed in her white lab coat and ready for her furry client to arrive.

She heard the phone ring and listened as Gramps answered it. "Furry Friends Veterinary Clinic. May I help you?"

Ally made a writing motion on the palm of her hand as a reminder for him to take notes. Gramps didn't always get his messages right, and she didn't relish feeling like a fool in front of her patients.

"Okay, I'll tell her." Gramps hung up without making a single note. Ally bit back the urge to snap at him. How hard was it to write something down? "That detective of yours is going to swing by later," Gramps said.

"He is?" She stared at him in surprise. "Why?"

Gramps shrugged. "He wouldn't say. Just asked if you could make sure to stick around this afternoon."

"Hmm." Ally wasn't sure this was good news. Especially since Noah had called the clinic, not her personal cell phone.

"Maybe you're still a suspect in Hilda Green's eyes," Gramps added.

"Gee, thanks for the vote of confidence," Ally said dryly.

"Hey, I know you're innocent, but it sounds like Hilda Green is looking for a scapegoat to blame."

"Maybe." Ally turned as the bell over the door jingled. A short round woman in her fifties walked in carrying a black-and-white tuxedo cat in her arms. Ally smiled warmly. "Hello, you must be Beverly and Tulip."

"Yes, this is Tulip. She's my baby," Beverly cooed.

"Right this way, please." Ally led the way into the first exam room, closing the door behind Beverly and Tulip. "I have Tulip's distemper shot ready to go; this is an immunization that actually covers her for three different diseases. Do you have any concerns you'd like to discuss?"

"No, Tulip has been very healthy—haven't you, precious? Yes you have."

Ally smiled. "Okay, then, hold on to Tulip for me so I can administer the injection."

"Tulip is a very good girl, aren't you? Yes you are."

Ally quickly injected the cat's flank. The feline let out an ear-splitting howl and turned out of Beverly's arms, clawing up Ally's lab coat and raking her paw down Ally's face.

"Ouch," Ally said as the cat's claws left four deep scratches on her face.

"Oh, now, that wasn't very nice, Tulip." Beverly plucked the cat off Ally and curled her against her ample bosom. "There, there, it's all over now."

Ally did her best to blink back tears as the scratches on her cheek burned. She was all for not having cats declawed, but wow, her face hurt.

"Excuse me for a moment." Ally ducked out of the exam room to wash her face at the sink. Looking in the small mirror, she grimaced at the blood welling from the scratches.

What was the chance they'd be healed up before her date with Noah? Slim to none.

Maybe it didn't matter. It was highly likely Noah was coming by later to cancel anyway. And seeing her face might be all the impetus he'd need. Apparently she wasn't going to get rid of her Calamity Jane persona anytime soon.

If ever.

Chapter Six

Ally returned to the lobby of her clinic to find Gramps chatting with Beverly. His eyes widened in surprise when he saw the scratches on her face, but the injury didn't prevent him from continuing the conversation.

"Oh, so Marlie is Fred and Darlene's granddaughter?" Gramps was saying, as if he knew exactly who Fred and Darlene were. Maybe he did; who knew? He wrinkled his brow and tapped his fingers on the counter top. "Remind me, Beverly, what's their last name again?"

"Crown," Beverly supplied. "Darlene told me Marlie has been a wreck since hearing the news. Marlie took Pricilla in, you know, after Hilda kicked Pricilla out, since the girl was coming and going at all hours and not working as much as Hilda thought she should."

"Really?" Gramps's lake-blue eyes gleamed with interest. "I didn't realize they lived together. I'm glad Marlie was kind enough to provide Pricilla a place to stay."

"Marlie is such a sweet girl," Darlene said. "Losing her mother at such a young age was very difficult for her. Especially since she never knew her father."

"I can certainly understand," Gramps agreed with a sympathetic smile. Ally couldn't believe how easily Gramps was able to get information from the ladies. Maybe Noah *should* let Gramps help with his investigation. "Do you know Steve Norris, a guy who works with Marlie?"

"I don't think so," Beverly said with a frown. She turned, and her abashed expression upon seeing Ally's face made her feel slightly better. "Oh dear, I'm very sorry, Dr. Winter. I don't know what got into Tulip." She turned to her pet. "Naughty kitty," she cooed in a way that hardly sent the message of wrongdoing.

"That's okay." Ally didn't smile, because it made her cheek hurt. She printed the invoice for Beverly and was relieved that she paid with a credit card that actually worked.

Always nice to have a paying customer. Even if she'd had to sacrifice her face in the process.

"Say bye-bye." Beverly moved Tulip's paw as if the cat were waving at them.

"Take care of yourself, Beverly," Gramps called. The minute the door shut behind the woman, he swung to look at Ally. "Her cat did that to your face?"

"Well, I didn't scratch myself," Ally retorted, short on patience. "Leave it up to you to pump her for information while I'm in the back, bleeding."

"I didn't know you were hurt," Gramps protested. Then he offered a sly grin. "But I did learn Marlie's last name is Crown and that she and Pricilla lived together, which could be very important." He waved a hand at her computer. "See if there are any Crown families in your client list."

Ally reluctantly did as he asked, relieved when she didn't find anyone by that name. "Nope, sorry."

"Ah well, it was worth a shot. And it's interesting that Hilda kicked her daughter out of the house." He narrowed his gaze, studying her face. "Those scratches look like they hurt."

They did, but there was no point in whining about it. "I'll be fine. Listen, I'm going to take Domino out for a quick break. Afterwards, we should head over to the Lakefront Café for lunch. We'll need to be back in time for Noah's visit."

"Are we bringing Roxy?" Gramps asked.

"Yes, I'd like to. Poor girl has been crated more than usual because of Domino."

"Sounds good," Gramps agreed.

Ally wrestled with keeping Domino on a short leash at her side during their brief outing. Maybe it was her imagination, but she thought he listened slightly better than usual. At least it seemed her arm didn't hurt as much.

Although maybe she was simply developing stronger muscles.

After crating Domino, she led Roxy out to the office area. "Ready, Gramps?"

"Yep." Leaning on his cane, he walked toward her.

"Are you sure you don't want me to drive?" Ally offered as she turned the sign from OPEN to CLOSED and locked the front door of her Furry Friends clinic.

"I'm not an invalid," Gramps said in a grumpy tone. "You're the one who told me I should go back to physical therapy. Walking is therapy."

She conceded to Gramps's stubborn streak and gave up the argument. Roxy trotted happily alongside them as they made their way slowly down Main Street. Ally had worked with Roxy enough that she could have taken the dog without a leash had the café not required one for their outdoor seating.

She bent to stroke Roxy's golden brown fur. "You're such a good girl, yes you are."

Roxy wagged her stubby tail in agreement.

"When are the Bentons coming to pick up Domino?" Gramps asked.

"Sometime late Sunday afternoon." She sent him a sidelong glance. "Why? It's not like Domino knows who murdered Pricilla."

"Maybe, maybe not," Gramps responded. "Dogs pick up all kinds of scents, don't they? Who's to say Domino didn't catch a whiff of the murderer from the scarf that was left around Pricilla's neck?"

Ally sighed and shook her head. Roxy had been a witness to the murder this past summer and had helped identify and bring down the killer.

But this wasn't the same situation. Gramps was grasping at straws, likely because they didn't have nearly as many clues to investigate this time.

Something she was secretly relieved about. At least this way, Gramps wouldn't get himself in trouble.

The café wasn't as busy as usual in the wake of the town's waning summer tourist season. It didn't take long for Ally and Gramps to be seated at a table.

"Sit, Roxy." The boxer instantly obeyed. "Good girl."

"Too bad Domino doesn't listen like that," Gramps said with a smile. "We could have brought both dogs with us."

Ally shuddered at the thought. "No way would I take a chance out in public with Domino and Roxy together. I may try to have them play together this afternoon inside the clinic."

Their server was someone different from yesterday, and Gramps actually looked disappointed that the young woman was wearing short sleeves.

"What can I get you to drink?" the woman, Cindy, asked.

"Iced tea for me," Ally said. "Gramps?"

"The same." He hesitated, then asked, "Cindy, did you know Pricilla?"

Cindy's face fell. "Yes, poor girl. I was sick to hear she'd been killed."

"She worked here, right?" Gramps pressed.

Now Cindy looked at him with suspicion. "Yes, in the kitchen. Why?"

"Just curious. Do you happen to know Steve Norris too? A guy with spiky brown hair who works at Electronics and More?"

Cindy frowned. "No. Excuse me, I'm very busy. I'll be back with your drinks shortly."

"What are you doing?" Ally demanded in a low whisper. "You can't ask everyone about Steve and Pricilla. It's rude."

"Why is it rude? It's a simple question, that's all." Gramps shifted in his seat. "How else are we going to learn more about these kids?"

Ally dropped her chin to her chest and mentally counted to five. Getting upset at Gramps for prying into a criminal investigation was like crying in the rain.

Nothing she could say or do would stop it.

"Speaking of which, why do you think Noah is coming by?" Gramps asked. He leaned forward eagerly. "Maybe he's uncovered more clues about Pricilla's murder."

"We'll find out soon enough," Ally said.

Cindy returned with their drinks, and they both placed their lunch orders: a Cobb salad for Ally, a cheeseburger for Gramps.

"What we need is a way to convince Noah to tell us more about the store robberies," Gramps said thoughtfully. "Or a way to trick him into telling us."

Ally glanced around the café, desperately trying to find a way to change the subject. Her gaze landed on Rosie Malone. The librarian loved to gossip; hadn't she already told Gramps about the mayor's fear that drug abuse was the cause of the robberies? Maybe it was the location of the library—close to city hall—but Rosie often knew what was going on before anyone else.

Even the police.

As if sensing Ally's gaze, Rosie looked at her. Instantly, the woman hurried toward them. "Ally, Oscar, how nice to see you."

"Hello, Rosie." Gramps struggled to his feet and greeted her with a nod. "How are you? What's new?"

"Oh, you know, murders and robberies." Rosie's eyes gleamed. "Never a dull moment in Willow Bluff."

Being the gentleman—and the nosy cop wannabe—he was, Gramps gestured to the empty chair. "You must be on a lunch break. Would you care to join us?"

"Oh, I'd love to!" Rosie smiled broadly. "If you don't mind."

"Please do," Ally said with a smile. "Although we already ordered, so we'll need to flag down our server."

Gramps waited until Rosie took her seat before easing into his own with a grimace. Ally could tell his hip was bothering him.

Rosie looked at Gramps with wide eyes. "Can you believe Pricilla Green is dead?"

"I know, it's a terrible tragedy." Gramps shook his head. "Any idea who did it?"

"None, and you know I've been keeping my ear to the ground, Oscar." Rosie leaned toward Gramps. "I'll be sure to let you know if I hear anything."

Gramps patted her hand. "I appreciate that, Rosie. Very much."

Ally was beginning to feel like she and Roxy were third wheels in this conversation, despite the fact that Rosie was in her late forties, far too young for Gramps at seventy-eight. Ally petted Roxy while trying to catch their server's eye.

There were more patrons in the café now, so it took almost fifteen minutes for Ally to flag Cindy down for Rosie's order.

"I'll bring out all the orders together, okay?" The wary expression on Cindy's face made Ally think the server hadn't put in her and Gramps's orders yet.

"Fine, fine," Gramps said with a wave of his hand. "No hurry."

Ally could tell he was enjoying himself. Which was nice, except she wanted to be back at the clinic well before Noah stopped in.

"Ally, what on earth happened to your face?" Rosie asked.

"Scratched by a cat." She resisted the urge to cover her injured cheek. She stirred her iced tea, glancing ruefully at her watch. Maybe she should be late for Noah's so-called appointment. Did she really want their date to be broken off in a face-to-face meeting?

Yeah, no.

"I learned Pricilla's best friend and roommate, Marlie Crown, is devastated about the murder," Gramps went on, as if he knew the family on a personal level. "And Steve Norris looked rough around the edges, too . . ." He paused, then said, "Do you know him?"

"Steve from Electronics and More?" Rosie nodded. "He helped me pick out a new computer a few weeks ago. Very nice young man."

"Yes, he seems to be." Gramps sent Ally a triumphant look. "I remember he has some amazing computer skills."

"Well, he sure seemed to know what he was doing. Helped me set the computer up for no charge." Rosie glanced around. "I only have a short time to eat. Where is our food?"

"I'm sure it will be here soon," Ally said, even though she was just as anxious to eat as Rosie was. Gramps, too, most likely, since he'd gotten the information he'd wanted.

By the time they'd finished eating, it was five minutes after one. Ally was anxious to go, knowing it would take Gramps extra time to walk back.

Gramps had paid for their meals, which was very sweet. Ally could tell Rosie was grateful; the woman held his hand longer than necessary.

"I've still got it." Gramps grinned as they headed back down Main Street.

Ally kept Roxy on her left so she could support Gramps with her right arm.

"You need to see if Steve's dog, Clancy, is due for his shots," Gramps said. "I'd like to grill him for more information."

"No way. Not happening." When he opened his mouth to argue, she held up a hand. "The Furry Friends clinic is my livelihood, Gramps. I'm not about to do something that might harm my reputation. Besides, Steve's dog was probably in recently, if he had to come by to get heartworm meds."

"Yeah, I guess." Gramps looked keenly disappointed.

Time to change the subject. "I'm going to take you home after our chat with Noah. The two dogs need exercise, and I don't want you getting hurt." The last thing she wanted was for the dogs to go berserk, bump into Gramps, and cause him to fall and break his other hip.

"Okay." The fact that he agreed so readily told her he was feeling tired. Darn it, she'd known three days in a row was too much for him.

As they drew closer to the clinic, she heard the agitated sound of Domino barking. Roxy whined in response, sensing something was amiss. Ally frowned, wondering what that was about. Domino hadn't loved being kenneled, but he hadn't barked like that before.

"Gramps, if you don't mind, let's go around back," she suggested. The back door to the clinic was closer to the kennels, and she thought Domino might need to be taken outside in a hurry.

"I don't mind," Gramps agreed.

She kept her right arm beneath his as they rounded the building. When she saw the back door hanging ajar, the area around the door handle badly damaged, she stopped short. "Not again!"

"No wonder Domino's barking," Gramps said.

Ally pulled out her phone and handed it to her grandfather. "Call 911, tell them about the break-in. I have to check on Domino."

"Take Roxy with you for protection," Gramps urged as he took the phone.

Ally swallowed hard and moved forward, tugging Roxy's leash. Using the hem of her shirt to avoid damaging any potential fingerprints, she carefully opened the door.

"Domino? Are you okay?" Ally called, gingerly crossing the threshold. Roxy wasn't growling, which she took as a good sign. The boxer had protected her in the past, and Ally believed she would again. Especially if there was someone still inside.

Domino's barking increased in volume. "I'm here, boy. It's okay, I'm here." She glanced around but didn't see anyone.

Had Domino's barking scared the burglar off? And why had someone tried to break in, anyway? Last summer, her clinic door had been smashed as a warning to back off from the murder investigation.

But this? It didn't make any sense. Especially during daytime hours.

Then again, she had put the CLOSED sign on the door. And their lunch had been prolonged by Rosie's joining them.

Ally ventured farther into the clinic with Roxy at her side. Nothing appeared disturbed.

The burglar had likely been scared off by Domino's barking. Which was a good thing.

"I'm coming, Domino," Ally said, returning to the rear portion of the clinic. Poor Domino had been barking for so long, there was foam around his mouth. "It's okay, boy." She quickly put Roxy in the empty crate next to his, then opened his door, clicking the leash onto his collar.

Even from here, she could hear Gramps yelling at the 911 operator—not in anger but to make himself heard.

Honestly, the man really needed to learn how to use a cell phone.

"Good boy, Domino, good boy." Ally took a moment to soothe the poodle. For once he didn't lunge at the leash or try to run off. Instead he began sniffing the floor as if picking up the burglar's scent.

But the intruder hadn't come all the way inside, had he? If he'd come in, he'd have seen Domino was in his crate and unable to hurt him.

Or her, she silently amended.

"Ally?" Gramps called. "You okay?"

"Fine, Gramps, the place is empty." Ally took Domino outside with her.

"The cops are on their way." Gramps returned her phone.

"That's good, thanks. Listen, go inside and get Roxy out of her crate. She'll protect you while I take Domino for a quick walk."

"I can do that," Gramps agreed. He frowned at the broken door. "I wonder why someone tried to break in. Do you think it's related to the Electronics and More robbery?"

"I highly doubt it." Ally had no idea what had possessed someone to try to break into her clinic. But as long as Domino was okay, she wasn't going to complain.

After Gramps headed inside, Ally walked the dog.

Rather than tugging on the leash, Domino kept his nose to the ground, sniffing with the intensity of a bloodhound. Ally had to pull him away from the broken clinic door, forcing him to empty his bladder.

But all too soon, Domino's nose was back on the ground. A chill rippled down the back of Ally's spine. Was it possible the poorly trained standard poodle had picked up the intruder's scent?

But—that would mean the burglar had gotten all the way inside.

She abruptly turned to stare at her clinic. Oh no! She hadn't checked her medication cabinet!

"Come, Domino," she said in a firm tone.

Domino eagerly followed the scent all the way back to her clinic. He'd have stayed in the doorway longer, but she dragged him inside.

Holding on to Domino's leash, she walked down to the end of the hall to her locked medication cabinet.

The cabinet was fine. She let out a deep sigh.

Then she remembered her petty cash drawer, located behind the main desk. Keeping Domino close, she strode through the lobby to where Gramps was sitting behind the counter.

"Everything okay?" Gramps asked as the two dogs greeted each other with wagging tails and licks. Domino must have been worn out from his frenzied barking, because he didn't try to chase Roxy.

"I'm not sure." Ally opened the drawer and sighed when she found it empty.

Apparently the intruder *had* come inside. At least far enough to clean out her petty cash.

Chapter Seven

A knock at the front door of the clinic reminded her that she hadn't unlocked it, having come in through the back. She hurried over to do so now, not surprised to see Noah standing there.

"What happened? Are you okay?" He frowned. "What happened to your face? Did the intruder hurt you?"

She'd almost forgotten her scratches. Amazing how a break-in and theft could do that. She put a hand up to her cheek. "Oh, this is from a cat I immunized earlier. I never saw the burglar. Come in, I'll show you the broken back door." She grimaced as Noah walked through the clinic behind her. "I was robbed. I'm missing about a hundred and fifty dollars from my petty cash drawer."

"You keep that much in the clinic?" Noah asked in surprise.

She shrugged. "Some customers pay cash." Like Valerie Wagner, Puddles's owner who'd tried to stiff her. "The bulk was in small bills, but whoever did this also stole all the change, too, which is weird."

Noah was inspecting the broken back door. He looked around, then asked, "Anything else missing?"

"No. My medication cabinet was untouched. Not that I have many narcotics in there, just a small amount for emergencies."

"Understandable," Noah agreed. He scowled and rubbed the back of his neck. "I'll have the door and your desk area dusted for prints."

"Uh, okay." She inwardly winced. "I'd better get Gramps away from the desk."

Noah groaned, and she knew he was already thinking about getting Gramps's fingerprints on file to rule out those of the burglar. Knowing Gramps, he'd be thrilled with the entire process.

"He was a Vietnam vet," she informed Noah. "I'm sure his prints are on file somewhere."

"No, unfortunately; military records that far back aren't in AFIS." Noah's expression was pained. "I'll need both you and Oscar to come in to have your fingerprints taken."

"Oh goody." She sighed.

"We can wait until your appointments are finished for the day," Noah offered.

"I don't have any." The blunt statement sounded worse than she'd intended. "This afternoon," she amended. After all, she'd immunized Tulip today and had the claw marks to prove it.

"Hey, both of you knock it off!" Gramps's raised voice along with thumps and bumps had Ally spinning around to see the dogs had begun to play, jumping on each other and nipping.

Not again?

"Roxy, heel!" Her sharp tone actually caught the boxer's attention. Domino ignored her as usual. "Roxy!"

The boxer loped toward her. Domino followed, but Ally grabbed Roxy's collar and shoved Domino back. "No, Domino. Sit!"

Of course, Domino didn't sit. Ally let go of Roxy's collar to grab his instead. He danced out of reach, then came around behind her to jump on Roxy again.

She wanted to scream, *Enough!* But suddenly Noah was there, pulling Domino away with a strong grip. She grabbed Roxy, then gestured toward the kennel area. "Will you please crate Domino in his kennel?"

"Sure. Come, Domino. You should know better than to misbehave in front of the ladies," Noah scolded.

His comment made her smile and also made her realize how nice it would be to employ a vet tech to help out. Not that she could afford one. Especially now. She wasn't rolling in clients, and what little cash she'd had on hand was gone.

She took Roxy upstairs, filled her water bowl, then closed the door to keep the dog in her apartment. When she returned, she overheard Gramps talking to Noah.

"We know Marlie Crown didn't show up for work today, and Steve Norris looks like he didn't sleep much, so why not just admit they're at the top of your suspect list?"

"Oscar, haven't I told you to stay out of my investigation?" Noah's tone was laced with exasperation.

"And haven't you figured out we can help you crack this thing? We did before, and we can do it again."

"We?" Noah echoed, pinning Ally with his intense green eyes as she crossed the lobby.

"Thanks for your assistance with Domino." Her attempt to change the subject didn't work.

"Ally, didn't Rosie Malone mention how Steve Norris helped set up her computer? I'm sure he's computer savvy enough to bypass a video feed. Isn't that how the robbers got away with several big-ticket items?" Gramps gave a curt nod. "Has to be an inside job, don't you think?"

And the eye tick was back. Ally closed her eyes and wished she didn't feel like a boxing referee between Gramps and Noah.

"What do you know about the store's video feed?" Noah demanded.

"I know plenty," Gramps retorted, although she knew he really didn't.

"Enough, Gramps. We need to head down to the police station to get our fingerprints taken and placed on file. When that's finished, I'll take you back to the Legacy House."

"Good idea," Noah muttered.

Gramps scowled. "You just wait until I solve this case for you."

Noah let out a snort of disgust.

"Why did you want to come to the clinic this afternoon, anyway?" Gramps asked. "Sounds like you're not here to fill us in on the case."

Her grandfather raised a good point. Ally swung to look at Noah. "Yeah, why did you want to stop in?"

For a moment Noah hesitated. Then he said, "I need to know where you were on Wednesday between five and eight PM."

It took her a minute to understand the implication. "You're asking if I have an alibi for the time frame of the murder?"

"Ally was with me," Gramps said firmly.

As much as Ally appreciated Gramps's support, his statement wasn't entirely true. "Is this because of Hilda's ridiculous allegations?"

"Ally, I just need to know where you were, okay?"

The way Noah avoided answering told her everything she needed to know. "Fine. I came back to the clinic around five. I ate a quick dinner in my apartment, then took Roxy for a walk. When I finished with that, I took Domino out to the Legacy House. I had pumpkin pie on the patio with Gramps. What time was that, Gramps, maybe seven fifteen or seven thirty? Then I took Domino down to the lakefront for his walk." A chill snaked down her spine. "Are you saying Pricilla was murdered shortly before I got there? I guess that could be right, although her body seemed cold when I checked for a pulse."

Noah sighed. "All I need to know is where you were, Ally. I can't talk about an ongoing investigation."

The time frame of the murder still rattled her. She'd truly believed the girl had been lying beneath the willow for a while, not just an hour or so. How long did it take a body to cool down after being murdered?

And why was she thinking such grisly thoughts?

She pulled herself together. "Well, Roxy can't vouch for me, but I'm sure someone must have seen me walking her." Ally turned toward Gramps. "And I have plenty of witnesses, like the widows, who saw me at the Legacy House eating pie."

"Okay, thank you. That helps a lot." Noah tucked his small notebook into the breast pocket of his dress shirt.

"Ridiculous," Gramps muttered in a hostile tone. "As if Ally would hurt a fly."

"Never mind, Gramps." Ally summoned a smile. "Are you ready? I'll drive us down to the police station."

"Speaking of which, your car has been parked behind the building all this time, right?" Gramps asked, a knowing gleam in his blue eyes.

"Yes, why?" Ally didn't understand where he was going with this.

"Don't you think it's odd the burglar chose to break in during the day, and while your car was parked right there?" Gramps demanded. "How did he or she know we were at the café for lunch when you could have just as easily been upstairs in the apartment?"

There was a brief silence as Gramps's question hung in the air.

She turned to look at Noah, arching a brow.

"You raise a good point, Oscar," Noah said with a thoughtful nod. "It seems likely the person who did this watched you and Ally walking away from the clinic, toward the café."

Ally didn't like the idea that she and Gramps had been watched. "It could be the burglar knew our routine was to eat lunch at the café each day." Maybe it would be smart to ask Harriet to make them a lunch for next week.

Unless Noah managed to solve the murder by then.

"See? I can be helpful, Detective." Gramps grinned with satisfaction.

"Oscar . . ." Noah pinched the bridge of his nose, then tried a different tack. "Ally, if it's okay with you, I'll stay here until the crime scene techs are finished."

"Fine." Who was she to argue? Even if Noah did manage to find and arrest the burglar, the cash would likely be long gone.

Maybe the whole drug theory wasn't so far off base. It would explain why someone would go to the effort of stealing her measly hundred and fifty bucks plus change.

"Let's go, Gramps." Ally crossed over to take her grandfather's arm.

Gramps glowered at Noah as they passed him to head outside to her car. Ally didn't see Noah's expression but felt certain the feeling was mutual.

The trip to the police station didn't take long. Gramps reveled in the process of being fingerprinted but then demanded that his prints be removed from the system as soon as they were finished being used to eliminate other prints from the crime scene.

"I'm not a criminal. No need for you to hold on to my personal information," Gramps said grumpily.

"We typically only keep them six months in cases like this," the female officer offered helpfully.

"Six months?" Gramps looked outraged as he dabbed at his dark fingertips with a tissue. "That's too long."

Ally tried not to show her frustration, but it wasn't easy. "What does it matter how long it takes? You're not going to embark on a crime spree, are you?"

"No, but I don't appreciate being treated like a criminal," Gramps said loudly, lifting his fist as they left the police station. "I have rights!"

She didn't bother to remind him that he'd loved being a suspect back in June after Marty Shawlin was murdered. Apparently, Gramps preferred to be on the legal side of crime fighting these days.

"Did you notice anyone watching us when we left the clinic?" Gramps asked, once she had him seated in the Honda.

"No, but I wasn't paying attention either." She'd enjoyed the recent lull in local crimes for Gramps to get all excited about. Before the murder this past June, Willow Bluff hadn't had a murder for over five years. After nearly becoming a victim herself, Ally realized, she'd been foolish to let down her guard.

Poor Pricilla. The girl might not have been the best worker in town, but she certainly hadn't deserved to die.

She thought again about how Domino had sniffed all along the back door where the burglar had broken in. Was the robbery of her petty cash related to Pricilla's murder? Or had Pricilla been killed by her boyfriend, Jake Hammond?

"Noah didn't mention anything about Pricilla's boyfriend, did he?" She glanced at Gramps.

"No, he didn't." Gramps tapped his hand on the armrest. "I wonder if the boy has a decent alibi. Otherwise, why was Noah at the clinic grilling you?"

"Maybe Noah wants to cover all possibilities." She sent Gramps a narrow look. "Isn't that what the cops do on *Dateline*?"

"Yeah, yeah," Gramps agreed. Ally didn't want to tell him that she'd begun watching the show too, just to see what he found so intriguing. From the few episodes she'd watched, the killer was almost always the victim's spouse or boyfriend/girlfriend.

Which meant Jake Hammond should have been Noah's prime suspect.

For that matter, Hilda should have been all over the possibility of Jake being involved in her daughter's death too.

So why all the scrutiny of Ally?

Especially from Noah?

* * *

After dropping Gramps off at the Legacy House and declining Harriet's invite to dinner, Ally returned to her clinic. Noah was still there, although it looked as though the crime scene techs were nearly finished.

"Sorry about the mess." Noah gestured to the fine black fingerprint powder that covered the back door and the entire area of her desk and counter.

"It's okay." She had plenty of time to clean these days—at least when she didn't have to walk two dogs.

Noah peered at her face. "Those scratches look painful."

She shrugged. What could she say? Being scratched, bitten, pooped on, and thrown up on was part of her life. It wasn't necessarily the animal's fault. She resisted the urge to touch her wounds. "I just hope they heal without a scar."

"Have you had a doctor look at them?" Noah asked.

"No need. They're not deep enough for sutures." Just enough to make her look like Ms. Frankenstein. "Noah, will you please explain why I seem to be a suspect in Pricilla's murder?"

"You're not," he said quickly. Too quickly.

"Because I have an alibi?" She wasn't sure why she was pressing the matter. She knew she hadn't killed the girl, and even if she had, why would she then take Domino for a walk there to find her?

"Ally, I can't talk about this with you." Noah actually looked upset. "I'm sorry, but this is rather—political."

"No, really? I hadn't guessed."

He didn't appreciate her sarcasm. "Once I verify your alibi, you'll be in the clear."

"I'm in the clear because I didn't do it!" she fired back in a rare spurt of anger. "Honestly, Noah, you're wasting time better spent finding the real culprit."

"I promise you, I'm working all angles," he responded mildly. He hesitated, then said, "Unfortunately, until I am able to verify your alibi, we can't be seen together, you know, outside of work-type stuff."

She'd expected him to break their date, but it still hurt. Far more than it should. "Fine. Now if you're finished here, I need to take care of the dogs and clean up."

"Ally, I'm sorry." Noah looked truly contrite.

"Whatever." She thrust a hand through her springy, out-of-control hair. "Just leave. I have things to do."

He looked as if he wanted to stay something more, but only nodded and turned away. Then he spun to face her. "What about your broken door?"

She'd forgotten about that. "I'll figure it out."

Noah frowned. "I don't think it's safe for you to stay here. Maybe you should go to the Legacy House for the night?"

"Harriet doesn't like dogs, and I'm responsible for two of them now." She waved a hand. "Just go. I'll figure something out."

Noah didn't appear satisfied but didn't argue. After he was gone, Ally blew out a breath and went over to examine the door for herself. The door handle was broken, the edge of the doorjamb splintered. The door closed but didn't stay that way because of the fractured frame. The entire thing needed to be replaced very soon, but not now.

She went up to her apartment and dug out her small tool kit, the one she'd purchased to make minor repairs. Picking up a hammer and nails, she returned to the broken door. Within minutes she had it nailed shut.

A temporary fix, and inconvenient as far as getting in and out of her apartment, but the best she could manage at the moment.

Using the front door, she took Roxy outside first, then Domino. She kept them in their side-by-side kennels as she cleaned the clinic.

Not the best way to spend a Friday night, but not the worst. She considered heading back to the Legacy House for dessert but decided against it.

The stress of the day had worn her down. Between Gramps's determination to help solve the case and being considered a suspect herself, she'd had enough.

And the thought of her and Gramps having been watched as they left the clinic to go to the café wouldn't leave her alone. Walking outside after dark wasn't something she looked forward to.

But she couldn't shirk her duties to the animals in her care either. Especially the naughty Domino.

Roxy had been able to get out for a bit at lunchtime, but poor Domino had spent more time in his crate than she liked. Granted, much of that was because he didn't know how to behave, but that wasn't entirely his fault either.

After heating and eating a frozen dinner, she decided to once again take Roxy out first, then Domino. As she had on Wednesday night, she'd take Domino for a longer walk, heading through town. At least that way he'd be less likely to stumble across another dead body.

She might never walk a dog at Lakefront Park again.

Thankfully, Main Street was well lit. Ally kept a wary eye out for anyone paying her too much attention as she walked Roxy. She didn't see anything but couldn't quite get rid of the itch along the back of her neck.

Then it was Domino's turn. She shortened the leash and struggled to keep him at her side. "Heel, Domino. Heel!" She wrenched him back.

His tongue lolled to the side, giving the impression that he was happy.

"You know, if you didn't play so rough with Roxy, we could walk together."

As they passed by the grocery store, Domino abruptly stopped and put his nose to the ground, sniffing intently.

Had he picked up the scent of the burglar? Ally swallowed hard and glanced around. No one was paying any attention that she could see.

She told herself she was imagining things. Domino was just finding interesting scents. He wasn't a police dog by any stretch of the imagination.

But he continued sniffing, veering away from the grocery store, down through the parking lot. Ally's pulse kicked up as she followed the poodle's lead.

He stopped and sniffed the empty parking space between two cars. He stood there for a good five minutes, just sniffing, which wasn't like him. Even though there was an empty french fry container lying on the ground.

Had Domino been following the enticing aroma of french fries? Or that of the burglar who'd left the container behind?

Chapter Eight

Ally woke up the following morning to Roxy's nose in her face. It was her typical greeting from the boxer, so it was difficult to be annoyed. Still, it would be nice to sleep in on a Saturday. "Yeah, yeah." She yawned and groaned, staggering through the apartment to get Roxy's leash.

She was down at the bottom of the stairs with Roxy before she remembered she'd hammered the back door shut. Dragging a hand through her unruly curls, she turned back upstairs to pull a hoodie over her ratty sleep shirt before heading downstairs again. Forced to take Roxy through the clinic to the front door, she grimaced as they passed Domino's crate, sending him into an excited barking frenzy.

"Your turn soon," she promised.

The fall temperatures were a little chilly in the early-morning hours, so she was grateful for the hoodie. Although being dressed in her sleepwear on Main Street wasn't fun. Thankfully, it was early enough that there weren't too many people out and about.

"I gotta get that back door fixed today, Roxy," she muttered as the dog did her business. "I don't want to be out here every morning where people can see me."

Roxy nudged her hand as if in agreement.

"Good girl." Ally took a moment to pet the dog, then headed back inside. After placing Roxy in a crate, she took Domino out.

He lunged forward, eager to get outside. "Heel! Domino, heel!"

She yanked the leash, forcing him to her side, but he didn't seem to notice, leaning forward with a strength that threatened to knock her flat on her face.

Just what she didn't need, a broken nose to go along with the scratches on her face.

"Domino!" She yanked again, harder, pulling him to her side. Then she stopped and forced him to sit.

He finally began to listen and was walking more calmly at her side by the time she returned to the clinic. She made a mental note to put a handful of training treats in her pocket for later. Domino had potential, and maybe if she kept working with him, he'd learn how to behave.

Of course, once Domino was back with the Bentons, he'd likely fall right back into his previous bad habits. Unless she could convince Kayla to keep him compliant.

Ally showered, changed, and ate breakfast, thinking about the fact that she didn't have any appointments scheduled for the day. She was glad the pets in Willow Bluff were healthy but really wished she had something to occupy her mind.

Anything to keep her from ruminating over Noah and Pricilla's murder.

She took Roxy with her down to the clinic and decided to let both dogs play together. They'd done fairly well yesterday, at least for a short while.

The dogs jumped and nipped at each other, making her wince. Yet she hoped they'd wear each other out, so she did her best to ignore them while she made arrangements with a local handyman to have her back door fixed. George had been recommended by Rosie Malone. George agreed to be there by two in the afternoon, which was a relief.

Next, she checked her computer for animals who were still overdue for immunizations. Pulling up her delinquents list, she gaped in surprise when she saw Clancy, the mixed-breed dog owned by Steve Norris, on the list. She'd placed a reminder call exactly four weeks ago. But Steve hadn't brought Clancy in, despite stopping in to buy his heartworm meds.

A crash drew her attention, and she jumped up when she realized the dogs had knocked over one of the chairs in the waiting room. "No! Sit!"

Roxy sat, but Domino didn't. He lunged at Roxy, but Ally shouted again, "*No!*"

Domino reared back, and when he sat, she pulled out a small treat. "Good boy."

He scarfed down the treat, then put his nose to the ground as if searching for more. Ally righted the chair, then stood with her hands on her hips. "Behave, Domino, or I'll have to put you back in your crate."

His tongue lolled to the side, as if he were smiling in agreement. The two dogs must have already worn each other out, because while they went back to playing, it wasn't nearly as out of control as before.

Ally knew it was too early for reminder calls, but she made a list of the pets who were overdue. There were only two, Clancy and

Frankie the Siamese cat. Several pets were due later in the month, though, so she performed the painstaking task of comparing those who were due to those who'd already made appointments.

By ten o'clock, she felt safe making calls. To her surprise, Clancy's owner picked up right away. "Hello?"

"Mr. Norris? This is Dr. Winter at Furry Friends. Your dog Clancy is overdue for his immunizations. I have openings today if you're not busy, or next week as well."

"Uh, yeah, okay. I'll see if we can get Clancy in today."

"Great!" Ally could barely contain her enthusiasm. Not just because she had a paying customer but also because Steve would come in while Gramps wasn't there to interrogate him. A win-win in her book. "Say ten thirty?"

"That should work. Clancy will be there soon." Steve disconnected, and Ally glanced over to where the two dogs were lying stretched out on the floor next to each other.

"I guess miracles can happen." She looked at them in awe. Yet as much as she'd liked having them out of their crates, she knew they'd have to go back inside before Clancy arrived. Adding a third dog, one she didn't know, to the mix was not a good idea.

She stood near the counter and said, "Roxy, come."

The boxer instantly got up on all fours and came over, dropping onto her haunches beside Ally. "Good girl." She slipped Roxy a treat.

Domino was already up too, but she held up her hand. "No, stay."

Domino looked at her uncertainly. "Stay," she warned again.

He didn't move.

"Domino, come." As she gave the command, she put her hand in her pocket for another treat. Domino bounded over, and while he didn't sit nicely like Roxy, he did well, so she rewarded him with a treat.

"You know, maybe I should take some training lessons myself so I can help teach dogs like you, Domino." Ally scratched his fur, and when Roxy nudged her, she provided the same treatment to her own dog.

She had both dogs back in their respective crates before she heard the bell over her door chime.

Ally frowned when she saw a woman in her early fifties standing there with a dog on a leash. "Ah, Clancy?" she asked questioningly.

"Dr. Winter? Yes, this is Clancy. My son said he's overdue for his shots?"

"Yes, he is. Thanks for bringing him in, Ms. Norris." Ally gestured toward the exam room. "This way, please."

"Come, Clancy." Ms. Norris tugged on the dog's leash. He was sniffing around the interior of the clinic, no doubt picking up Roxy's and Domino's scents.

"I just spoke to your son, Steve. I expected him to bring Clancy in."

"Oh yeah, well, he was already running late for work, so I told him to go ahead and I'd bring the dog." The woman rolled her eyes. "Not like he can afford the immunizations anyway."

Even though he had a job? Ally simply nodded, understanding that Steve still lived with his parents. The way a lot of the younger generation did nowadays.

Good thing Gramps wasn't here. He'd have been very disappointed not to be able to grill a suspect for information.

If Steve Norris even was a suspect at all.

"I understand Steve was close to Pricilla," Ally said after she finished immunizing Clancy. He'd taken the injection with only a small whimper and eagerly gobbled up the treat she provided when he was finished.

"What?" Ms. Norris looked surprised. "Well, I guess the kids all hung out together, but I wouldn't say they were really close. They weren't seeing each other or anything." She lifted Clancy to the floor.

"Oh, sorry, I must have confused him with someone else, then," Ally said hastily. She knew her interrogation skills weren't on par with Gramps's, although she'd tried.

"Steve mentioned that Colin Felton was close to Pricilla." Ms. Norris shrugged. "It's such a shock to have something like that happen right here in Willow Bluff!"

"I know, it's terrible." Ally led the way back to the main counter.

Ms. Norris didn't say anything more about her son or Pricilla as Ally printed the invoice. Thankfully, the woman paid the bill and took Clancy on his way.

Ally wrote the name *Colin Felton* on a slip of paper, feeling good about having gotten some key information from Ms. Norris.

Wait a minute. She wasn't actually trying to help Gramps solve this thing, was she? Ally reached over to crumple the note in a ball, then drew her hand back.

Did Colin Felton work at Electronics and More? Did it matter if he did? Gramps would likely come up with some new wild theory, despite the fact that there was no hard evidence indicating that the robberies were related to Pricilla's murder. Still, Pricilla's car being in the store's parking lot was strange.

Ally took a moment to wash down the exam room. She heard the bell over her door ring and hurried into the lobby. She stopped short when she saw Gramps standing there.

"What—how did you get here?"

"Caught a ride from Rosie Malone." Using his cane, Gramps thumped toward the desk. "I've been trying to come up with ways to find out more about the robberies. I think we need to take another trip over there."

"Gramps," Ally said with a sigh. What was it with Rosie and her grandfather? "Noah will be upset if we poke around."

"Why? It's a free country." Gramps sat down behind the desk, and she immediately winced when he picked up the slip of paper. "Who's Colin Felton?"

Against her better judgment, Ally filled Gramps in, telling him that Steve Norris lived at home with his parents and apparently hadn't been as close to Pricilla as they'd been led to believe. But a kid named Colin Felton was known to be close with the victim.

"But I thought her boyfriend's name was Jake Hammond," Gramps said.

"He is, but guys and girls can be friends without, you know . . ." She waved a hand, feeling her cheeks flush.

"I suppose." Gramps eyed her keenly. "That's good work there, Ally. I wonder if Colin was the guy with the dark hair we overheard talking yesterday. The one who mentioned how they were instructed to cooperate with the police."

"No idea," Ally said. "Although if so, he didn't sound too broken up about Pricilla's death."

Gramps tapped the note thoughtfully. "If Steve Norris isn't close to Pricilla, why did he look like something Domino dragged in two days after her murder? Unless he was the one who did the deed?"

"Gramps," she warned, "you need to stop jumping to conclusions."

"Who, me?" he asked innocently. "I'm just doing my best to help that detective of yours."

Noah was far from being hers; they hadn't even gone on one date by themselves and wouldn't anytime soon, but she didn't bother to correct her grandfather.

"Electronics and More, then lunch," Gramps said firmly. "Come on, Ally. I didn't convince Rosie to bring me out here for nothing."

"Fine." What could she do? Gramps might just ask Rosie to take him to the stupid store regardless. "But I have to be back in time for George to fix the back door."

"What time is that?" Gramps asked.

"At two o'clock." She glanced around the clinic. "Let me take the dogs out first, then we can go."

The dogs were still tired from their romp, so it didn't take her long to get them outside for their respective bathroom breaks. Ally had Gramps wait for her out front while she went around back to get the car.

"Just what do you think this trip is going to accomplish?" she asked him as he was latching his seat belt.

"I don't know, but we need *something* to go on," Gramps said with a sigh. "This case is flailing in the wind."

"How do you know that?" Ally tried not to sound irritated. "Noah might already have a suspect in custody."

"Is your date back on?" Gramps arched a brow.

"No." No date tonight or any other night. She scowled and dropped the subject. Going to Electronics and More would be a waste of time, but these days she had more time than she knew what to do with.

Definitely time to look into training options. Maybe Kayla would be her first client. It had been Gramps's idea originally, but she was seriously thinking it would be a great income stream for her business.

No job to small . . . or too big, she mused silently.

Ally pulled into the parking lot, noting that the yellow crime scene tape had been removed. As had Pricilla's rusty brown car. She wondered if Noah had gotten any sort of DNA evidence from it but knew that if she asked, he wouldn't tell her.

Despite it being a Saturday, the store wasn't crowded. At least, not yet.

She helped her grandfather from the car. He leaned on his cane as they headed inside.

"Keep your eyes peeled for Jake Hammond or Colin Felton," Gramps said in a loud whisper.

"Shhh." At this rate, he might as well use the store intercom to track the guys down.

They didn't see anyone for several minutes as Ally wandered aimlessly down one aisle, then the next. Nothing grabbed her interest, partially because she didn't have extra money to spend.

Then again, she was more apt to buy doggy toys and treats than items for herself.

"Over there." Gramps nudged her with his elbow. She saw a red-haired young man with a freckled face near the phone section. Gramps immediately headed toward him, leaving Ally little choice but to follow in his wake.

"Young man?" Gramps called. Freckle Face turned toward them. Ally inwardly groaned when she noticed that his name tag read Colin.

"I have a problem with my phone," Gramps said as Colin stepped forward.

"Sure. What seems to be the issue?" Colin's eyes were swollen as if he'd been crying, but his tone was polite.

"People keep saying I'm talking too loud." Gramps glanced at Ally, then turned back to Colin.

"You probably have the volume set too high. I can take a look if you'd like," Colin offered.

"Say, aren't you one of Pricilla's friends?" Gramps put a sincere and compassionate expression on his face. "I'm so sorry for your loss."

"I am—er—*was* her friend." Colin swallowed hard, his expression full of sorrow. "I still can't believe she's gone. How did you know Cilla?"

Cilla? Ally guessed it was no surprise they had a nickname for her. Pricilla was quite an old-fashioned name for a twenty-one-year-old.

"She cleaned the Legacy House where I live." Gramps offered an expression full of grave concern. "Such a nice girl."

Personally, she thought Gramps was laying it on a bit thick. No one who knew Pricilla was likely to call her a nice girl. But he was leading this interrogation of Colin Felton, not her.

"Yeah, she was cool," Colin agreed. "I—we were close." He had the puppy-dog eyes that made her think Colin had some unrequited feelings for Pricilla. "Oh, er, did you want me to look at your phone?"

"Oh, yeah." Gramps patted his pockets and pulled out the small disposable flip phone she'd given him. It was a little embarrassing, but it wasn't as if Gramps knew anything about using a smartphone.

"Oh, uh, hmm." The simple phone seemed to have stumped Colin. "I'm not sure how to use this one, sorry." The kid looked at Ally, who shrugged.

"Well, that's okay, I guess." Gramps tucked the phone in his pocket. "Say, is Jake working today? He's a friend of my great-nephew."

"Uh, no. Jake doesn't work here. Even so, he's barely left our apartment since Pricilla died. I've been trying to help cheer him up."

"Oh, you live with him, then?" Gramps asked. "I have a card— or, well, it might be in the car." He patted his pockets again. "Yeah, I left the card in my car."

"I can bring him the card if you want to grab it," Colin offered. A woman approached from the other side of the aisle, grabbing Colin's attention. "Excuse me."

Colin left, and Gramps put a gnarled hand on Ally's arm. "Did you hear that? Those two share an apartment! Just like Marlie and Pricilla!"

"Yes, I heard, but what does that mean as far as the investigation?" Ally asked, subtly pulling Gramps farther away from Colin and the customer so as not to draw their attention.

"Well, you were saying that Steve fella lives with his mother, which got me to thinking about the other kids who work here. Might be harder for a kid who lives with his parents to sneak away to kill someone."

"Maybe." Ally hadn't done much sneaking out as a teenager. She'd been the nerdy science geek, not part of the cool crowd of cheerleaders and football players. "But you're the one who said Steve had the computer skills needed to bypass the video feed."

"True." Gramps glanced around the store, obviously looking for another employee to chat with. "Maybe a group of them are working together on the robberies."

"That just means less cash to go around," Ally pointed out. She thought about her missing hundred and fifty dollars. "And really, it seems silly for a group of them to rob the store where they work. Pretty obvious, if you ask me. How much do you think they're getting for the stolen items anyway? It can't be much. Not enough to risk going to jail over."

Gramps waved an impatient hand. "I don't know how much those newfangled phones and computers cost. That's not the point. The robberies are secondary to finding out who murdered Pricilla Green."

Professor Plum killed her with a knife in the library. Ally had enjoyed playing the board game Clue, but in fun, not in real life. She gave herself a mental shake.

"Let's go, Gramps. Time for lunch." She gently tugged on his arm.

"Okay, fine," Gramps grumbled. "But we didn't learn very much. I'd like to know where Jake and Colin's apartment is."

"Well, we can't ask for his address. I doubt he'd tell us anyway," Ally pointed out.

Gramps brightened. "I have an idea." He shook off her arm and clumped back over to where Colin was finishing up with his customer.

"Colin, would you do me a favor?" Gramps asked.

The freckled kid eyed him warily. "Like what?"

Gramps pulled a crumped piece of paper from his pocket— remnants of a receipt, Ally noted. "I forgot the card for Jake; it's not in the car after all. If you'd give me your address, I'll mail it. I sure do feel bad for that young man losing his girlfriend like that."

Colin hesitated, then reluctantly took the paper. He scribbled the address and handed it back. "Yeah, it's a sad day. The funeral is scheduled for next Monday, if you're interested."

"Oh, I'm very interested. Thanks, Colin." Gramps tucked the address away and followed Ally outside.

"I can't believe you did that," she scolded.

"It's a lead we can't afford to ignore," Gramps said firmly. "And it's to your benefit as well, Ally. The sooner we catch the murderer, the sooner you and that detective of yours can have your dinner date."

Ally shook her head wryly but couldn't help being intrigued by the idea. Maybe Gramps was right. Solving this case meant life could get back to normal.

And secretly, she very much wanted to have that dinner date with Noah.

Chapter Nine

G ramps insisted on doing a drive-by past Jake and Colin's apartment building. It was a small structure, a four-family unit that appeared to be in decent shape. The building was only a few blocks down from the grocery store, and Ally remembered how Domino had sniffed all around the empty parking spot there yesterday.

Logically, she knew everyone in town went to the grocery store at some point, so the apartment's proximity didn't necessarily mean anything. Domino had likely been looking for food, not a suspect in Pricilla's murder.

"Slow down," Gramps said, lowering his window.

Ally noticed he was staring at a dark-haired girl, wearing a blue Electronics and More shirt, who was in an intense conversation with Steve Norris.

"You owe me," she was saying harshly.

"I know, I know." The young man hunched his shoulders. "I'll catch you later, I promise." Steve quickly dodged around the girl and strode away.

The girl scowled and stalked toward a black sedan that sported more rust than Pricilla's Dodge. Seconds later, she drove away.

"You think that was Marlie?" Gramps asked. "She's wearing the same shirt as the other employees."

Ally shrugged. "I have no idea. And it's not against the law for Marlie to talk to Steve about a favor. Are you hungry or not?"

"I'm hungry," Gramps agreed, although he gazed thoughtfully after the black sedan as they drove to lunch.

Ally parked as close as possible to the Lakeview Café, then helped Gramps out of the Honda.

"Thanks," Gramps muttered, leaning heavily on his cane.

Ally glanced warily up at the dark clouds gathering overhead. "We don't have Roxy, so we may as well head inside to eat today. Looks like a storm is coming in from the lake."

"Fine with me." Gramps hadn't said much on the drive over, and she sensed his brain was working hard to come up with a new theory around the crime.

The hostess sat them in a small booth. Gramps wanted to face the doorway, no doubt to keep his eye out for someone new to inter-rogate, so she slid in across from him. "I'm going to take you home after lunch, okay, Gramps?"

"Not yet. We still have more work to do on the case," he protested.

"Gramps, I know very well you coming to the clinic all those days in a row has been exhausting. Maybe you should spend some time with Tillie. How is her arm doing?"

"She's fine, and we played cribbage after breakfast this morn-ing, so it's not like she's being neglected." He waited as their server, a woman named Mags, brought their drinks and took their order. Then he leaned forward to pin Ally with an intense gaze. "Here's what we've learned. Jake and Colin share an apartment and it could be that Colin has feelings for Pricilla, despite the fact she was dating

Jake. What if Pricilla was in the process of breaking up with Jake, intending to date Colin instead, so Jake gets mad, they have a fight, and he strangles her?"

"That's pure supposition, Gramps." She glanced around the interior of the café, hoping no one could overhear their conversation. She lowered her voice. "Noah needs a pesky little thing called proof."

"I know, but having a theory helps you to focus on where to find that proof." Gramps gave a stubborn nod. "That's what the cops do on *Dateline* all the time. You'll find out that I'm onto something soon enough."

She couldn't deny that some of Gramps's theories had worked out fairly well in the past. But Roxy had been the real heroine in closing that last case. Without Roxy's keen scent and courage, Ally knew she might not be sitting across from Gramps today.

Suppressing a shiver, she took a sip of her iced tea.

"We need to go to Pricilla's funeral," Gramps said.

Ally gasped. Her tea went down the wrong pipe, sending her into a coughing fit.

"You okay?" Gramps laboriously stood and came over to thump her on the back. "Do ya need the Heimlich?"

"I'm fine," she wheezed between coughs. She waved him back to his seat. "Sit down." *Cough, cough.* "I'm fine." *Cough.* Tears welled in her eyes and coursed down her cheeks. She brushed them away, then winced as she accidently pulled a small scab off the cat scratches.

"You don't look fine." Gramps eyed her critically as he sat back in his seat.

Gee, thanks. Ally took a cautious sip of her iced tea this time. The coughing eased, which was good. "There's no reason to attend Pricilla's funeral."

"Oh yes there is. The murderer often attends the funeral of their victim. Besides, your detective will likely be there too." Gramps's gaze focused on a spot over her shoulder. "Well, well, speak of the devil. Hello, Detective Jorgenson."

Ally turned in her seat, mortified to see Noah heading toward them. He wasn't smiling, indicating that this wasn't a social visit.

At least his eye wasn't twitching. *Yet.*

"Oscar, Ally." Noah made an imposing figure standing next to their table. "Do you have a minute?"

"Not really," Ally said.

At the exact same time, Gramps responded, "Sure, have a seat."

She leveled a sour look at her grandfather but scooted over to give Noah room to sit beside her. She hugged the wall; the bench wasn't wide enough for both of them. Noah's enticing woodsy scent filled her senses, making her dizzy.

"I saw you leave the store," Noah said, his expression serious. "Second day in a row you went there and came out without buying anything."

"So?" Gramps shrugged. "It's not a crime to shop without purchasing something."

"No, but it is a crime to interfere with an ongoing criminal investigation," Noah shot back. "I've told you to stay out of it. Don't force me to arrest you."

"You wouldn't," Gramps said.

"Don't bet on it." Noah turned to look at Ally. "Why are you encouraging him?"

His disparaging tone put her back up. "Gramps has a right to go to the store if he wants. And we haven't done anything to mess up your precious investigation."

Noah's green eyes held hers for a long moment. Her mouth went dry, and she told herself to ignore the surge of attraction she always felt around him.

Noah finally looked away and softened his tone. "Listen, I care about both of you and don't want either of you to get hurt."

Like last time. The unspoken words hung in the air between them.

She didn't want anyone to get hurt either. Especially not Gramps. "I understand, Noah, and appreciate your concern. But we really haven't done anything. Don't worry, I'm taking Gramps back to the Legacy House after lunch."

"Don't forget you have George coming to fix your door at two," Gramps reminded her.

"I'll have you home well before then," Ally retorted.

"Yeah? Well, I can always get a ride back into town if needed," Gramps said with a scowl. "Got myself to your clinic today, didn't I?"

Ally sighed. "Yes, you sure did."

Their conversation was interrupted when Mayor Cromlin approached their table. "Detective, I hope the Willow Bluff Police are checking the abandoned farmhouse on a routine basis, as I've requested."

"Yes, ma'am," Noah agreed. "The patrol officers swing by at least once per night."

"Only once?" The mayor frowned. "I told the chief of police I will not tolerate drug use in this town."

"I don't want to see drug use here either," Noah assured her. "Trust me, we're keeping an eye on the place. There's been no sign of drug use, and no one has been arrested for drug possession."

"That's something, I guess." The mayor sniffed, glancing at Ally and Gramps. "I'm hopeful the place will be leveled before the snow flies. It's about time that land was put to good use."

"That would certainly help curtail any activities going on there," Noah conceded.

"Well." Mayor Cromlin forced a tight smile. "Enjoy your lunch."

"What's going on at the abandoned farmhouse?" Gramps asked.

"Nothing for you to worry about," Noah said firmly.

Mags brought their meals, frowning at Noah. "I didn't realize you had someone joining you. Do you need a menu, Detective?"

"No, thanks." Noah rose to his feet. Ally instantly missed his warmth. "Take care, Ally. Oscar."

The minute Noah left the café, Gramps grinned. "We're onto something, Ally."

"What are you talking about?"

"We must be on the right track, or that detective of yours wouldn't have bothered to warn us off." Gramps's blue eyes gleamed. "He's been at the store both days we were there, which makes me think the robberies are connected to Pricilla's murder. That means we absolutely have to go to Pricilla's funeral. You know, pay our respects."

"Pay our respects?" Ally narrowed her gaze. "Yeah, right. You didn't like the girl, Gramps."

He waved a finger at her. "Now, now, don't speak ill of the dead."

Good grief. She rolled her eyes and took a bite of her salad. As much as she didn't want Gramps to be anywhere near Pricilla's funeral, she'd feel better if she was with him to help keep him in line.

Although keeping Gramps from crossing the line would be a monumental task. One she wasn't likely to succeed in carrying out.

* * *

Ally's cell phone rang as she was paying their tab. She put on her best professional voice. "This is Dr. Winter at the Furry Friends Veterinary Clinic. How may I help you?"

"I think Goldie had a stroke!" The woman's voice on the other end of the line was trembling.

"Okay, what's your name?"

"Nikki Jo Shoofs."

"Okay, Nikki Jo, what kind of pet is Goldie?" Ally finished with the bill and gestured for Gramps to follow her outside. A slight drizzle was falling, but she was too focused on the call to care.

"Goldie's a golden retriever." Nikki Jo let out a sob. "Oh, it's awful. She's drooling and won't eat and just lays around doing nothing. I afraid something terrible has happened to her."

"Bring Goldie to the clinic. I'll be happy to examine her, okay?" Ally pinched the phone between her ear and her shoulder to help Gramps into the Honda. "I'll be there in less than five minutes."

"Thanks, Dr. Winter."

Ally quickly disconnected and went around to the driver's side. She was glad to have a paying customer but sincerely hoped the golden hadn't actually suffered a stroke. The drooling could be the result of a foreign object being lodged in the back of the animal's throat, or something worse, like something caught in her intestines that would require surgery.

"Guess I'm not heading back to the Legacy House after all," Gramps said with a satisfied smile.

"Not yet." She glared at him. "But you will be as soon as I'm finished with Goldie."

"Sure, sure." Gramps sat back in his seat. "Unless it takes longer than you expect. And George might show up early."

According to Rosie, George did good work, but in his own sweet time, so Ally didn't argue. She pulled up in front of the clinic and unlocked the door before helping Gramps out of the car and inside. The drizzle was still falling, and she hoped it would blow over soon. She took a minute to drive the Honda around back to its parking spot. Dodging raindrops, she raced back around to enter through the front.

The sooner George fixed her back door, the better.

Ally heard Roxy and Domino barking as she entered. Glancing at her watch, she winced. There wasn't enough time to take them outside.

If Gramps were steadier on his feet and Domino weren't so poorly trained, she'd ask him for help. Again, she thought wistfully of the days when she had employed veterinary techs.

Telling herself the dogs would be fine for a little while, she went around to the computer and searched for Goldie and Nikki Jo Shoofs.

She found them and quickly scanned what little information Dr. Hanson had on file. The man had taken a minimalist approach to record keeping, so there wasn't much. Goldie was two years old and up-to-date on all her shots.

The bell over the door rang, and Ally turned to greet her client. "Nikki Jo? I'm Dr. Winter."

The woman, who was roughly her own age, had obviously been crying, and her clothes were damp from the rain. She had Goldie on a leash, but the animal was clearly lethargic.

Not good. Ally came around and let the dog sniff her before leading them into the exam room.

Ally helped Nikki Jo lift the golden onto the exam table. She pulled out her stethoscope and quickly listened to the animal's heart and lungs. Goldie's heart rate was a bit too high, but not dangerously so.

"When did this start?" Ally asked. She picked up a flashlight and gently pried the dog's jaw open.

"Earlier this morning." Nikki Jo's eyes filled with fresh tears. "I should have called right away, but I thought she'd get better."

"Ah, I see the problem." Ally flashed Nikki Jo a reassuring smile. "Goldie has a stick lodged in the back of her throat. This sometimes happens with golden retrievers and Labs; they tend to grab and carry sticks. They also chew on them."

"Really? A stick is lodged in her throat?" Nikki Jo looked dumbfounded.

"Yes, but this is easily taken care of." Ally was relieved that the problem wasn't too serious. "I'm going to give Goldie some medication to relax her so I can remove it, okay?"

"Okay." Nikki Jo looked relieved. "I think I can handle that."

"Hold on to her, please." Ally stepped away from the exam table and went into the back to her medication cabinet. Again Roxy and Domino began to bark, each seemingly trying to outdo the other.

"Hang on, I'll be there very soon," she called. Not that the dogs could understand, but it made her feel better to talk to them.

Returning to the exam room, Ally took a moment to smile at how Nikki Jo was hugging Goldie. This was why she'd become a veterinarian.

"Hold her for me, okay?" she repeated. She waited until Nikki Jo had a good grip and injected the dog with a sedative. Goldie didn't whimper, as if sensing Ally only wanted to help.

Without a vet tech, Ally had little choice but to use owners to help hold their pets. When Goldie's eyes drifted shut, Ally pulled forceps from a drawer.

"Hold her steady," Ally said as she once again pried open the golden's mouth. It took two tries to remove the stick. "There we go," she said in satisfaction. She dropped the five-inch stick on the metal tray beside her.

Nikki Jo looked surprised. "How did she get that stuck in there?"

"It's a mystery," Ally said with a sigh. "All I can suggest is that you try to keep her from carrying sticks in her mouth."

"That won't be easy. Goldie loves sticks," Nikki Jo said wryly. She stroked Goldie's fur. "Thanks, Dr. Winter."

"You're very welcome." Ally washed her hands at the sink. "It will take a while for the medication to wear off. Do you want to leave Goldie here for a while? If not, I can help carry her to your car."

Nikki Jo hesitated, then said, "Maybe keep her here for a little while."

"Not a problem." Ally opened the back door of the exam room. "I'll put Goldie in a crate for a bit."

"Thanks." Nikki Jo looked wiped out. No doubt all the stress of thinking the worst had gotten to her.

Goldie was seventy-five pounds of dead weight, but between the two of them, Ally and Nikki Jo managed to get the dog from the exam room into one of the kennels. Of course Roxy and Domino began barking again.

"Soon," she called, hurrying back to the lobby. She wanted to get Nikki Jo's bill taken care of before she took the dogs out.

Ally printed the invoice and handed it to Nikki Jo. The woman paid without batting an eye, likely prepared for something much worse.

"Okay, you can have a seat in the lobby," Ally said. "I have two dogs that need to go outside. I'll be back soon."

"Okay. Thanks again." Nikki Jo dropped into the closest chair.

"Gramps, you doing okay?" Ally paused a second to glance at him. "I need to take the dogs out."

"I'm good," Gramps assured her.

Ally took Roxy out first, knowing it would be less of a hassle. The drizzle had faded, but the air was damp and heavy with humidity. She could feel her hair springing out of control. She swapped Roxy for Domino, who was once again straining at the leash.

"Heel," she said, holding tight. "Heel!"

Domino didn't listen. Discouraged at how quickly he'd seemed to forget their brief training, she tried again with the treats in her pocket.

"Heel," she said sternly. When Domino returned to her side, she gave him a treat. "Good boy."

The rest of the walk went better, giving her hope that all was not lost. She returned to the clinic and put Domino back in his crate. No sense taking the risk of hurting a customer by letting them out together.

Ally took a moment to check on Goldie. The dog was resting comfortably and stirred very briefly when Ally reached out to stroke her. The meds were just beginning to wear off.

A quick glance at her watch confirmed it was already going on two o'clock in the afternoon. Ally knew there was no way to get Gramps back to the Legacy House before George arrived to fix the back door.

She was tempted to call Rosie Malone to demand that she leave the library right this minute to take Gramps back to the Legacy House. Why had the librarian gone to pick him up, anyway? Ally made a silent vow to have a stern chat with the woman next Wednesday, during Gramps's weekly visit. It was one thing for Rosie to find the true-crime novels he loved, but driving out of her way to pick him up and cart him around town was over-the-top.

As Ally returned to the lobby, she frowned when she saw Gramps sitting right next to Nikki Jo.

Uh-oh.

"You knew Pricilla?" Gramps was asking.

"Well, I know her mother better," Nikki Jo said. "Hilda works with my Aunt Martha."

"Oh, you're Mayor Cromlin's niece?" Gramps's entire face lit up as if he'd won the lottery.

"Yes, my mom is her sister." Nikki Jo looked at Gramps quizzically. "Why? Are you friends with Martha?"

"Well, not really, but I did vote for her," Gramps said. "And we've talked on occasion too. Wonderful woman. Has a good vision for our city, doesn't she?"

Ally barely refrained from rolling her eyes.

"Very much so," Nikki Jo agreed. "Aunt Martha has been so upset by Pricilla's murder. It doesn't look good for our town to have people dying every couple of months. She's worried they'll scare the tourists away."

"I'm sure it's been awful for her," Gramps agreed. "And for poor Hilda, too. I can't imagine losing a daughter like that. I know she's devastated."

"Yes, she's been racked with guilt over it," Nikki Jo said with a sigh.

"Guilt?" Gramps pounced on the word. "Why would Hilda feel guilty over her daughter's murder?"

Ally stepped forward, expecting Nikki Jo to be annoyed with her grandfather's line of questioning, but she needn't have worried.

"Well, according to Aunt Martha, Hilda kicked Pricilla out of the house just two days before the murder." Nikki Jo shook her head and lifted a hand. "Now mind you, Pricilla wasn't easy to live with. Coming and going at all hours, refusing to follow Hilda's rules. Hilda knew Pricilla was sneaking out at night to see her boyfriend and finally snapped. Told Cilla to get out and find her own place to live."

"Really?" Gramps looked intrigued.

"Yes, but to kick your one and only child to the curb, only to have her become a murder victim two days later . . ." Nikki Jo made a *tsk-tsk* sound. "Terrible. It's just terrible."

"I can see how she'd feel guilty about that," Gramps agreed.

Ally stood stock-still, absorbing the news. If Hilda Green felt guilty for kicking Pricilla out of the house right before she was murdered, then why was she so determined to blame Ally for her daughter's death?

Unless Hilda was deflecting attention from herself because she'd had something to do with her daughter's demise?

Chapter Ten

"Goldie is almost ready for you," Ally said brightly.

Nikki Jo smiled in relief. "Thanks, Dr. Winter. I really appreciate you taking such good care of her."

"Of course. That's what I'm here for," Ally assured her. *And send your friends and neighbors*, she added silently.

After another fifteen minutes, Goldie was ready to go. Ally helped carry the large dog out to Nikki Jo's car, grateful the dog would be okay. And that she'd had another paying customer.

The rain held off, and Ally hoped it would stay that way until her door was repaired.

"Did you hear that?" Gramps shot her a smug grin. "Hilda kicked Pricilla out of the house two days before the murder."

"I heard." Ally was intrigued in spite of herself. "This is a small town. I'm surprised Rosie didn't give us the scoop on that."

"Yeah, me too." Gramps stroked his chin. "I'm wondering if there was more to the fight between Hilda and her daughter."

"The good news is that it couldn't be related to her lack of cleaning at the Legacy House, since she'd already been kicked out by then." Ally changed the subject, knowing she shouldn't encourage him. "Are you okay for a little while longer, Gramps? George should be here in fifteen minutes or so."

"I'm fine." There was a hint of exhaustion in his gaze, but she knew he'd never admit it. Gramps preferred to believe he was the young, strong soldier he'd once been rather than the guy who'd slipped on the ice and broken his hip and was now forced to walk with a cane.

Ally bleached down the exam room. It occurred to her that she hadn't had a grooming appointment in a while—other than Molly, whose owner had turned and left after watching her wrestle with Roxy and Domino.

Maybe she should run a grooming sale of some sort to bring customers in. She decided to put something up on her website and social media pages.

No job too small.

When she returned to the front desk, Gramps was scribbling on a notepad. Hope flared. "Do I have another customer?"

"Huh?" He looked confused, then shook his head. "No, I just had another theory about the crime. Wanna hear it?"

"Gramps." She sighed. "I'm sure Noah has the investigation under control."

"Bah. I'm not convinced." Gramps tapped the paper in front of him with the pen. "Pricilla was coming home at all hours because she was spending so much time with Jake. Maybe Pricilla learned about the robberies from Jake and Colin, only she didn't want anything to do with stealing. She pleaded with Jake to turn himself in, but he got mad and strangled her."

Seemed a bit farfetched. "Didn't you say something about Colin having a thing for Pricilla? I doubt he'd stand by doing nothing while Jake and Pricilla argued about the robberies."

"I'm sure Colin wasn't there. No way would Jake have killed Pricilla in front of a witness." Gramps waggled the pen. "But it could be that Colin suspects Jake killed her and is wrestling with guilt over what happened. Probably thinks if he'd been there that night, Pricilla would still be alive."

Despite wanting to stay out of the investigation, Ally felt compelled to share her own theory. "I'm wondering if Hilda had something to do with Pricilla's murder. Maybe Pricilla returned, begging her mother to take her back, and they had a fight. Hilda killed her, then disposed of the body in the park, hoping no one would find it."

"That's another possibility," Gramps agreed. "Although it seems harsh. It sounds as if Hilda kicked her out as a way to force the girl to grow up. Regardless, I wish that detective of yours would clue us in as to what evidence he's collected. He must know *something* by now."

"Yeah, well, don't hold your breath." Ally still hadn't told Gramps about Domino sniffing around the outside of the clinic after the burglar broke in. The poodle hadn't seemed to be interested in following a particular scent since the night outside the grocery store, so she felt certain Domino had only been interested in the french fry container.

He wasn't a bloodhound, not by a long shot. Time to stop putting so much credence in Domino's ability to help solve the crime.

Ally heard banging on the rear door of the clinic. She hurried back, passing Roxy's and Domino's kennels, which made them bark.

"George?" Ally shouted over the dogs. "Come around to the front?"

"What?"

"COME TO THE FRONT!" Ally felt as if she were speaking to Gramps's twin brother. If Gramps had a twin brother.

There were more sounds, then nothing but barking. Hoping George had heard her, she went back through the clinic and opened the main door.

"Dr. Winter? I thought you needed the back door repaired," George said with a frown. He was probably ten years younger than Gramps and wore baggy jeans cinched with a belt beneath his wide girth. He was bald except for a dusting of white hair over his ears.

"Yes, I do. Thanks for coming." She gestured for him to come inside. George lugged a large toolbox with him, setting it down with a loud thud. "I'm sorry, but I nailed the back door shut, so you'll have to pull the nails out before you can repair it."

George's eyes goggled. "You can't nail a door shut. That's a fire hazard!"

"I know, but so is being attacked in the middle of the night." Truthfully, Ally hadn't considered the fire angle. Which she probably should have after nearly burning down the chemistry lab back when she was in high school. "Whatever, it doesn't matter. You're here to fix it now anyway."

"You took a big chance, missy," George scolded.

Hmm. In a heartbeat she'd gone from Dr. Winter to missy. It seemed to be an ongoing struggle to be taken seriously as a doctor of veterinary medicine in her hometown. She forced a smile. "Please, George, just repair the door, okay? I'll show you where I nailed it shut."

George hitched up his jeans and picked up his toolbox. Ally walked him around the building to show him what she'd done. He muttered under his breath about how foolish she'd been, but she ignored him. "Thanks again!" Without waiting for a response, she left him to work and returned to the clinic.

"Maybe Pricilla's murder wasn't about the robberies at all," Gramps said thoughtfully, as if there hadn't been any interruption in their conversation. "Maybe Jake noticed how chummy Colin and Pricilla were getting and killed her out of pure jealousy."

"Listen, Gramps, I want to take both dogs out again for a bit, okay? I'm feeling bad about how much time they've been spending in their crates. I'll lock the door and put the CLOSED sign out so no one stops in to bother you."

"Leave it open," Gramps said firmly. "I don't mind having visitors."

Ally knew he was anxious for more people to talk to about Pricilla's murder. And honestly, Gramps had managed to ferret out some interesting information, first learning how Colin and Jake lived together in an apartment and now how Hilda had kicked Pricilla out of the house. It made her think once again that Noah should use Gramps's ability to get the scoop on things to his advantage rather than fighting against him.

She took Roxy out first, then placed her in the kennel temporarily, until the back door was fixed. Then she reached for Domino. George was banging on the door, which in turn made the dogs bark madly.

A headache formed at Ally's temples, but she did her best to stay focused. George wouldn't be there too long, would he?

Domino was excited to be out of the kennel and went back to his usual lunging against the leash.

"Heel," Ally said sternly, pulling him back. Domino eased up on the leash, so she gave him a treat. "Good boy."

As she turned around to head home, the rain started up again in earnest. Not a drizzle but a downpour. Ally broke into a jog, Domino keeping pace beside her.

Her foot landed in a large puddle and she slipped, falling forward. Domino kept going, tugging her farther off-balance. Ally hit the sidewalk on her hands and knees, shouting at the top of her lungs, "Heel! Heel!"

Domino finally stopped and came back to sniff at her. Drenched from head to toe, her palms and knees stinging from the impact, she pushed herself upright.

"Ally? Are you okay?"

She turned to see Noah rushing toward her. She inwardly groaned, wishing she were wearing a rain slicker like his. "Fine, I'm fine."

"That was a bad fall," Noah said, helping her up.

"I'm okay." She winced as she put weight on her left ankle. She didn't have time for an injury, not when she had two dogs to care for.

"I'll walk you back," Noah said.

"No need," she protested. Noah ignored her comment, taking the leash from her hand.

"Heel," he said firmly, and miraculously, Domino came to his side.

Traitor, Ally thought, grinding her back molars together. How was it that Domino listened to Noah, someone he barely knew? Maybe Kayla's husband, Mark, disciplined the dog, so Domino only listened to men.

"What are you doing here?" Ally asked, trying not to sound ungrateful.

Noah didn't respond until they were safely inside the clinic. Ally was glad there wasn't a mirror handy, although seeing Domino's coiled wet fur told her what her hair probably looked like.

"Detective," Gramps said with a nod. "Ally, what on earth happened to you?"

"I slipped in a puddle and fell." Ally hoped no one other than Noah had seen her hit the pavement. "Give me a minute to take care of Domino. I need to towel him off."

And myself too, she thought wryly.

Leaving Noah and Gramps alone probably wasn't the best idea, but she didn't have another option. In the back area of the clinic, she pulled out a towel and began drying Domino. Then she frowned when she realized there was no noise coming from her back door. With a frown, she headed over to investigate.

The door was still broken, hanging open an inch, allowing the rain to seep in, and there was no sign of George.

Ally put Domino in his crate and marched into the clinic. "Gramps, where did George go?"

"Uh? Oh, he said he'd come back tomorrow. The rain should be gone by then."

Seriously? Ally scowled. "But he took the nails out and now the door is hanging open and water is everywhere."

"I could ask Jim Kirby to take a look if you like," Noah offered.

"I'm sure he's busy," Ally said, although she felt certain Erica's husband, who ran his father's construction company, would do a better job than George.

Noah already had his phone out and was making the call. "Hey, Ally Winter needs help. Her clinic was broken into and the back door won't close properly. She's got rain coming in. Can you give a quick hand? I'm sure it won't take too long." Noah paused, then said, "That would be great, thanks. She'll appreciate it. See you soon." Noah lowered the phone. "He's on his way."

She gaped. "Just like that?"

"Well, I happen to know his current job can't be done in the rain," Noah said modestly.

"Thanks, that's wonderful." She glanced at Gramps. "I need one more favor, Noah. Will you stay here while I run Gramps back to the Legacy House?"

"I'm fine," Gramps protested, although she could tell he was fatigued.

"Sure," Noah agreed.

She hesitated, then asked, "Were you coming to see me for any reason in particular?"

"Oh, yeah. Your alibi checked out fine. No need to be concerned."

"I wasn't concerned, because I didn't do anything. Which is more than Hilda can say."

Noah's gaze sharpened. "What do you mean?"

"We know Hilda tossed Pricilla out of the house two days before the murder," Gramps said smugly. "Have you asked for her alibi?"

Noah's jaw tightened, and Ally put a hand on his arm. "I'm sure you're doing a fine job, Noah, right, Gramps? Now if you'll stay here, I'll take Gramps home."

"Hrmph." Gramps looked annoyed, but he must have been exhausted, because he didn't keep arguing.

Ally ran out through the back to get her car. When she pulled up in the front of the clinic, she was surprised to see Noah helping Gramps outside.

"You should have worn a raincoat," Noah said.

"The weather lady didn't say anything about storms," Gramps said grouchily.

Ally glanced at her grandfather as she navigated the short ride home. "You okay?"

"That detective of yours makes me mad," Gramps admitted. "I'd like to know if Hilda has an alibi, but do ya think he'd tell me? Oh, no."

Ally was wet, cold, and sore from her fall, so she wasn't in the mood to argue. She took Gramps to the Legacy House and helped him inside. By the time she returned to the clinic, Jim Kirby was there, repairing her broken door.

She was so happy to see him, she could have kissed him. "Thanks for coming on short notice, Jim," she said gratefully. "If you'll excuse me a minute, I need to change."

Ally limped up the stairs to her apartment, where she put on dry clothes. She tried to tame her hair too, but it was useless. She peered at the scratches on her face and sighed. They looked just as bad as they had earlier.

Since Noah was always seeing her at her worst, she told herself to get over it. When she returned to the main floor, she frowned when she saw Noah was gone. "Uh, did something come up?" she asked Jim.

"Huh? Oh, yeah, Noah said he'd be in touch with you later."

Later tonight? Later tomorrow? Later in a few months?

Stifling her disappointment, Ally went to get her checkbook to pay Jim for his work. He was surprisingly fast, and within the hour her back doorjamb was repaired, the handle replaced, and a new dead bolt installed.

"Jim, I can't thank you enough for this. How much do I owe you? You saved me from nailing the door shut again."

He winced at that. "No problem. And consider this my contribution to the cause."

"What cause?" Flustered, she gaped at him. "Seriously, I don't expect you to work for free."

Jim rubbed the back of his neck. "I know business hasn't been very good lately, so consider this a gift from a friend."

Friend. Tears pricked her eyes, and she had to brush them away before Jim noticed. "I have a better idea: you tell Erica to bring Tink in for free grooming, and I'll buy her lunch. Okay?"

"Deal." Jim grabbed his tool belt and lifted a hand. "Take care, Ally."

She closed the door behind him, shooting the dead bolt home. For a moment she stood there, humbled by Jim Kirby's kindness. It almost made up for the fact that he and Noah had dubbed her Hot Pants after the fire ant incident.

Ally ate another frozen meal heated up in the microwave, thinking of how she and Noah should have been out somewhere sharing dinner. Deep down, she'd secretly hoped that after he'd verified her alibi, he'd ask her to dinner again.

Instead, he'd vanished without even saying good-bye.

Men. Who needs them? Ally preferred animals, and this was the reason why.

After dinner, she went down to care for the dogs. With the clinic all to herself, she let them loose, staying well out of the way of their playing.

When they'd tired themselves out, she donned her raincoat and took them both outside one last time. Domino was more mellow than usual, which was a nice change.

Ally took Roxy upstairs with her, feeling guilty about leaving Domino down in his kennel. But no way was she going to have the two dogs running loose in her small apartment.

She needed sleep.

After downing some ibuprofen to help with her sore knees and ankle, Ally crawled into bed and snuggled with Roxy, who was stretched beside her.

Sleep didn't come easily, her thoughts circling from Noah to Gramps's stubborn determination to investigate Pricilla's murder. Those moments when Hilda had yelled at her in the emergency department replayed in her mind. Had to have been guilt over kicking Pricilla out that had caused the woman to lash out like that.

And how had Pricilla's body ended up beneath the weeping willow?

When her phone rang, Ally groaned and pressed her face into the pillow. Then, realizing it could be a call for emergency veterinary services, she blindly groped for her phone. "This is Dr. Winter," she mumbled.

"ALLY?" Gramps's shouting in her ear brought her fully awake.

Sitting up, she pushed her hair out of her face, squinting at the clock. Two in the morning? All sleepiness evaporated. "What's wrong? Are you okay?"

"SOMEONE BROKE INTO THE HOUSE."

"What? The Legacy House? Are you hurt?" She leaped from the bed and pulled clothes out of her closet.

"I'M FINE. POLICE ARE ON THEIR WAY."

She sent up a silent prayer of thanks that Gramps wasn't hurt. At least, judging by the shouting, he wasn't. "I'll be there in a few minutes."

"OKAY!"

Ally disconnected the call, pulling on a pair of jeans and her University of Madison sweatshirt. She took Roxy outside briefly, then Domino, then put both dogs in their respective kennels to keep each other company. "I'll be back soon."

The dogs touched noses through the wire mesh, making her grin.

But her smile faded as she jumped into the Honda and drove to the Legacy House. Thankfully, there was no traffic so early in the morning, so she made it in record time.

Her heart squeezed with concern. Gramps would have told her if any of the women were injured, wouldn't he?

She rushed inside, finding everyone in the kitchen—Noah, a uniformed officer she didn't recognize, all the widows, and her grandfather. She immediately crossed over and drew Gramps into a tight hug.

She didn't want to imagine her life without Gramps. Or the WBWs.

Chapter Eleven

"What happened?" Ally asked after releasing her grandfather. She stayed close to his side, raking her gaze over the widows.

Harriet and Lydia were dressed in long flannel nightgowns, and Harriet's hair was up in tiny pin curls. Tillie was wearing a flannel pajama top and matching bottoms, her casted left arm still in a sling.

"Oh, Ally, it was so awful," Lydia said, her eyes wide with fear.

"Very scary," Harriet agreed in a soft voice.

Ally couldn't help herself; she went over and gave each of the widows a reassuring hug. "I'm just glad you're all okay." She had to brush tears from her eyes.

"Oscar, I'd like to talk to you about what happened here tonight," Noah said.

Ally glanced at Noah, offering a smile of gratitude. Thank goodness he'd come to the Legacy House tonight. Most attempted break-ins probably didn't warrant a detective's response, especially in the middle of the night.

But Noah had come. Because of her and Gramps.

"Yeah, okay." Gramps moved to sit at the table, but Noah stopped him. "I'd like to talk to you each separately, if that's okay. Let's go into the living room while the ladies wait here."

"Fine with me." Gramps reached for his walker, and Ally knew his hip must be sore for him to have succumbed to using the dreaded thing. He preferred his cane.

"I'm coming, too." Ally followed Gramps into the living room.

Noah didn't argue, likely knowing it would be useless. He sat across from Gramps, a small notebook on his knee. "I understand you heard something that woke you up?"

"I did." Gramps looked calm despite the frightening event, and Ally knew that, despite his age, Gramps saw himself as the widows' protector. She reached out to take his hand—to comfort herself more than anything.

"Care to start at the beginning?" Noah asked.

Gramps took a moment to think. "I heard a loud thud. I didn't think much of it at first, but then I heard it again. I got out of bed and silently made my way into the hallway. At first I didn't see anything, but after my eyes adjusted to the dim light, I saw a shadow standing in the hallway."

Ally gasped, tightening her grip on Gramps's hand. "You saw him?"

"I saw someone," Gramps corrected. "Shape of a person, but I can't say for sure if it was a man or a woman."

"Go on," Noah encouraged.

"I shouted at the person to get out and used my walker to bash him or her over the head." A fleeting grin crossed Gramps's features. "It wasn't heavy enough to do any damage, but it scared the idiot. In a flash, he or she was gone."

"You hit him with your walker?" Ally could hardly believe what she was hearing. "Gramps, you should have gone back to your room, locked the door, and called 911!"

"I did call 911, after I bashed him with my walker," Gramps said reasonably. "To be honest, I was more worried about falling and breaking my other hip than anything else. Besides, I needed to check on the WBWs." Gramps's expression turned grim. "I wanted to make sure they weren't hurt."

Or worse. The unspoken words brought a lump to her throat.

"How did the intruder get in?" Ally asked, perplexed. "You keep the house locked, don't you?"

"Glass cutter on the patio door." Noah gestured to his left. "Silent and effective."

The round hole in the glass made her shiver, and not because of the cool autumn air drifting in. It had been all too easy for someone to break in.

And why?

"Was anything stolen?" She glanced from Gramps to Noah.

"Not from me," Gramps said. He swept a gaze over the room. "And the TV is still here, along with Tillie's computer."

The TV was at least ten years old, and the computer was far from new. Had the intruder figured the items weren't worth the hassle?

Couldn't they have seen that through the window? If so, why bother breaking in at all?

"Oscar, can you give me any idea of how tall this person was, how much they weighed?" Noah asked.

Gramps looked thoughtful again. "I would say four to five inches shorter than me and slender, not heavy at all." He shook his head ruefully. "I wish I'd gotten a closer look."

"That's very helpful," Noah assured him.

Ally was just grateful Gramps hadn't been hurt by his attempt to protect the widows. Thinking of Gramps using his walker to smack the intruder over the head would have been funny if it hadn't been so serious.

"Have you seen anyone suspicious hanging around the house the past few days?" Noah asked.

Gramps shook his head. "No, and other than yesterday when it was raining, we spent several evenings out on the patio."

"Think back," Noah advised. "Could be the person who did this came by and checked things out ahead of the break-in."

"Casing the joint," Gramps said, sounding like someone from an old gangster movie. "I pay attention, Detective, and didn't see anyone lurking around. Woulda called you if I did."

"Okay, anything else?" Noah asked.

"Nah. You can talk to the widows, but I don't think they heard much," Gramps said. "Harriet and Tillie were sleeping when I went to check on them. Lydia was just waking up, said she heard noises from the hall, which was probably me bashing the intruder with my walker."

"I understand, but I'd still like to check with each of them. If you'd send Lydia in next?" Noah looked at Ally expectantly.

"Come on, Gramps." Ally helped her grandfather to his feet and escorted him to the kitchen. Harriet, bless her heart, had brewed a large pot of coffee and was bustling around the kitchen, pulling items from the fridge to make breakfast. "Harriet, you do realize it's still the middle of the night."

"No one will be sleeping anymore after this," Harriet said briskly. Ally had the impression the woman needed to stay busy or fall apart. "And I'm sure your detective is hungry, as is Officer Slavic."

"Lydia, Noah would like to talk to you next." Ally helped the woman up and escorted her into the living room. Then she went over to see what Officer Slavic was doing. He was in the hallway, examining the walls and the floor in front of the hallway closet. The closet door was hanging ajar, and she wondered if the officer had opened it or if the intruder had. Maybe he'd thought the closet was a bedroom.

"Find anything?" She frowned, noting there was a small dent in the wall, maybe where Gramps's walker had hit it. Or maybe the intruder's head or elbow had made the mark. Served him right, breaking into an assisted-living home. Trying to take advantage of the older generation.

Thinking about it made her angrier by the minute.

"Time will tell," Officer Slavic answered cryptically.

"Look, my grandfather is the victim here. I want to know what, if anything, you find, understand?" She gave him a narrow glare. "Now what do you think caused that small dent in the wall there?"

Officer Slavic eyed her warily. "I don't know, but the crime scene tech will be here soon to dust for prints. Maybe they'll have an idea. In the meantime, I need you to stay back so as not to destroy any evidence."

Ally reined in her temper. "Of course I don't want to destroy any evidence, but I would like to know if you found something."

"No, ma'am."

"Was the linen closet door open when you got here?"

He hesitated, then nodded. "Yes."

She wasn't sure if that was a key element to the crime or not but was glad he'd given her something. She spun on her heel and returned to the living room.

"Oscar was so brave, wasn't he?" Lydia was saying, resting her hand on Noah's arm. "We're so lucky to have him here with us. I can't imagine what might have happened if Oscar hadn't scared him away."

"Yes, Oscar was very brave," Noah agreed. "Are you sure you didn't see anything, Ms. Schneider?"

"I'm sure."

Noah glanced at Ally. "I'd like to talk to Tillie now."

Feeling a bit like a game-show hostess, Ally escorted Lydia back to the kitchen and brought Tillie out. That interview was short, as Tillie hadn't heard anything other than Gramps waking her up after it was all over.

Noah repeated his question about noticing anyone hanging around the house, but Tillie shook her head. "No, I didn't see anyone."

Ally brought Harriet in, and Noah's questions produced the same result. "Breakfast will be ready shortly," Harriet said, patting her pinned curls as if embarrassed to be entertaining in that state. "I hope you and Officer Slavic can stay for a bit."

Noah looked surprised. "Oh, that's very kind, but we're working."

Harriet looked crestfallen. "But—I made extra. I'm sure you can eat while you work."

Noah glanced at Ally for help. She shrugged. "Harriet is the best cook I know."

"Thank you, dear," Harriet preened. "Now, Detective, you and Officer Slavic must have some of my French toast. It's rather amazing, if I do say so myself."

"I'm sure it is," Noah said. He hesitated, then said, "Thanks, Harriet, but maybe another time. We need to talk to the neighbors, see if they noticed anything out of the ordinary. We can't risk missing something important."

"Oh, okay." Harriet waved a hand. "When you're finished chatting with the neighbors, come back. I'll keep a couple of plates warm for you."

"That would be wonderful," Noah said, giving in to the pressure. He rose and went over to the hallway to speak with Officer Slavic. Ally paused near the hallway, trying to eavesdrop, but couldn't make out what they were saying.

When Noah turned and saw her standing there, he frowned. "Do you need something?"

"Yes. I need to know Gramps and the widows are safe." Ally stepped closer, pinning him with a knowing gaze. "You need to find out who did this and arrest him or her ASAP. And I'd like Jim to come out as soon as possible to fix the patio door."

"Gave up on George, huh?" Noah's attempt at humor didn't make her smile. "Okay, Ally, I'm sure Jim will be happy to help. And I want your grandfather and the women to be safe here too. I've asked for another officer to be sent here to stand guard until the patio door has been fixed."

That made her feel slightly better. "Thank you. But I want to know what you find out about who did this, Noah. Breaking into my clinic is one thing, but breaking in here and harming the widows is unacceptable."

"You believe the same person committed both break-ins?" Noah asked.

"Well, yeah. Don't you?"

"Maybe." Noah didn't look convinced.

"Why wouldn't they be related?" Ally pressed.

"The motive for the clinic break-in was money. Someone obviously knew you kept cash in a drawer at your desk. A client did the deed or mentioned it to someone in passing; otherwise, how would they know to look there?"

"True," Ally agreed.

"What was the motive here?" Noah threw out his arm, encompassing the tidy but modest home. "I'm not sure I'd target this place looking for easy cash."

She hated to admit it, but he had a point. Gramps never kept a lot of cash on him, and neither did Lydia or Tillie. Harriet barely left the house, so Ally didn't know if she had money in her purse, but she doubted it.

If not money, then what? The only chilling reason Ally could come up with was that the intruder wanted to silence Gramps because he'd been asking too many questions about Pricilla's murder.

And that was far worse than someone looking for a quick and easy buck.

* * *

By the time dawn was peeking over the horizon, Ally knew she had to get back to the clinic to take care of the dogs.

"Thanks for breakfast, Harriet." Ally gave the woman a warm hug. "It was delicious."

"Anytime, dear. But are you sure you have to go so soon?" Harriet glanced nervously at where the glass had been cut in the patio door.

"Noah promised there would be a cop stationed outside until the door is repaired. I wouldn't leave, but I have two dogs to take care of."

"You could bring them here." Harriet's offer was so out of character, Ally thought she'd misunderstood. The woman was not fond of dogs, although she had mellowed where Roxy was concerned.

"Harriet, I would if I could. But Roxy and Domino get a little out of control when they play together." She hesitated, then added, "I'll come back later, maybe with one dog at a time, okay?"

"Okay." Harriet put on a brave smile. She'd taken the pins out of her hair, and her gray curls were looser than normal.

"You'll be fine." Ally desperately wanted to take Gramps to the clinic with her but sensed the women would feel better if he stayed here with them. "I'll be back as soon as I can."

Ally drove back to the clinic. She was physically exhausted, but her mind kept whirling about the break-in. The glass cutter had made for a silent entry into the house. She really had no idea how Gramps had heard the intruder moving out in the hallway. Must be his old soldier instincts had roused him, warning of danger.

She shivered and tried not to dwell on how close she'd come to losing her grandfather.

The dogs greeted her exuberantly, easing some of the tension in her shoulders. Even Domino seemed well behaved, heeling better than normal. She left them both out to roam around the clinic, wincing as they once again turned over one of the waiting room chairs.

Good thing the chairs were plastic and basically indestructible.

Sunday wasn't a usual day for clients, although emergencies could happen at any time. When her cell phone rang, she pounced on it. "This is Dr. Winter at Furry Friends Veterinary Clinic. May I help you?"

"Ally? It's Erica. Are you okay?"

"Oh, Erica." Ally sank into the chair behind the desk, grateful to hear her friend's voice. "You heard from Noah?"

"Yes, Jim went straight over to repair the door. What on earth happened?"

Ally filled her in on the details, belatedly remembering they were supposed to have lunch together later that day. "I don't know if I'll make lunch, Erica. I was thinking of heading back over to the Legacy House after giving the dogs a break."

"Don't worry about it, although I'd like to hear how your date went."

Ally sighed. "No date. Noah canceled."

"Oh, Ally. I'm so sorry to hear that. But I don't understand; why would he back out on you like that?"

"He claims it's related to the case, but who knows? I'm sure he was having second thoughts." She touched her injured cheek. "It's fine, really. We're better off staying friends."

"That doesn't make sense, Ally. Why would Noah tell Jim how much he likes you if he wasn't interested?"

Ally sat up straighter. "He did? Jim told you that?"

"Yes, but I wasn't supposed to say anything, so don't mention it, okay?"

"I won't." A tiny bud of hope bloomed in her heart. Maybe Noah really had called off the date because of the case. To make sure there was no way he could be accused of interfering with a witness. Not that she'd witnessed anything other than Pricilla's dead body, but still.

"Listen, I have to feed the hoodlums before things get ugly, but keep in touch, Ally. We'll schedule another lunch soon, okay?"

"Okay, thanks, Erica. And thank Jim, too, for repairing my door. I still owe you lunch and a free grooming for Tink."

"And I plan to take you up on both," Erica assured her. "Especially the grooming; Tinker Bell could use one. Talk to you later."

Ally hung up and stared blindly at the dogs, thinking about the fact that Noah had actually confided in Jim about being how much he liked her.

He liked her!

Hopefully that meant he would ask her out again, once the stupid case was over. Ally realized she was grinning like a fool, which was crazy, considering the grim break-in at the Legacy House.

She needed to get her head out of the clouds and stay focused on taking care of Gramps and the WBWs. The danger was escalating, yet she had no idea why.

Which of Gramps's questions had sent someone out to the Legacy House?

Gramps had spoken to Rosie Malone, but Ally found it difficult to believe the librarian had anything to do with the burglaries. Or with Pricilla's murder.

Hilda had been acting very strangely, but Ally was having trouble picturing the city executive cutting a hole in the patio door and sneaking in.

Although the city executive could have hired someone to do her dirty work.

Yes, Hilda was still a suspect in her mind. Nikki Jo, on the other hand, seemed harmless.

What about Colin Felton? Gramps had theorized that the young man was secretly in love with Pricilla, which the kid had almost admitted. Maybe Colin wasn't happy with how Jake had treated her and Jake had gotten upset with him for pointing it out. Jealousy could cause a boyfriend to act irrationally and lash out in anger.

In her mind, Pricilla's boyfriend, Jake Hammond, was a prime suspect. Along with Steve Norris, the computer geek. And she couldn't forget Pricilla's mother, Hilda Green. Any one of them could have lost their temper and killed Pricilla. And really, any of them could be responsible for the break-in at the Legacy House.

Either Jake or Steve could have done it himself, or Hilda could have hired someone to do it.

It would be helpful to know what Noah was thinking.

She brought herself up short. Wait a minute, she was acting like Gramps. Creating a suspect list and thinking through all possible aspects of the crime.

Her chosen career was veterinary doctor, not detective wannabe.

Still, she couldn't shake off the desire to help solve Pricilla's murder. Gramps becoming one of the victims changed the rules.

She'd do whatever was necessary to protect him and the widows.

Even if that meant upsetting Noah by trying to figure out who was behind this and why.

Chapter Twelve

Ally took both dogs outside for another bathroom break while waiting for Kayla Benton to come pick up Domino. The young mom of twins had said she'd be back on Sunday late in the afternoon.

The hour was heading toward five o'clock, and she frowned, thinking it wasn't like Kayla to be late.

When her phone rang, she hoped the caller was Noah, but no such luck. "This is Dr. Winter from the Furry Friends Veterinary Clinic. How may I help you?"

"Dr. Winter? It's Kayla Benton."

"Oh yes, hi. I hope you and Mark had a nice weekend getaway."

"We did, but Brooke is sick with the flu, and there's no way I can get over there to pick up Domino. I'm so sorry, but would you mind keeping him for another day or two? I'd really appreciate it."

"Of course, that's no problem." Ally smiled down at Domino. He'd come a long way in the past few days. She didn't mind continuing to work with him. "Why don't you call me when you're ready to pick him up?"

"Thanks so much." Kayla sounded harried. "We had such a nice time; then to come home to one puking kid—soon, I'm sure, to be followed by the other—was a bit of a reality check."

"I can imagine." Ally could tell Kayla had her hands full. "Domino has been great, so don't worry about him."

"You're awesome. Thanks again." Kayla disconnected the call.

"Well, Domino, what do you think of that?" Ally bent down to stroke the dog's springy curls. "I guess you and Roxy are going to be playmates a while longer. Just try not to break anything, okay?"

Domino wagged his tail in agreement.

She decided to put Roxy upstairs in her apartment and take Domino to the Legacy House with her. It was a risk, but she hoped Domino was tired enough from his romp with Roxy to behave.

If he became too wild, she'd bring him back and kennel him. It just hardly seemed fair that he ended up spending so much time in his crate.

"Don't make me regret this," she warned, opening the back hatch of her Honda. Domino leaped inside, then sniffed the area, no doubt intrigued by Roxy's scent.

As Ally pulled up in front of the Legacy House, she recognized Noah's SUV. She frowned. Had something happened? She quickly released Domino and put him on his leash.

"Heel," she said sternly before heading inside.

She stopped short when she realized the widows were all seated at the kitchen table with a crime scene tech taking their finger-prints. Gramps's, of course, were already on file.

"Find something?" Ally glanced at Noah.

He shrugged. "Picked up a few fingerprints off the closet door handle, but it's likely one of the women. We're checking just to be sure."

"Hey, Ally." Gramps greeted her with a tired smile. "How come you still have Domino?"

"One of Kayla's twins has the flu, so I'm keeping him a couple extra days." Domino strained at his leash, eager to explore the new surroundings. "Has the patio door been repaired?"

"Jim is finishing up with that now. Had to replace the whole thing." Gramps shook his head. "What a waste. We wouldn't have done that in the old days."

"You didn't have argon-gas-treated doors back then, did you?" Noah asked.

"Bah." Gramps waved a hand. "New technology is fine, but to toss out a perfectly good set of doors because of a hole in the glass is still wasteful."

"No other problems while I was gone?" Ally asked, taking Domino over to sniff at the widows. Lydia and Tillie both bent down to pet him, but Harriet twisted her hands in her lap. "Nice doggy," she said with a smile that looked more like a grimace. The way Harriet avoided touching him made Ally wonder if the woman had once suffered a traumatic experience related to a dog.

It would explain a lot and made Ally feel bad for being impatient with Harriet's aversion to animals.

"Last one," the tech said, moving over to take Tillie's fingerprints.

Ally edged into the living room to take a look at the door herself. It looked great, better quality than what they'd had before.

Domino sniffed along the carpet, and Ally shortened the leash. "Don't even think about lifting your leg to mark this place."

"I had to send the officer on guard duty home," Noah said from behind her.

Ally turned to look at him in shocked surprised. "Why? I want Gramps protected."

Noah lifted his hand. "I know, Ally, and I'm doing my best. But with the door repaired, I can't justify the expense."

"Expense?" She let out a harsh laugh. "Gramps deserves better, Noah, and you know it." Then she frowned. "You're not doing this to get back at him for interfering in your investigation, are you?"

"How can you say that?" Noah looked wounded by her accusation. "I care about Oscar and you." He blew out a breath and said, "I'll sleep on the sofa tonight."

Really? Her heart melted. "I know it's a lot to ask, Noah, but I'd be grateful if you would. Just for tonight," she hastily added. "I'm hoping the Benton twins recover quickly and they'll pick up Domino soon. Once I don't have to worry about caring for Domino, I'll be able to stay here with Roxy."

"I know, and I don't mind." Noah gave her a look of reproach. "I still can't believe you'd think I'd do something so petty."

"I don't." She wished now she could take it back. "I—look, we're both exhausted and stressed from lack of sleep. Despite your threats to arrest Gramps for interfering with a criminal investigation, I know you really wouldn't follow through."

Noah lifted a brow. "I wouldn't pull a cop off duty out of spite, but understand that I *will* arrest Oscar if he continues to interfere."

Ally narrowed her gaze. "Maybe you should just keep focusing your efforts on getting to the bottom of this thing. Then Gramps wouldn't need to interfere, or almost be killed during a break-in."

Noah's lips thinned, but she didn't release her intense stare. In the end, he looked away first.

"Ally, please," he finally said in a resigned tone. "Help me out here. Keep your grandfather at home."

"Yeah, as if it were so easy," she muttered. Noah turned and left the room, leaving Ally feeling deflated.

As she led Domino back toward the kitchen, he yanked hard on the leash, sniffing in the direction of the hallway. With a frown, she tugged him back.

"Heel."

Domino ignored her, lunging forward again, nearly pulling her off-balance. His nose was still on the floor, as if he'd picked up some intriguing scent.

Roxy's scent? She'd had Roxy in the Legacy House several times over the past month. And Pricilla hadn't been the best housecleaner on the planet.

She gave Domino more leash, and he continued down the hall. When he stopped in front of the linen closet—which now had a layer of fine black fingerprint powder all over it—she became intrigued.

"What is it, boy?"

Domino sniffed and sniffed all around the door. On the floor and up the edge of the door, which still hung ajar. Before she could stop him, Domino nosed the door open.

"Hey, what is it?" The standard poodle was acting very strangely.

Domino leaped up and placed his front paws on the shelf, where there were several folded towels. They tumbled off the shelf and onto the ground.

"Uh-oh." She quickly bent down to grab them, intending to put them back, when she saw it.

A small red bound diary.

Ally stared for a moment, trying to understand. Did the diary belong to one of the WBWs? Not Gramps. She couldn't imagine him keeping one, but maybe Harriet? The woman spent a lot of time in the house.

She reached for it, something telling her to only touch the edges. After carefully opening the book, she gaped at the loopy script.

The first line read: *I think Jake's cheating on me.*

Pricilla's diary? Intrigued, Ally turned another page, and another. *I hate my mother more than anyone on earth* was another entry.

As much as she wanted to read more, Ally quickly set the diary down on the towel and stepped back. "Noah?" she called loudly, staring at the red book as if it were a snake that would bite her.

"What is it?" Noah frowned when he saw the open door. "Ally, what are you doing?"

"Look what I found. Or rather, what Domino found." She gestured toward the book. "It's Pricilla's diary."

"You've got to be kidding me." Noah sounded half angry, half excited. "Did you touch it?"

"Only on the edges." When his scowl deepened, she lifted up a hand in defense. "How was I supposed to know it belonged to Pricilla? Could have been placed there by one of the widows." She avoided his gaze, knowing she was guilty of reading more of the entries than she should have.

Noah pulled an evidence bag out of his pocket and carefully scooped up the diary. "I don't understand why Pricilla would have left it here."

"To keep it away from her mother?" Ally suggested. "We know they didn't get along. Not to mention Hilda threw her out of the house two days before she was found dead. Pricilla probably didn't want anyone, even her friend Marlie, to read it."

"Why does that matter?" Noah asked.

She rolled her eyes. "You've never been a young adult woman writing about her hopes, dreams, and fears."

"Clearly not," Noah said dryly.

"The first line of the diary was something about Jake cheating on her, and she also mentions how much she hates her mother." Ally shrugged. "Have you verified Jake's alibi and Hilda's for the time frame of the murder?"

Noah didn't answer, not that she'd really expected him too. But his gaze was thoughtful as he looked at the diary. "This is a good clue, Ally. Nice work."

She was ridiculously happy with his praise. "Thanks, but Domino gets the credit."

Noah eyed the poodle. "Don't even try to convince me he'd make a good police dog."

"He's not well trained, but that doesn't mean he's useless," Ally protested. "He came sniffing at the closet for a reason."

"Maybe." Noah took a moment to shuffle through the rest of the items in the closet but didn't find anything more. "I'll get this to the lab, see if they can find any prints."

"What did you find?" Gramps asked, clumping toward them.

"Pricilla's diary," she answered when Noah remained stubbornly silent.

"Her diary?" Gramps looked flummoxed. "You think she hid it here to keep it away from her mother?"

"I don't think anything yet," Noah said, his jaw tense. "I'll take it from here, Oscar."

"He's going to check it for fingerprints," Ally said helpfully.

"More fingerprints?" Gramps looked annoyed. "I hardly think you're going to find the murderer's fingerprints on the girl's diary. Otherwise, why would it be hidden in our linen closet? The murderer wouldn't have taken it, then broken into the Legacy House in order to return it to the closet. Makes no sense."

Ally hated to admit Gramps had a point. Was it possible the linen closet had been the ultimate destination of the burglar? Had the person known the diary was in there? If so, how? Ally had hoped for more evidence, yet the words written in Pricilla's diary kept flashing in her mind.

I think Jake is cheating on me.

I hate my mother more than anyone on earth.

Were the statements just typical young adult angst? Or something more?

*   *   *

Ally didn't want to leave Gramps and the WBWs but needed to get Domino home and take care of Roxy. Gramps wanted to come with her, but she insisted he stay back with the others.

"Will you at least come for dinner?" Gramps asked. "You can bring Roxy."

"Sure," she agreed.

"Great. Noah is going to have dinner too," Gramps said with a gleam in his eye.

Oh boy. She should have considered that possibility. Maybe she'd get an emergency vet call? Nah, she wouldn't be that lucky.

"He'll love Harriet's cooking," Ally said, hoping Gramps and the other WBWs weren't trying to play matchmaker. Their interference in her love life—or lack thereof—was likely to have the opposite of the intended effect. It would probably send Noah running as far away from her as he could possibly get.

"See you soon, Ally," Gramps said as she walked Domino out.

Back at the clinic, Ally let the dogs play together for a bit, then worked with Domino on basic training. Pleased with his progress, she placed him in his kennel, then took Roxy for a long walk to make up for the lack of attention.

"Sorry, girl, but we're getting another day or two of boarding fees out of this, right?"

Roxy wagged her stumpy tail in agreement.

Ally showered and changed before heading back to the Legacy House. She told herself it wasn't a date, but knowing Noah would be there was enough to make her spend extra time trying to tame her wild hair and add a light dusting of makeup to help cover the scratches on her cheek.

She took Domino out for a quick walk, then grabbed Roxy's leash. "Your turn, Rox. Let's go see Gramps."

Ignoring the slight nervousness in her stomach, Ally drove to the Legacy House. Seeing Noah's SUV parked outside made the butterflies worse.

Stop it. This is not a date! He's doing you a favor by staying here tonight with Gramps. That's it. Nothing more.

"Ally, it's so nice to see you." Harriet greeted her warmly. Her smile barely faltered when she saw Roxy at Ally's side. "Come in, dear. Dinner will be ready shortly."

"Thanks, Harriet." Ally came inside and gave the woman a quick hug. After all, the three women had become a part of her family.

"Hi, Ally." Gramps grinned as she entered the kitchen. "Have a seat."

The only empty seat was right between Gramps and Noah, which had likely been arranged by Gramps. Ally bent down to take Roxy off her leash.

Roxy adored Noah and greeted him like a lost-long friend. Then Roxy moved on to nose and lick the others before taking up her normal spot beneath the kitchen table.

"Something smells great, Harriet." Ally's stomach rumbled with hunger. "What did you make this time?"

"Bavarian pot roast with German potato dumplings." Harriet stood at the stove, a long apron over her flowered dress. She was clearly in her element having a full table to feed.

"Sounds amazing." Ally took the empty seat between Noah and Gramps, the scent of Harriet's pot roast almost overpowering that of Noah's woodsy aftershave.

Almost.

Harriet placed all the food on the table, then helped her sister Tillie by cutting up the meat and dumplings for her so she could eat one-handed.

"Need anything else, Tillie?" Harriet asked when she'd finished.

"No, thanks." Tillie gingerly set her casted arm on the edge of the table. "I'm so sorry I can't help you at the clinic for the next eight weeks, Ally."

"Oh, don't worry. I'll be fine," Ally assured her.

"I can pick up an extra day if needed," Lydia offered.

"Me too," Gramps said.

The way the widows wanted to help was sweet. "I'm not that busy at the moment, so I'll be fine."

"Well, if business picks up, let me know." Lydia beamed. "I enjoy our days together."

"Me too," Ally said, although there were times the widows were more of a hindrance than a help. They tried hard, though, and it was nice to have someone answering the phone while she was caring for her furry patients. When she had actual appointments, that is.

"Did that puppy ever find a home?" Noah asked.

"Bandit?" She glanced at Noah in surprise. Had he been more interested in the puppy than he'd let on? "I'm not sure. I haven't heard from Wendy lately."

"You should take him in, Noah," Gramps said, waving his fork. "That little pup needs a good home."

"My schedule is a bit erratic for a pet," Noah protested.

"I'm sure Ally would be willing to help you out as needed." Gramps jabbed her with his elbow as if to say, *See? I'm helping you two get together.*

She barely refrained from jabbing him back.

"Another dog?" Harriet looked slightly horrified.

"Don't worry," Ally tried to assure her. "I'm sure Bandit will find a good home."

"With Detective Jorgenson," Gramps added with a wink.

"Oscar," Noah said in a warning tone. "Don't push."

"Who, me?" Gramps attempted to look innocent.

"Did anything come through on the fingerprints?" Ally asked, changing the subject. "On the diary or the door handle here and at the clinic?"

Noah filled his mouth with food to avoid answering. When he finished chewing, he looked at Harriet. "You are a wonderful cook, Harriet. This is fantastic."

"Oh, it's nothing," Harriet said modestly. "And the least I can do, since you've agreed to sleep on our sofa to keep us all safe and sound."

"I don't mind getting your meals as reimbursement," Noah said with a charming smile.

Ally tried not to think about how Noah didn't smile at her like that. All the proof she needed that this was nothing more than a simple meal among friends.

When they finished eating, Ally helped clear the table. "I can take it from here, dear," Harriet insisted, shooing her off.

"Okay. I should get back to the clinic anyway. Domino still needs to go out tonight."

"I'll walk you out," Noah offered.

She eyed him curiously for a moment, wondering if he had news he didn't want to share in front of Gramps, then decided he simply wanted her to be safe. "Okay, thanks. Bye, Gramps." She gave her grandfather a hug and a kiss on his cheek.

"Don't forget to come and get me for the funeral," Gramps said.

"You're attending Pricilla's funeral?" Noah scowled.

"It's a free country," Gramps said, jutting his chin. "We're going to pay our respects, right, Ally?"

"Right." She took Roxy's leash. "Come on, girl."

Noah didn't speak until they were outside. "Ally, you have to convince your grandfather to stay away from the case."

"It's a funeral, Noah." She opened the back hatch for Roxy. "And if I don't take him, he'll find someone else who will."

Noah rubbed the back of his neck. "Ally, I'm worried about him. And you. This break-in was a close call."

"I know." She opened the driver's side door, then faced him. "I'm worried about Gramps, but I can't control him either. Please find out who did this before Gramps gets hurt."

Noah gazed into her eyes for a long moment. Then he surprised her by pulling her close and capturing her mouth with his in a toe-curling kiss.

Chapter Thirteen

"Be safe," Noah murmured after they'd both come up for air. "Hmm?" Ally was having trouble gathering her thoughts. She honestly could have stayed nestled in Noah's strong arms forever.

He chuckled, sending a shiver down her spine, but then stepped back. "I better head inside before your grandfather comes to see what's taking so long."

She reluctantly nodded and somehow managed to stand on her own two feet without Noah holding her upright. "See you later, then."

"Yes. But keep your grandfather away from the funeral," Noah added as he stood, waiting for her to slide into the Honda.

She frowned and shook her head. They'd already had this discussion. Controlling Gramps was impossible. Was that why Noah had kissed her? To help sway her into doing what he wanted?

She'd enjoyed every moment of Noah's kiss. Wanted nothing more than to kiss him again, very soon. But his comment didn't sit well.

Irritated, Ally closed her car door and started the engine. Roxy's breathing had steamed up the windows, so she had to lower hers in order to see.

Ignoring Noah, she backed out of the parking spot and headed back to the clinic. She needed to take both dogs out for one last walk before heading to bed.

Because as sure as the sun rose in the east, come morning, Gramps would be calling to find out when she'd be picking him up to attend Pricilla's funeral.

She could all too easily imagine Noah's reaction to seeing them in attendance.

When she took Domino on his walk, he tugged on the leash more than usual, maybe annoyed that he'd been left alone while she'd had dinner at the Legacy House, but she continued using treats to convince him to heel.

Ally had trouble sleeping that night, primarily because of Noah's kiss. She didn't want to believe he'd kissed her with an ulterior motive but couldn't entirely discount the possibility either.

By the time Roxy woke her at six o'clock on the dot the following morning, Ally had barely gotten five hours of sleep. Feeling cranky, she glared at Roxy.

"You need to learn to sleep in."

Roxy licked her face and waved her stumpy tail, making it difficult to stay mad.

"Come on, then. You first, then Domino."

Once she'd finished caring for both dogs, including feeding them, Ally took a shower and eyed her closet. Was it still a thing to wear black to a funeral? Thankfully, she hadn't been to many over the years. She pulled out a black skirt and a patterned black-and-white blouse. The skirt was a tad snug around the waist, but she sucked in her stomach and figured it would be fine for a few hours.

She was finishing her oatmeal when Gramps called on his cell phone. "ALLY? WHAT TIME ARE YOU COMING TO GET ME?"

"Gramps, don't yell." Lack of sleep had given her a nagging headache, and his shouting only made it worse. "The funeral visitation starts at ten o'clock, so I'll be there around nine forty-five."

"OKAY! I'LL BE READY."

She put down her phone and wondered how Noah's night had been. Harriet was in her element, likely feeding him breakfast right now, something better than instant oatmeal. Noah could easily give Gramps a ride to the clinic, but Ally knew that even if she called to ask him to do her the favor, he wouldn't.

Sipping her coffee, she wondered what information Gramps thought he'd get from attending Pricilla's funeral. According to the few *Dateline* episodes she'd watched, the cops tended to go to see how people reacted.

Personally, she was dreading seeing Hilda Green again. The woman's ridiculous and embarrassing accusation in the hospital waiting room still burned, even though Ally suspected it had just been Hilda's knee-jerk reaction to guilt over kicking Pricilla out two days before her murder. Still, the diary made it sound as if there had been a lot of emotional turmoil between mother and daughter. Something more than simply breaking the rules.

Ally finished her coffee and headed down to take both dogs out. They weren't thrilled with being placed back in their respective kennels, but there was nothing she could do about it.

"I'll give you some playtime later, okay?" She glanced from Domino's dark curly face to Roxy's brown one, telling herself there was no reproach in their dark eyes.

They were dogs; they didn't hold their owners in contempt. Did they?

When Ally arrived at the Legacy House, there was no sign of Noah's SUV. Grumbling to herself about Noah's stubbornness, she stepped up on the porch and knocked.

"Ally, dear, it's nice to see you." Harriet was wearing her usual flowered dress and dark support stockings. "Oscar has been waiting."

"Hi, Harriet. Hey, Gramps." Ally was glad she'd chosen the skirt when she saw Gramps was wearing black dress slacks and a long-sleeved black shirt with a blue tie. "You look sharp."

"So do you." Gramps struggled to his feet. "Although I must say, I'm disappointed in that detective of yours. I asked him to give me a ride into town, but he said he couldn't do that."

"Yeah." Ally scowled. "He's being difficult about our decision to attend the funeral."

Gramps waved a hand. "He can't stop us."

"I know." Ally forced a smile. "Let's go, then."

The trip to the Willow Bluff Funeral Home didn't take long. Ally was surprised to see how crowded the parking lot was but understood that a lot of townsfolk had come out of respect to their city executive. There was an hour of visitation prior to the formal service.

"What exactly are you planning to do, Gramps?" Ally asked as she escorted him inside.

"Not sure yet." Gramps stood and looked through the room. "Let me know when you spot Jake Hammond."

Oh boy. She did not want Gramps to interrogate Pricilla's boyfriend at the funeral. Maybe it was a good thing there were so many people in attendance; it would limit Gramps's ability to speak privately to those on his suspect list.

A young woman with mascara smeared beneath her puffy red-rimmed eyes was standing next to Hilda Green. Ally stared in surprise; it was the same woman they'd seen talking to Steve outside the apartment building. Marlie Crown? If so, the girl was dressed vastly differently from the way Pricilla had been. Her hair was a normal chocolate brown, and other than a small stud nose ring, she didn't have any visible piercings or tattoos. She was dressed conservatively in black slacks and a scoop-necked black sweater. There were red blotches all over her neck, as if she were having some sort of allergic reaction.

Or maybe it was just the stress of being here to say a final good-bye to her friend.

Ally nudged Gramps. "Check out the young woman standing beside Hilda."

He lifted a brow. "The same woman we saw chatting with Steve. Let's get closer."

Ally kept a grip on Gramps's arm, keeping him nearby as they threaded their way through the crowd. When they drew closer, Ally's suspicions were confirmed.

"Marlie has been wonderfully supportive during this difficult time," Hilda was saying to the older couple who'd stopped to pay their respects. "I always felt like I had two daughters, Pricilla and Marlie."

Really? Did you kick Marlie out of the house too?

As soon as the sarcastic question popped into her mind, Ally pushed it away. It wasn't her place to judge Hilda's actions. Ally wasn't the mother of a troubled young adult and very well might have given Pricilla the same ultimatum: find a way to follow the rules or get out.

Still, the way Marlie stayed so close to Hilda's side seemed odd, as if she were Pricilla's sister rather than her best friend. Ally thought about her friend Erica. Would she be this supportive of Erica's mother if something happened to her friend? Maybe.

She remembered how Marlie had lost her mother when she was young. It was possible the girl saw Hilda as some sort of surrogate mother. Giving herself a mental shake, Ally told herself to stop looking at everyone with suspicious eyes. She was letting Gramps and his crazy theories get to her.

A tall, lean man with salt-and-pepper hair came over to put his arm around Hilda. Ally wondered if he was just a friend of the city executive or something more.

"What happened to Pricilla's father?" Ally asked.

"I heard he took off when Pricilla was young. They're divorced now," Gramps answered in an absent tone, his gaze on the crowd. "I haven't seen Jake yet, have you?"

"No." And really, the kid should be easy to spot. He dressed outrageously, just like Pricilla, and had dyed pitch-black hair, a lip ring, and some sort of colorful tattoo on his neck.

"He's too racked with guilt to show up," Gramps said in a loud whisper.

"Oscar. Ally." Noah's deep voice came from behind them.

She wanted to ignore him, but Gramps was already turning around. "Detective. Have you noticed the glaring absence of Jake Hammond too?"

"Oscar, don't go there," Noah warned.

"Why? Have you already cleared him as a suspect?" Gramps demanded.

Ally turned to glare at Noah, who should know better than to confront Gramps. "We're not hurting anything, so why not just leave us alone?"

Noah's brow shot up at her irritated tone. But before he could say anything, Ally caught a glimpse of Jake, his black hair a dead giveaway. "There he is, Gramps. Just came in the front door."

"I see him." Gramps nodded and glanced at her. "Let's go."

"Where?" Noah demanded.

"To pay our respects." Gramps clearly wasn't leaving without at least attempting to speak to Jake. Ally avoided Noah's gaze as she followed her grandfather. "Too bad you didn't bring Domino. I'd have liked to see the dog's reaction."

"Can you imagine Domino in a group this size? Talk about utter chaos."

Ally continued clearing a path toward Pricilla's boyfriend, but they were a few seconds too late. Marlie beat them to it, taking Jake's arm and yanking him down a hallway and away from the crowd. Ally had only gotten a glimpse of the annoyed expression on Marlie's face but wondered if Hilda had asked the girl to get Jake out of there.

Gramps didn't hesitate to trail them into the hallway, forcing Ally to follow.

"Why are you here?" Marlie's voice was low and tense. "Mrs. Green is going to cause a scene when she sees you."

"She can't keep me away," Jake protested.

"Why do you have to cause trouble?" Marlie asked. "You're being selfish."

"Me?" Jake let out a harsh laugh. "You should talk."

Marlie's face flushed scarlet, the blotches on her neck turning just as bright. "That's not fair!"

"The truth hurts," Jake said snidely.

"Stop it." Marlie's sharp tone abruptly softened. "Get out of here, Jake, before Detective Jorgenson decides to question you again."

"I don't have anything to hide. I told the detective everything I know." Jake hesitated, then sighed. "Fine. I'll leave, but you know me, Marlie. Better than anyone. It wasn't my fault Cilla was kicked out. You know I didn't do anything to hurt her."

"I know, and I'm sure Mrs. Green will calm down eventually." Ally peered around the corner in time to catch Jake and Marlie in a quick embrace. "I'll talk to you later, okay?"

"Yeah, okay." Jake sounded completely defeated. Marlie came down the hallway, looking a little surprised to see Ally and Gramps hovering nearby.

"Marlie?" Ally smiled and stepped forward. "Do you remember me? I'm Dr. Winter, the local veterinarian. I wanted to let you know how sorry I am for your loss."

"Oh, uh, thanks." Marlie looked a bit flustered and avoided Ally's direct gaze. "Nice to see you again, but I have to go."

Before she or Gramps could say anything more, Marlie brushed past them. The girl returned to Hilda's side, looking like a sentinel protecting her post.

"Hmm," Gramps mused. "That was interesting."

Ally tried to resist being drawn in. "They're friends, and Marlie is supporting Hilda. Nothing unusual about that."

"What was all that about being selfish? And why does Marlie know Jake better than anyone?" Gramps countered. "Why wouldn't his buddy and roommate Colin know him the best? Not to mention Pricilla?"

She frowned, glancing after the disappearing figure of Jake Hammond. "Probably because guys don't talk to each other about their feelings. A guy is far more likely to open up about something like that with a girl. And maybe Jake expressed some frustrations about Pricilla to Marlie."

"They seemed closer than friends," Gramps said thoughtfully. "You think Jake was cheating on Pricilla with Marlie?" His blue eyes gleamed with suspicion.

"No way." She hesitated, then asked, "Why would Marlie cheat with her best friend's boyfriend?"

"You should have looked through that diary to see if Pricilla mentioned her suspected cheater by name."

"That would be tampering with evidence, Oscar," Noah said in a terse tone.

"Which I didn't," Ally shot back, belatedly realizing Noah had come up behind them. She should have anticipated he would. "But maybe you should just tell us what you found, Noah, since Domino uncovered the diary in the first place. Did Pricilla mention who she believed was seeing Jake?"

Noah looked pained. "You know I can't tell you that."

"So it is Marlie," Gramps said with satisfaction. "That's why you're here, to figure out what the girl is up to."

"No, Pricilla didn't mention any names," Noah finally admitted. "And I'm only telling you so you stay out of it."

Ally knew Noah expected them to be grateful for learning something, but she was still irked at how he'd kissed her, then told her to keep Gramps away from the funeral. "Well, that's something, I guess." She took Gramps by the arm. "Are you ready to leave?"

"Not yet." Gramps kept his keen blue gaze locked on Noah's. "I still think there are more clues yet to be uncovered."

Ally wanted to groan in frustration, especially when she noticed that the small tick had returned to the corner of Noah's left eye.

"Come on, Gramps." She tugged on his arm, anxious to get him away from Noah. "Let's mingle."

This time, Noah let them go without saying a word. But as they walked through the crowd of mourners, Ally could feel Noah's annoyed green gaze boring into her back.

As if that incredible kiss between them had never happened.

*   *   *

Ally managed to drag Gramps away from the funeral after forty minutes, which included listening to people chatting about the horror of another murder taking place in Willow Bluff. They hadn't learned anything new after the conversation between Marlie and Jake, and Ally was weary of the whole thing.

Last night she'd wanted nothing more than to help crack the case to protect Gramps, but today she yearned to stay far away.

Too bad she didn't have enough clients coming to the clinic to take her mind off the murder.

"I have an idea," Gramps said, after she'd gotten him settled in the car.

She inwardly groaned. "No more ideas, Gramps, please? I'm exhausted."

"This one is easy," Gramps insisted. "Remember what I said about having Domino at the funeral?"

"Yes, why?"

"I think we should take Domino for a walk toward Jake's apartment, see how he responds to the kid's scent." Gramps eyed her curiously. "Maybe that would be enough for that detective of yours to take him into custody."

"It's not enough, Gramps." Although she couldn't deny his idea had merit. "And I don't think today's a good day."

"But we have to take the dog over there today. The Bentons are picking him up sometime soon, aren't they?"

Again, he had a point. In fact, she was rather surprised she hadn't heard from Kayla already.

Domino and Roxy did both need to be walked. She really didn't want to do this, but she hoped that if she did, then maybe Gramps would return to the Legacy House without complaint.

And maybe I'm the Mad Hatter in Alice in Wonderland.

"Come on, Ally," Gramps pressed. "It won't take that long."

"Fine." She caved the way she always did. "But after that, I take you home, okay?"

There was a slight hesitation before Gramps agreed. "Okay."

She shot him a narrow look. "I mean it, Gramps. I'll humor you for a while longer, but then I need to focus on my business. I haven't had a grooming appointment all week and need to run some sort of fall special to draw in some new customers."

"Okay, okay." Gramps threw up his hands. "This is the last thing I'll ask of you."

She snorted. "Yeah, right."

"The last thing I'll ask of you today," Gramps clarified with a wry grin.

"Now that I believe." Ally shook her head and drove back to the clinic. "Stay in the car. I'll get Domino out and put him in the back."

"Sounds good," Gramps agreed. Of course, he was always agreeable once he'd gotten his way.

Cagey old man, she thought with affection. As much as he drove her crazy, she'd be devastated and heartbroken without him.

Taking Domino out of his kennel, she winced at Roxy's reproachful gaze. "I'll put you upstairs in the apartment while you wait for your turn, okay?"

Roxy stood at the top of the stairs, watching as she led Domino outside.

Ally put Domino in the back hatch, then slid behind the wheel. "We can't be too long. Roxy needs to go out too."

"I know." Gramps leaned forward eagerly. "I hope Jake is at the apartment."

"Where else would he be?" Ally knew it wasn't likely Jake was working today. And he wasn't at the funeral.

The trip to the four-family apartment building didn't take long. She decided to park at the grocery store. "Do you want to wait here, Gramps?"

"No, I'm coming with you."

Of course he was. Ally helped him out, handed him the cane, and then took Domino out of the back. The dog yanked at the leash, and she bemoaned the fact that she didn't have any treats. Her black skirt didn't have pockets.

"Heel!" She shortened the leash and held tight.

As they approached the four-family, Domino didn't react any differently. He didn't sniff at the ground or seem to pick up any particular scent. He watered several patches of grass as they walked but otherwise couldn't have cared less.

"This doesn't look promising," Ally said to Gramps.

"Let's go inside," Gramps suggested.

"I'm sure it's locked," Ally protested. But to her surprise, the front door wasn't locked. When they walked inside the small lobby area, there were four slender metal mailboxes on the wall, each with a name written above it.

"Here he is." Gramps tapped on the number 3. "I think that's on the second floor."

"Wait here," Ally said, not wanting Gramps to navigate the stairs. She quickly took Domino up to the next floor and easily found apartment number three.

She looked down at the dog. "Well?"

Domino looked up at her as if to say, *Well, what?*

Muttering to herself, she knocked at the door.

No answer.

She leaned in, listening intently. She didn't hear anything.

Knocking again, she listened for sounds of movement from inside.

She turned and took Domino back down the stairs to Gramps.

"Well?" he asked.

She shook her head. "No one is home, and Domino didn't pick up any intriguing scents, from what I can tell."

Gramps looked dejected. "Maybe Jake didn't kill Pricilla."

"Yeah." Or maybe Domino was just a lousy police dog.

Chapter Fourteen

As Ally drove back to the clinic, her phone rang. Not recognizing the number, she answered in a professional tone. "This is Dr. Winter at Furry Friends Veterinary Clinic. May I help you?"

"Hi. You left me a message about Lulu's shots?"

Ally searched her memory for a Lulu. Then it clicked: Lulu was a Pomeranian belonging to a Harry Parker. "Oh yes, Mr. Parker. Would you care to schedule an appointment?"

"I don't suppose you have time today?"

"I do, actually. What works for you?" Ally pulled into the parking space behind the clinic and scrambled for a paper and pencil.

"I can be there in thirty minutes," Mr. Parker said.

"Perfect." She glanced at Gramps, who winked. "Noon works fine."

"See you soon."

"Hot diggity," Ally said with satisfaction. "I have another appointment." She frowned. "Although this means you have to wait a while before I can take you back to the Legacy House."

"I don't mind." Gramps grinned. "Now we can have lunch at the Lakeview Café before heading back."

"Gramps." Ally sighed. Gramps would give up one of Harriet's scrumptious meals only if he had a reason to go to the café. Like pumping people for information. "Noah is doing a fine job of working the investigation."

"With our help," Gramps insisted.

Ally shook her head and helped Gramps from the car. Then she freed Domino from the hatch.

Her newly repaired door looked great, and she was reminded again of how she owed Erica a grooming and a lunch. "Do me a favor and unlock the front door of the clinic, would you? Then sit down for a bit while I take Roxy out."

"Okay." He thumped across the clinic lobby to do as she asked.

Ally put Domino back in his kennel and took Roxy out. "Domino isn't nearly as good at tracking criminals as you are, Roxy."

Roxy wagged her stumpy tail.

"Don't worry." Ally bent over to scratch the boxer's silky ears. "When Domino goes home, things can get back to normal."

Roxy cocked her head to the side as if thinking about her statement. Oh, Ally knew the dog couldn't understand her ramblings, but talking to Roxy was probably better than talking to herself.

Ally took Roxy back inside and decided to put her in the kennel next to Domino. If they had to be crated, the least she could do was put them next to each other.

After a quick wipe-down of the exam room and grabbing the vaccinations she needed from the medicine cabinet, she was ready. When she returned to the lobby, she found Gramps using his two index fingers to peck at the keyboard.

"What are you looking for?" She peered curiously over his shoulder.

"They still have local news posted online, don't they?" Gramps asked, punching one key at a time. "I wanna see what they have posted about the robberies."

"Here, let me pull it up for you." At this rate, it would take him ten minutes. She turned the keyboard toward her and quickly typed in a search for the local newspaper. In seconds, she had an article on the robbery up on the screen.

"Thanks, Ally." Gramps peered at the screen and began to read. She was curious what he'd find out but turned away when the bell over the door chimed.

A very skinny, tall man came in holding a ball of fluffy fur in his arms. The dog's hair was so long Ally could barely see her eyes.

"Hello. You must be Mr. Parker and Lulu." Ally stepped forward with a smile. "I'm Dr. Winter." She held out her hand for Lulu to sniff. "Thanks for bringing her in."

"Sure." He frowned. "What happened to your face?"

"Oh, just a mishap with a cat." Ally's cheeks burned with embarrassment, even though the injuries she sustained taking care of animals were rarely her fault. "Come this way, please."

She led him into exam room number one and closed the door.

Mr. Parker set Lulu on the stainless-steel table as Ally pulled on gloves. "Do you have any concerns about Lulu? Is she eating well?"

"She seems fine," Mr. Parker assured her.

Ally did a very basic exam before reaching for the syringe. "You know, I offer grooming services as well. I think Lulu could use a little trim. She needs to see where she's going, doesn't she?"

"Well, I suppose that's true." Parker looked at his watch. "If you have time now, I could wait."

Yes! Ally wasn't about to give up the opportunity to make more money. Gramps and lunch would have to wait. "That's not a problem. Hold her firmly now; this will pinch a bit."

"I've got her," Parker said.

Lulu tolerated the injection like a champ. It was always surprising to Ally how some small dogs handled the pain better than some of the larger dogs.

Ally dropped the needle into the sharps container and stripped off her gloves. "Do you have a leash for her?"

"Uh, no." Parker looked chagrined. "I carry her everywhere I go."

"That's okay, I have disposable ones." Ally pulled out a neon-pink leash from one of the drawers. She clipped it to Lulu's collar, then set the dog on the floor. "This shouldn't take long."

Parker followed her out of the exam room. He took a chair in the waiting room while Ally led Lulu over to the front desk, where Gramps was still squinting at the computer.

"I'm doing a grooming too, so lunch will be a bit late."

Gramps blinked. "Not a problem, Ally. I'm learning a few things here I didn't know."

Oh boy. She sighed. "You can fill me in later." She led the dog into the grooming suite.

She picked the dog up and set her into the washtub. "Okay, girl, here's the rule. No biting."

The dog was squirmy, as if she wasn't used to being washed or having her anal glands released, one of Ally's least favorite but necessary tasks. Soon the dog smelled fresh and clean. She let the dog air-dry for a few moments in a crate and returned to the main lobby.

"I just washed her and will clip her soon," Ally informed Mr. Parker. "I'll just get your invoice ready."

He nodded and went back to reading the nine-month-old *People* magazine.

"Excuse me, Gramps. I need to create an invoice." Ally quickly included the grooming fee with the vaccination and printed it for Harry Parker.

She handed it to him, then returned to the grooming suite. Normally she preferred to let dogs air-dry, but since Mr. Parker was waiting, she used the cool setting on the dryer to hurry the process along.

Clipping Lulu didn't take long. Ally finished with the dog's face and smiled when she could see Lulu's beautiful dark eyes. "There you are."

She tied a bow around a small topknot on the dog's head, then led her out to reunite with her owner. "Any questions about the invoice?" Ally asked.

"No, it's good." Parker took Lulu into his arms. "She smells great."

"Yes, grooming is important, especially for smaller breeds. I recommend once every couple of months." She maintained a professional smile, but inside she was doing a happy tap dance.

Parker paid the bill without complaint, and she was happy to have the possibility of a return customer.

"There were only two robberies," Gramps announced after Parker and Lulu left.

"Only two? At the same store?" Ally asked.

"Yeah, over the course of two weeks. There were a couple of stolen items taken each week." Gramps tapped the computer screen. "The article says that the security video was tampered with, so the robberies weren't noticed until the inventory was checked."

Since that had been the rumor all along, it wasn't surprising. "Any particular day of the week?"

"Nope."

"Hmm. It might be difficult to narrow down the date, since the security feed was tampered with," Ally mused.

Gramps wagged his finger at her. "Very good point, young lady. See? You're starting to think like me."

That wasn't exactly her life's mission, and Ally decided it was well past time to change the subject. "If we're going to eat, we need to go. I want to do some updates to my website and social media to offer a special on grooming services."

"I'm ready." Gramps reached for his cane.

As much as she longed to bring Roxy along, she decided it was better to leave both dogs together. After dropping Gramps back at the Legacy House, she'd give them some playtime.

But speaking of the Legacy House brought up her concerns about the break-in. "Do you feel safe at the Legacy House?"

To her surprise, Gramps didn't shrug off her question. "I'm safe enough but worry about the WBWs."

"If Kayla picks up Domino tonight, I'll stay on the sofa with Roxy." Although it was odd that she hadn't heard from the Bentons. Were the twins doing worse? She made a mental note to call Kayla after lunch.

The weather had improved, and they were able to sit on the patio today. Ally and Gramps both ordered their usual.

"Hey, isn't that Marlie talking to that server?" Gramps nudged her.

"Yes, that's Marlie talking to Darla." Ally noticed that Darla looked upset. "I wonder if they're discussing Pricilla."

"I still think there's something more going on here," Gramps declared. "You heard Mayor Cromlin. Those kids were hanging out at the farmhouse for some reason."

Ally suppressed a sigh. "We don't know who was hanging out there. Besides, you heard Noah say there were no arrests for drugs, Gramps."

"I know. There must be something else that would explain why someone is stealing from the store," Gramps insisted. "Maybe they just need money to buy booze."

"You think this is all about making a quick buck?" Ally grimaced. "I'd hate to think Pricilla was murdered for a couple hundred dollars."

"Yeah, I hear you," Gramps agreed. "Who knows, the whole Jake-cheating-on-Pricilla deal could be the cause of the murder, and maybe the robberies aren't related after all."

Their meals came quickly, as the lunch crowd had already dissipated. Ally had just taken a huge bite of her salad when her phone rang.

Another customer? She chewed quickly, looking at the screen. She belatedly recognized Kayla Benton's number. "Hello?" she said with her mouth still half full of food.

"Dr. Winter?" Kayla's voice was so soft Ally could barely hear her.

"Yes, this is Dr. Winter. Kayla? Are you okay?"

"No. Sick. Flu." Suddenly she heard the sound of retching in the background.

Ally put a hand to her own stomach and pulled the phone from her ear. *Ugh.*

"Keep Domino longer?" Kayla's voice came through.

"Of course. You just feel better." Ally hit the end button before she could overhear anything more.

"Who was that?" Gramps asked.

"Kayla Benton has the flu. She wants me to keep Domino longer." Ally picked at her salad with her fork. "I really wanted to spend the night at the Legacy House, Gramps. Do you think Domino will be okay at the clinic alone?"

He shrugged, his appetite still going strong as he bit into his burger. "Why not?"

"I don't know." She couldn't bear the thought of anything bad happening to a dog in her care. What if there was a fire in the clinic? No, she couldn't do it. "I'll call Noah, see if he'll sleep on the sofa one more night."

"I don't need a babysitter," Gramps said testily.

"He'd stay as a way to keep the WBWs safe." *And you, Gramps,* although she didn't add that thought out loud. Ally forced herself to make the call, because Gramps's safety was more important than her ego. Noah didn't pick up, so she left a message, then finished her salad. If Noah didn't agree to stay one more night at the Legacy House, she wasn't sure what she'd do.

*   *   *

Ally dropped Gramps off and had already returned to the clinic to let the dogs play when Noah returned her call. "Hey, Ally. I'd be happy to stay at the Legacy House with the widows."

"You would?" His agreement was a huge load of guilt off her shoulders. "Thanks. Kayla has the flu—sounds like a twenty-four-hour bug—so I'll have Domino longer than planned. I didn't feel right leaving him in the clinic all alone so I could stay with Gramps."

"Understandable." Noah paused, then added, "How is your grandfather?"

"He's fine. Why?"

"No reason, just curious. I can talk to him later tonight."

It took a minute for his intent to register in her brain. "Noah, you can't have it both ways," Ally said irritably. "First you tell him to stay away, then you grill him about what he's learned. You know that's just encouraging him to keep nosing around."

"It's not as if he listens to me, so I may as well take advantage of his nosiness." There was the sound of a radio squawking in the background. "Sorry, Ally, have to go."

"Thanks, Noah." She dropped the phone on the counter and watched the dogs playing. When her phone rang again, she quickly answered. "Furry Friends Veterinary Clinic. How may I help you?"

"Dr. Winter? This is Wendy Granger. You know, Patsy's owner?"

There was no way in the world Ally would ever forget Wendy Granger. "Yes, of course, Wendy. How are the puppies doing? Did you find a home for Bandit yet?"

"A very nice young man by the name of Jake Hammond came to see Bandit on Saturday. He said the dog cheered him up. But he was supposed to show up an hour ago and isn't answering his cell phone. After hearing of that poor girl's murder, I'm worried about him. Do you think he's missing?"

Ally remembered seeing Jake at the funeral a few hours earlier. "No, I saw him at Pricilla Green's funeral this morning. I'm sure he's having a hard time with his loss. Maybe give him an extra day or two, okay?"

"Oh, that makes me feel better," Wendy declared. "Thanks, Dr. Winter."

"No problem." Ally set her phone aside, smiling ruefully. Somehow she'd become Wendy Granger's confidant, which wasn't necessarily a bad thing. Ally checked her schedule and verified that Wendy was bringing Patsy in to be spayed the following week.

Maybe once there wasn't a litter of puppies for Wendy to deal with, she'd settle down.

Interesting that Jake had agreed to take a puppy, especially after Pricilla's murder. Living in a second-story apartment would add some complexity to getting the puppy house-trained, but it wasn't impossible. Still, she hoped Jake wasn't taking on a bigger responsibility than he was ready for. Getting a puppy after losing someone you were close to probably wasn't smart.

Not her problem. Unless, of course, Bandit ended up at the shelter.

Ally decided to take Domino and Roxy out for a walk at the same time. But within five minutes, she was wrapped up in their leashes to the point that she almost fell on her face.

"Fine. One at a time, then." She took Roxy out first, then Domino. The poodle seemed eager to be outside, so she decided to take a longer walk. Instead of heading into town, she chose to head out toward the empty farmland on the edge of town.

Seeing the abandoned old farmhouse off in the distance made Ally think about the concerns Mayor Cromlin had mentioned to Noah. She ended up walking toward it, out of curiosity more than anything. The place was certainly in a state of disrepair. Ally warily eyed the peeling paint and the saggy steps leading to the front of the home. It looked as if a strong wind would blow it over.

Her intent was to work with Domino on basic commands, but he started that eerie sniffing-the-ground thing again.

And there wasn't a french fry packet in sight.

Her imagination? Maybe. After all, she was pretty sure Domino would never make it as a police dog. Not like Roxy. Still, she decided to give him some leeway.

Suddenly Domino lunged forward, yanking hard on the leash. Her foot slipped in some mud from the recent rain, forcing her to let go or fall on her face.

"Domino, heel!" she shouted, regaining her footing and taking off after him. "Heel!"

She had treats in her pocket, but Domino wasn't close enough to smell them. He approached the abandoned farmhouse, barking his head off.

"There's no one in there," she called. At least she hoped there wasn't. Surely Domino's barking would scare anyone who might be lurking around. Especially since Noah had mentioned that the cops were keeping an eye on the place.

"Domino, heel!" Ally frowned when she noticed him scratching at the front door. "Heel!"

The dog ignored her. Curious now, she gingerly walked up the sagging steps, being careful to stay near the edges where there was more support.

"Domino, heel." She found herself whispering, which was crazy. It was broad daylight, and there was no reason to think someone was hiding inside.

The dog kept scratching at the door, sniffing along the bottom. Ally reached for the door handle and turned it. The unlocked door only opened partway because the wood was warped.

"Hello?" she called loudly, wrinkling her nose at the musty odor.

Domino slipped through the opening, sniffing around the interior of the farmhouse. Ally took a few steps before realizing the place wasn't as abandoned as she'd thought. There were empty beer bottles, soda cans, and cigarette butts on the floor.

It was a party house, exactly as Mayor Cromlin had mentioned. No signs of drug use, which aligned with Noah's statement.

Her gaze landed on a playing card lying near a beer bottle. The ace of spades. She picked it up and looked at it curiously.

The dog was still sniffing, but there wasn't anything else of interest that she could see. She grabbed his leash. "Come on, Domino. Let's get out of here."

Domino didn't want to go, but offering a treat helped. Outside, Ally drew in a deep breath of fresh air.

Noah obviously knew about this place, must have checked it for clues at some point. Yet she couldn't help but wonder who'd been in the place most recently. Domino had picked up some sort of recognizable scent.

Had the group of partyers included Pricilla?

Chapter Fifteen

When Ally returned to the clinic, she decided to let both Domino and Roxy out to play. They were getting so used to each other by now that their romping had toned down a bit.

Crash! Or maybe not. One of her plastic waiting room chairs toppled over. Ally sighed, righted it, and scolded the dogs.

"Behave. Both of you." While they continued to play, she moved to the front desk, pulled out her cell phone, and called Noah.

"What's up, Ally?"

His deep, husky voice was balm to her frayed nerves. The man could sell audio recordings of his voice to people who owned yoga studios. No one would ever leave; they'd just listen to Noah's voice over and over and over . . .

Realizing she was getting off track, she pulled herself together. "I was just out at the abandoned farmhouse with Domino."

"Why on earth would you go out to the old Thompson place?" There was a pause before he added, "Did you take your grandfather with you?"

"No, I did not." She remembered now that Abe Thompson had once owned the property. He'd been in his eighties when she was in high school, so it was no wonder the place had been abandoned.

"I was walking Domino, and he went straight toward the house, sniffing along the door as if he recognized the scent."

"Ally . . ." Noah sighed. "Domino is not a police dog."

"I know, but it's still strange," she insisted. "And while I can see why Mayor Cromlin was concerned about parties being held there, I found a playing card, the ace of spades."

"I know there have been parties there—thankfully no drugs. At least, that was the word from the patrol cops checking the place," Noah admitted. "The cops swung past last night, in fact. No one was there."

"Seeing the playing card made me wonder if there could be illegal gambling going on." Ally didn't want to sound too much like Gramps. "I mean, robberies and gambling could go hand in hand."

"Could be, but it's not really your concern, Ally," Noah said gently. "Please have faith in my investigation."

"I do," she insisted. "But Domino acted weird, more so than usual."

"Thanks for telling me, but you know as well as I do, that dog is far from well trained."

"Hey, he's doing much better," Ally protested, even as she rubbed the ache in her right shoulder from Domino's pulling. The two dogs had finally settled down and were resting next to each other. Ally eyed Domino warily. "He listens some of the time."

"You keep telling yourself that." Noah's voice was laced with humor. "Bye."

"Bye." Ally slid her phone back in her pocket and thought about the old Thompson place. Gramps might have more information about it, so she made a mental note to ask him for details.

Ally's phone rang again, and she smiled when she recognized Erica's number. "Hey, Erica, what's up?"

"Ally, I know it's last-minute, but any chance you can meet me for dinner?" It sounded as if Erica was upset about something.

"Of course. Where would you like to go?"

"Somewhere away from town." Erica sniffled loudly. "My mom agreed to watch the kids."

"How about Gino's?" Ally had never eaten there but had heard the food was good. Although Helen Ryerson, not Gino, did most of the cooking. Then she remembered it was Monday. "Never mind, they're closed today. How about that small Italian place? Alfonzo's?"

"That works. I'll meet you there."

"No, listen, Erica, I'll come pick you up. Just give me a few minutes to take care of the dogs."

"Okay, see you soon."

Erica had not sounded good, and Ally worried about her as she quickly took each of the dogs outside, then placed them in their kennels. She locked up the clinic and darted outside to her car.

Erica and Jim had a beautiful house on the other side of Willow Bluff. She knew Jim had built the place himself, with some help from some of his company of construction workers.

Erica was outside on the sidewalk waiting. When Ally pulled up, she didn't hesitate to jump in. "Thanks, Ally."

"What's going on?"

"Jim and I had a fight." Erica swiped at her eyes.

"What kind of fight?" Ally was surprised to see Erica like this. She'd always been envious of Erica and Jim's marriage, their two adorable kids, and their small schnauzer Tinker Bell, named by Erica's daughter LeAnn. The thought of their marriage being on the rocks bothered her.

"Oh, the usual." Erica waved an impatient hand. "He came home late tonight because he stopped to have a drink with Noah.

Does he ever think I might want to get out to see someone? No, he does whatever he wants and expects me to be waiting with a warm meal when he decides to show up."

"I'm sorry, Erica." Some of the tightness in Ally's chest eased. As upset as Erica was, at least there wasn't any hint of Jim cheating on her.

"I told him to get out," Erica said softly. "So he left."

Ally gasped. "He didn't walk out on your marriage?"

Erica shrugged. "I don't know, but that's why I had to get my mom to watch the kids." She let out a harsh laugh. "I should have told him to stay home and that I was leaving."

"Oh, Erica." This was sounding worse than Ally had thought. "I'm sure this is just a temporary thing."

"Maybe." Erica sniffed again and drew in a deep breath. "I just wanted him to apologize for leaving me hanging there, wondering where he was. He told me not to make such a big deal out of it, but he's not getting that I've been home with the kids all day and could use a break too."

"Of course you need a break too." Ally wanted to smack Jim for making Erica cry. She thought about the Bentons taking a long weekend away. Granted, their trip had ended with everyone coming down with the flu, but still, Erica and Jim certainly needed to have some time to themselves.

"I'm sorry, let's talk about something else." Erica pasted a smile on her face. "Tell me how things are going with Noah."

"They're not, unless you count having dinner together with the widows at the Legacy House a date."

"Oh, Ally." Erica reached over to pat her arm. "Trust me, I know Noah is interested."

Ally pulled into the parking lot of the small Italian restaurant on the outskirts of town. They didn't have a reservation, but since it was a Monday night, Ally hoped it didn't matter.

The parking lot wasn't that full, and soon they were seated in a small booth in a corner of the room. From her vantage point, Ally could see everyone who came in and out the door.

Before they had a chance to order, Ally saw Jim Kirby walk into the room. He stood in the doorway, looking around, obviously searching for his wife.

Ally reached over and patted Erica's arm. "Wait here a moment, okay?"

"Okay." Erica was staring blindly down at the menu.

Ally headed straight over to Jim, who looked upset. "Hey, Ally. Have you seen Erica? Her mom told me she was here."

She pulled him off to the side. "Yes, she's here. And I want you to go over there and have a nice romantic meal with your wife, understand?"

Jim's gaze filled with relief. He nodded. "I can do that."

"Good. Now get over there and apologize for being a jerk."

He looked taken aback by her tone but didn't argue. "Thanks, Ally. I owe you one."

"Nah, you've been wonderful in helping to fix my clinic door and replacing the patio doors on the Legacy House. Now go fix your marriage."

Jim didn't need to be asked twice. He brushed past her and crossed over to the booth. Ally smiled when he bent down and whispered something into Erica's ear.

Even though she was starving, Ally left the restaurant, knowing it was best for Jim and Erica to be alone. She wondered how

Jim had found them there, then figured Erica's mother might have mentioned where they were.

The idea of eating another frozen dinner didn't appeal to her, especially since she'd been anticipating Italian, so Ally headed to the Legacy House. Normally it was rude to show up at dinnertime, but she knew Harriet loved to feed people, the more the merrier.

Besides, she wanted to fill Gramps in on finding the playing card at the Thompson house.

She rang the bell.

"Ally, dear, you're just in time." Harriet beamed. "Dinner is just about ready."

"Thanks, Harriet, I hope you don't mind." Ally stepped inside and gave the sturdy, rectangle-shaped woman a hug. "I had dinner plans with a friend, but things changed and I'm hungry."

"Ally, you're welcome anytime." Harriet turned, and Ally followed her into the kitchen.

"Hey, Gramps." Ally's smile faltered when she saw Noah sitting at the table. She should have known he'd be there but had thought he'd be out looking through the Thompson property.

"Ally, have a seat." Gramps patted the empty seat beside him. "I'm glad you decided to join us."

"Thanks, Gramps." Ally dropped beside him and sent Noah a sidelong glance. "I was supposed to have dinner with Erica, but she and Jim are eating together instead."

"That's nice," Noah said, as if he was clueless about the argument between Erica and Jim.

"Yeah, it is," Ally agreed. "But next time you decide to hang out with Jim after work, make sure he calls his wife."

"Me?" Noah looked surprised, and her stomach dropped. Had Jim lied about being with Noah? Was Jim having an affair after all?

"Why should I have to tell him to call his wife? Shouldn't he know to do that on his own?"

"Yes, but do me a favor and remind him anyway." Ally turned toward Harriet and sniffed the air appreciatively. "Something smells good."

"It's nothing fancy, just my apple-and-spice pork tenderloin," Harriet said demurely.

It wasn't Italian, but Ally almost drooled anyway. "Sounds delicious."

"And for dessert, Harriet made a German chocolate cake," Tillie added. "My sister's cake is the best."

Ally swallowed hard, knowing she'd never in a million years be able to resist German chocolate cake. At this point, she didn't care if her jeans were tight.

"I'm surprised to see you here, Noah," Ally said as Harriet passed serving plates heaped with food.

"What do you mean?" He looked puzzled. "I told you I'd stay the night to keep an eye on things."

"Yes, and thanks for that," Ally agreed. "But I thought maybe you had gone to check out the Thompson farmhouse."

"What about the Thompson place?" Gramps pounced on the information like a dog on a fresh bone.

"There's no reason to go," Noah said, his gaze narrowing.

"You already checked it out?" Gramps practically rubbed his hands together with glee. "You're sure that isn't where Pricilla was murdered?"

"Oscar, please," Harriet scolded. "No talk of murder while we're eating."

Gramps ignored her. "Well?"

Noah's jaw tightened. "There's no evidence a crime has taken place at the Thompson farmhouse."

"So you *have* ruled it out as a crime scene," Gramps said with satisfaction.

"This is delicious, Harriet, thank you," Noah said, ignoring him.

"I bet Jake and Pricilla had many a rendezvous over there," Gramps said with a chuckle.

Ally decided to leave that one alone. She sampled the pork and almost moaned out loud. "Harriet, I agree with Noah. This is incredible. Probably your best yet."

"Why thank you, dear." Harriet preened and eyed Lydia and Tillie as if to imply she was at the top of the food chain as far as currying favor with Ally's grandfather.

And she was probably right. Gramps usually defended his beloved late wife Amelia's cooking, but these days he seemed to simply enjoy what was in front of him. Based on the meals she'd eaten, Ally couldn't blame him.

"I'd like to check the farmhouse out for myself," Gramps declared.

"No!" Ally and Noah exclaimed at the same time. "It's too dangerous," Ally added. "And not easy to get to."

"Hrmph." Gramps looked put out and pinned her with a narrowed gaze. "Sounds like you were out there, Ally."

She could easily read the rebuke—*without me*—in his eyes. "By the way, who owns the property?" she asked, hoping that getting more information would soothe Gramps's ruffled feathers. "Mayor Cromlin said something about being glad the land would be put to good use. Did old man Thompson leave behind any family members?"

Noah filled his mouth with food, likely to avoid participating in the conversation.

"I'm pretty sure Thompson had a son, but I think there was a falling-out between them," Gramps mused, his annoyance fading. "What was that young man's name? Travis? Timothy?"

"Trevor," Noah supplied. "The old man was Abe Thompson and he had one son, Trevor."

"That's it. Trevor." Gramps arched a brow at Noah. "Why hasn't Trevor come to claim the property?"

"How do you know he hasn't?" Noah asked.

"Well, he's certainly not living there. The house is a complete disaster," Ally said. "Those kids are taking a risk by hanging out there to play cards. I wouldn't be surprised if the roof caved in on top of them during a storm."

"The land must be worth a pretty penny." Gramps frowned. "Maybe Trevor is waiting for the house to fall apart on its own so he doesn't have to pay the expense of tearing it down."

"But if the house collapsed on top of kids, he'd be responsible for any injuries, wouldn't he?" Ally countered. "Does he even carry homeowner's insurance on the property? Doubtful, based on how the interior looked." She took another bite of Harriet's masterpiece. "No way would I want to take on that level of risk."

A moment of silence hung in the air. Ally looked at Noah, who appeared to be focused on his meal.

"I have an idea," Gramps said.

Ally heard Noah let out a low groan. "What?" she asked.

"We should go down to city hall tomorrow and find out if Trevor has any plans for the place." Gramps's blue eyes widened. "Maybe he's going to work with a developer to create a new subdivision of residential housing."

"Maybe," Ally admitted. "That could be why Martha Cromlin mentioned the place is going to be leveled soon, hopefully before the snow flies."

"Yeah." Gramps drummed his fingers on the table. "Maybe Pricilla's murder is linked in some way to the land deal?"

"Okay, okay." Noah lifted a hand in surrender. "This is public knowledge, so I may as well tell you that yes, Trevor owns the land, and yes, he's been trying to connect with a developer to build on it." He pinned Ally and Gramps with a narrow look. "But no decisions have been made, because Trevor hasn't found anyone to partner with. So there's no point in you and Oscar traipsing down to city hall. Pricilla's murder has nothing to do with the Thompson property."

"How do you know that?" Gramps asked.

"Oscar, leave it alone." Noah's tone was curt.

Ally put a hand on her grandfather's arm. "Your theory is pretty far out there, Gramps."

"Someone has to come up with one, because Pricilla's murderer is still walking the streets," Gramps shot back.

A loud *thunk* cut through the tension building between Gramps and Noah. Ally glanced in surprise at Tillie, who was holding her casted arm, which she'd banged on the table. "Are you okay?"

"I'm fine, but I agree with my sister. No more talk of murder at the dinner table."

Gramps scowled and hunched his shoulders. Noah looked relieved.

"Oh, Ally, I'm finished with your sweater," Lydia chimed in. "I'd like you to try it on after dinner in case it needs some altering."

"Thanks, Lydia." Ally summoned a pained smile. She didn't need a hand-knitted sweater but couldn't bear to say anything negative to Lydia. Sensing Noah's curious gaze, she gave him a warning look.

When dinner was finished, Ally carried the dirty dishes to the sink.

"Who's ready for dessert?" Harriet asked with a broad smile.

"Me," Gramps said heartily.

"Count me in." Noah grinned.

"Me too." Ally caved.

Harriet cut generous portions, and Ally helped to distribute them. As she handed him a plate, Noah's fingers brushed hers, sending a tingle of awareness up her arm.

Ally took her seat last and sampled the cake. Like the meal, it was delicious. "Excellent, Harriet."

"Thank you, dear."

It didn't take them long to eat their cake. Ally hoped Lydia would forget about the sweater, but no such luck.

"Come with me, Ally." Lydia took her arm and led her down the hall past Gramps's room to her small bedroom. She picked up the sweater and held it up against Ally's frame. "I think it's going to fit perfectly."

"I'm sure it will." The sweater was soft to the touch and looked nicer than she'd expected. Maybe it wouldn't itch like mad.

"I'll wait for you in the living room." Lydia stepped out to give her privacy.

Ally pulled off her shirt and donned the sweater. She knew the color matched the blue eyes she'd inherited from Gramps. The soft yarn wasn't the least bit itchy. Feeling self-conscious, she walked into the living room. "It's beautiful, Lydia. Thank you very much."

"You're welcome, dear." Lydia eyed her with satisfaction. "I knew it would fit you perfectly."

Ally had no idea how the woman could know such a thing but couldn't deny the sweater was flattering. She appreciated Noah's appraising gaze.

She ran her fingers down the knitted garment and felt the edge of the playing card in her back pocket. She pulled it out and handed it to Noah. "Oh, this is the card I found at the Thompson farmhouse."

"Let me see that." Gramps took the card from Noah's fingers. He turned it around and peered at the back. "You found this card at the house?"

"Yes, why?"

Gramps handed it back to Noah. "It's from a marked deck."

Her jaw dropped. "What, like used for cheating?"

Gramps nodded. "Exactly."

Ally could tell Noah was surprised by the news. Was the marked deck of playing cards part of the motive for the robberies as well as Pricilla's murder?

Chapter Sixteen

Ally changed out of Lydia's sweater, her thoughts whirling. When she returned to the living room, she gave the widow a hug. "Thanks again for the sweater. It's lovely."

"You're welcome, dear." Lydia shot a satisfied smile at Harriet and Tillie.

"I better get home to the dogs." Ally glanced at Gramps, who still held the playing card in his hand. "You should probably give that to Noah."

"I'd like to take it," Noah agreed. "The techs might have found other playing cards in the mess."

With obvious reluctance, Gramps handed the ace of spades to Noah. "Looks like someone was cheating at cards."

"Maybe, maybe not." Noah pinned him with a stern look. "It's not your concern, remember?"

"Bah." Gramps scowled. "It seems obvious to me that there was gambling going on at the Thompson place. Which could be linked to the robberies and to Pricilla's murder."

"And they may not be connected at all," Noah countered.

Ally suppressed a sigh and glanced at her watch. These two could go at it like this all night. "I really have to go take care of the dogs. I'll check in with you tomorrow."

"Sure, sure." Gramps struggled to his feet and reached for his cane. Ally gave him a hug, silently grateful that Noah was spending the night on the sofa again. "Bye, Ally."

"I'll walk you out," Noah offered.

Ally lifted a brow, remembering what had happened the last time he'd walked her out. The mere memory of their heated kiss made her tremble. "Okay."

She gave each of the other WBWs a hug, thanked Harriet again for dinner and dessert, and walked outside. The cool September air made her wish she'd kept the sweater on.

"I'm disappointed in you, Ally," Noah said.

Stung, she swung to face him. "Because of the playing card?"

"Because you're poking your nose into my case." Noah's gaze, even in the dim light, was full of reproach. "It's bad enough that your grandfather keeps interfering, but I was hoping you'd learned your lesson after what happened this past summer."

"I'm not trying to interfere." Her protest was weak, because she had in fact been curious about the farmhouse. "And I have no desire to be in danger. But tell me this, Noah, did those patrol cops checking the place out know that a marked deck was being used by the kids there? Or was Gramps the first one to mention that?"

He frowned and didn't answer.

"Whatever." Ally turned away, suspecting that Noah felt guilty about not knowing about the cheating. "I have to go."

"I'm sorry, Ally. I shouldn't have come down so hard on you. But you and your grandfather really need to stay out of this from here on in."

"I'll do my best." She unlocked her car, then glanced at him. "Thanks again for staying here tonight. I feel better knowing you're keeping an eye on them."

"It's not a problem." Noah rubbed the small of his back. "Well, other than the sofa is a little too soft for me. By the way, did Jim and Erica really have a fight over his having a drink with me after work?"

"They really did," Ally confirmed. "I like Jim, he's a great guy, but it seems he's taking Erica for granted. Assuming she's fine sitting home all day with two kids and a dog." She shrugged. "I'm glad they were able to have dinner together tonight, just the two of them."

"Yeah." Noah held her gaze for a long moment, then stepped back. Apparently, no good-night kiss would be forthcoming. "Good night, Ally. I'll see you tomorrow."

"Good-night." Deeply disappointed, Ally slid behind the wheel. Before she could close her door, though, Noah was there, his woodsy scent filling her senses as he bent down to kiss her cheek.

Not exactly what she'd been hoping for, but sweet all the same.

"I'd like to take you out for dinner alone, too, Ally." Noah's low, husky voice was back. "But I think it's best if we do that after the investigation is finished."

"Uh, okay." She didn't totally understand his reasoning, but at least he'd asked her out. "Let me know when you arrest the murderer."

"Somehow I think you'll know the minute I do," Noah said dryly. "Oscar knows more than anyone about what goes on in this community."

"True. Good-night, Noah."

"Good-night, Ally." He stepped back so she could close her door.

Ally returned to the clinic, thinking about the marked playing card, the party house, and of course Noah.

Always Noah.

After taking both dogs out for their respective walks, she pulled out her phone and sent Erica a text.

Hope dinner went well.

Within seconds, Erica texted back: *Amazing.* ♥ *Fill u in tomorrow.*

Ally smiled and replied, *Can't wait.*

Relieved to know that Jim and Erica had found a way to work out their differences, she headed to bed. When Roxy jumped up beside her, Ally snuggled her close.

"It's just you and me, Rox," she whispered. "Just you and me."

For now.

* * *

The following morning, Ally took Roxy out first, then went to free Domino. The poodle was thrilled to see her. Making sure she had some treats in her pocket, she took him outside. Of course, he went back to his bad habit of pulling hard on the leash.

"Heel," she commanded.

He glanced up at her, then came to her side. She gave him a treat, which he inhaled without chewing.

"Behave," she scolded as they walked down Main Street. The hour was early, thanks to Roxy's internal alarm clock. Still, Ally noticed that several people were out and about, running errands or heading to work.

The latter made her think about her veterinary business. The past week had been better than expected, but she still didn't have many appointments scheduled. It wasn't easy paying her bills month to month when there was no way to estimate how much cash she'd have coming in.

Yet she was far better off now than she had been in Madison. At least the income and the bills were hers alone.

She'd put up the fall grooming special on her website yesterday but hadn't received a single call. Clearly people weren't searching online for grooming services.

Hadn't she put up a flyer at the library a few months back? Maybe Rosie had taken it down. Ally made a mental note to create new flyers and plaster them all around town.

If business was this slow in the summer and autumn, she dreaded to think what it would be like in the dead of winter.

She was so lost in her thoughts, she didn't notice a woman walking briskly toward her. When she recognized Hilda Green, Ally abruptly stopped, but of course Domino didn't.

"Heel!" Her sharp tone had the dog retreating to her side. She gave him a treat, hoping Pricilla's mother would simply walk past.

She didn't.

"Dr. Winter." Hilda's frosty tone made her inwardly groan. It was too early to deal with the woman's ridiculous accusations. She hadn't even had any coffee yet.

"Ms. Green." Ally gave a curt nod.

"I owe you an apology," Hilda said in a tone that was anything but apologetic. "I shouldn't have said anything when we ran into each other in the emergency department."

Ally wanted to ask why she had but decided a drawn-out conversation with the woman wasn't worth it. Hilda was dressed in a navy-blue business suit with a bright red–and–blue paisley scarf wrapped in a bow around her neck, clearly already back to work despite burying her daughter just yesterday. Ally forced a smile. "I understand. Grief can make us do and say things we might later regret."

"Grief," Hilda echoed, her stern tone fading to one of wistfulness. "Yes, I've been grieving my daughter. It's the worst thing I've suffered through in my entire life. And honestly, I still have trouble believing she's gone."

"I'm very sorry for your loss," Ally murmured, her gaze full of compassion. No matter what she thought of Hilda Green, the woman certainly hadn't deserved to lose her daughter at the young age of twenty-one. Especially since the person who'd killed Pricilla was still at large. "I'm glad you have Marlie's support through this difficult time."

"Marlie? Oh yes. She's been wonderful. They were close, and Marlie was really counting on having Cilla as a roommate after her previous roommate moved to Madison." Hilda rummaged in her purse for a tissue and blotted her eyes. "Again, please accept my apology."

"Of course. Take care of yourself." Ally watched as Hilda spun and retraced her steps, heading back toward the municipal building that housed city hall along with the other city council offices.

It was only then that Ally thought about the red-and-blue paisley scarf Hilda had been wearing.

She frowned, a sick feeling settling in her stomach. She'd seen a similar scarf not that long ago. Not exactly the same—the colors had been different—but close enough.

Only the paisley scarf she'd seen had been wrapped tightly around Pricilla Green's neck.

*　*　*

Ally practically ran with Domino back to the clinic. She needed to talk to Noah right away. Did he know the scarf that had been used to murder Pricilla was similar to the ones her mother wore?

It was a detail a man could easily miss.

She fed both dogs, then unlocked the clinic door before going around to the front desk. She needed to check her schedule, because she thought she had one more immunization coming in at some point.

Scheduled for tomorrow morning, not today. She sighed, then logged off and reached for her phone. The doorbell gave a little jingle. Ally glanced up and saw Wendy Granger standing there, holding Bandit. The adorable black Labradane looked as if he'd grown a full inch since the last time she'd seen him.

"Wendy, what's going on? Is Bandit hurt?"

"No, he's fine, but I really need you to help me find Bandit a home." Wendy's eyes were bright with tears. "That no-good Jake Hammond hasn't answered his phone and never showed up to claim Bandit." She made an annoyed clucking sound. "I called the police to report him for animal abuse."

"You what?" Ally gaped at her. "But he didn't touch the puppy."

Wendy sniffed. "He's completely irresponsible. I don't care if he was looking for a pet to love; he should have had the decency to call. Even if he came to get Bandit now, I wouldn't give him the dog. I doubt that boy would remember to feed Bandit three times a day."

Ally didn't know what to say. "Okay, but still, failing to pick up a puppy doesn't constitute animal abuse." She felt certain the Willow Bluff cop who'd taken her call was still laughing about it.

"Well, I don't care. That boy is worthless."

Ally sighed and rubbed her temple. "I'll keep trying to find Bandit a home, but I've had your flyer posted on my counter for the past several weeks with no takers." Although in truth, she hadn't had that many people coming in for appointments over that time frame, either.

"But you have to do something," Wendy said plaintively. "I can't bear the thought of taking him to the shelter."

"I understand." Ally didn't particularly want to see Bandit end up with Jeri Smith at the shelter either, but she wasn't the one who hadn't spayed her dog.

"What about that handsome detective of yours?" Wendy asked with a gleam in her eye. "I think he and Bandit would be perfect for each other."

"He's not my detective," Ally said, silently wishing he were. "I need to give Detective Jorgenson a call anyway, so I'll ask him again, okay?"

"Okay." Wendy looked deflated. "This poor little guy is the last one, and he's so cute. I just need to make sure he goes to a good home."

"Of course." Ally forced a smile.

Wendy nodded and spoke in baby talk to the puppy as she left. Personally, Ally thought Wendy should just keep the puppy for herself. But that wasn't her concern.

She picked up the phone and called Noah. Imagining him eating breakfast with the WBWs and Gramps, she expected him to answer, but the call when to voice mail.

"Noah? It's Ally. I need to talk to you about the scarf that was used to murder Pricilla. Call me, okay? Thanks."

She set her cell phone on the counter, staring at it for a long moment. Fully expecting he'd call back very quickly, especially after listening to her message, she waited.

After ten minutes, she gave up. She let both dogs out of their kennels, wondering when Kayla Benton would be by to get Domino.

The only good thing about his extended stay was that she'd get almost a full week of boarding fees.

Tailing Trouble

No job too small.

While the dogs played, Ally began typing an invoice for Kayla Benton, leaving the date of pickup open just in case it changed. Then she updated her grooming flyers and printed ten color copies.

With a frown, she looked down at her phone. Still no answer from Noah. Because he was busy looking into the marked card she'd found at the Thompson place?

Even as a teenager, Ally didn't think she'd have gone to the creepy, dilapidated farmhouse to party.

Although she'd bet Noah and Jim, along with the other football players and cheerleaders, would have.

Which brought her thoughts right back to Noah. When her cell rang, she pounced on it, but the caller was Erica.

"Erica? Tell me everything," Ally demanded.

"Oh, Ally. It was so nice. Jim apologized and told me he didn't want to leave."

"Of course not. He loves you, Erica, and the kids."

"We had a really nice dinner, Ally, thanks to you. And he agreed that he needed to call me when he's going to be late, and he insisted that I spend some time with you too."

"Me?" Ally was surprised to hear that. "Personally, I think the two of you need to have a weekly date night." It was on the tip of her tongue to offer to babysit, but the possibility of having a veterinary emergency held her back.

"We are," Erica said with a giggle. "We agreed to get a babysitter so that we can go out on Friday nights."

"Good." Ally was glad to hear Jim had stepped up. As he should.

"But I told Jim that I'd like to see more of my friends, so he agreed to help watch the kids on the weekends," Erica went on.

197

"I know last weekend didn't work out, but can we try again for this weekend? Maybe on Saturday?"

"I'd like that," Ally agreed. "And he *should* take a turn watching the kids. He's their father."

"Right?" Erica laughed. "Honestly, once he spends more time with them, he'll understand where I'm coming from."

"Exactly."

"Okay, so Saturday at noon?"

"It's a date, Erica. My treat, remember?"

"After last night, you don't owe me anything," Erica insisted. "Jim and I had the best night together in a long time."

Ally could easily read between the lines and had to squash a flash of jealousy. She was truly happy for her friend and hoped maybe someday she'd have a family of her own. "You deserve it. Take care, Erica; I'll see you Saturday."

"Bye, Ally."

After she set her phone down, Ally realized she hadn't told Erica about Noah's kiss or their sometime-in-the-future-when-the-case-was-closed dinner date.

Considering the last date hadn't happened, it was probably better to wait to tell Erica.

Not that she was superstitious or anything.

The dogs chose that moment to crash into the window, making her wince. "Stop! Heel!"

They chased each other around the room. Ally grabbed the teetering lobby chair before it could topple over. Again. Finally, the dogs dropped to the floor, stretched out beside each other, panting happily.

Good grief. Even though she would be glad to have Domino back with the Bentons were he belonged, Ally knew Roxy would miss him.

Maybe she could arrange for doggy playdates? Pathetic—Roxy was having better luck with her love life with Domino than Ally was with Noah.

After checking to make sure the window wasn't cracked or broken, she took both dogs out for a bathroom break. It had been over an hour since she'd left that message for Noah. What on earth was taking him so long to get back to her?

It couldn't be a coincidence that Hilda Green was wearing a paisley scarf that was almost exactly the same as the one used to kill Pricilla.

Was that why the woman had apologized to her? Because she was playing the part of the grieving mother to hide the fact that she'd murdered her own daughter?

Ally grabbed her phone and called Noah again. He picked up, but his tone was curt. "I can't talk right now, Ally, I'll call you back later."

"Did you get my message?" She couldn't believe he'd blown her off.

"Yes, and like I said, I'll call you back later."

"But Noah . . ." She realized she was talking to dead air.

What in the world? "Can you believe he hung up on me?" she asked the dogs incredulously. Domino thumped his tail in agreement.

Her phone rang again. This time the caller was Gramps, once again on his cell phone. She braced herself for the high volume and kept the phone three inches from her ear. "Hi, Gramps."

"ALLY! DID YOU HEAR THE NEWS?"

Uh-oh. A sliver of dread sank deep. "What news?"

"THERE'S BEEN ANOTHER MURDER!" Gramps was shouting so loud the dogs rose to their feet and trotted over to her, ears perked forward.

"Who?" Ally asked, now understanding why Noah hadn't had time to talk to her. Had he been standing at the crime scene? At the Thompson farmhouse? Or the weeping willow?

"JAKE HAMMOND WAS FOUND DEAD IN HIS APARTMENT!"

Jake? Dead in his apartment? She thought about Wendy's nuisance call to the police. Had that sparked an investigation?

Still, Jake had been their prime suspect in Pricilla's murder. Until she'd seen Hilda wearing the paisley scarf. Now she had doubts.

Could the city executive have murdered her own daughter and Pricilla's boyfriend too?

If so, why?

Chapter Seventeen

"I'm coming to pick you up, Gramps." Ally worried that if she didn't get her grandfather, he'd find someone else like Rosie Malone to give him a ride.

Better that she be the one in control of where he went. She didn't trust him being off on his own.

Especially not after the recent break-in at the Legacy House.

"I'LL BE WAITING!"

Ally shoved her phone in her pocket and looked at the two dogs. "Unfortunately, it's back in your kennels for a while."

After locking up the clinic, she gave each of them a treat as she put them in their respective crates.

Grabbing her keys, she headed out through the back of the clinic to her Honda. She could hardly believe Jake Hammond was dead. Had he been strangled too? No way to know, and she doubted Noah would give her and Gramps any details.

Just a few months ago there had been two murders on the same street, Appletree Lane. Now there had been another two murders, maybe not located near each other, but the two victims had been in a relationship.

She remembered Pricilla's diary and the girl's fears over Jake cheating on her. Didn't seem relevant now that they were both dead.

Gramps was waiting outside on the front porch of the Legacy House, leaning on his cane. The minute Ally pulled up, he began making his way toward her.

Ally jumped out to help him. "How did you hear the news about Jake's murder?"

Gramps settled into the passenger seat, his cane tucked between his legs. "Rosie overheard someone in the library saying something about the police being outside Jake's four-family apartment building."

"Okay, but how did you hear that Jake had been murdered?" Ally asked, perplexed.

Gramps flashed a grin. "Susie James lives across the hall from Jake, and she caught a glimpse of his dead body. His roommate, Colin Felton, screamed like a girl, so she came out to see what was going on."

Ally was still trying to piece the puzzle together. "Susie went into the library to tell Rosie?"

"Oh no, I think Susie told Marcus Andrews, who told Rosie."

It was all rather confusing, especially as she'd been gone from Willow Bluff for so long and didn't know half the people he was talking about. The names were all a blur, but she did her best to stay focused. "Okay, so Susie James saw Jake's body with her own eyes."

"Yep." Gramps gave a nod. "Because Colin screamed when he came home."

"So that means Jake might not have been dead for very long," Ally mused. "I mean, Colin lives in the apartment with him. It couldn't have happened in the middle of the night, or Colin would have heard something."

"If Colin was there," Gramps agreed. "But he might have been staying somewhere else."

"Like where?" Ally slanted him a glance.

"The Thompson farmhouse?" Gramps offered.

"Doubtful. The police have been making routine visits there, and it was empty when I was there too." Ally frowned. "Do you know something about Colin that I don't?"

"No, I'm just trying to keep an open mind." Gramps looked thoughtful. "If Colin decided to kill his roommate, he'd try to arrange to have an alibi, right?"

Gramps's wild theories were giving her a headache. "And why would Colin want to kill Jake?"

"Because Jake killed Pricilla and Colin secretly loved her." Gramps gave a nod of satisfaction. "I think Colin arranged to be gone but sneaked back in to do the deed. Then he came home this morning screaming for all to hear that he'd found his roommate dead."

"You have no proof that Colin did any such thing." She hated to admit that his idea was plausible. Totally pulled out of thin air, in her humble opinion, but still possible.

"Your detective is the one who needs to find the proof," Gramps pointed out.

Ally pulled into the parking space behind her clinic and helped Gramps out of the car. "I'll get you inside, then I need to take care of the dogs."

"Domino still with you?" Gramps asked as she unlocked the door.

"Yes, the flu bug has hit the Benton home hard." Deep down, Ally hoped that Domino wouldn't end up like Roxy, with owners who didn't want him. She hadn't minded taking custody of Roxy, but she couldn't keep taking in stray animals.

That was young Amanda Cartwright's goal in life, not hers.

As Ally took both dogs out for quick bathroom breaks, she realized she hadn't filled Gramps in on Hilda Green's paisley scarf.

The one Noah hadn't seemed very interested in.

No, that isn't fair, she silently amended. The paisley scarf wasn't nearly as important as finding Jake Hammond's dead body.

After returning to the clinic, she let both dogs out in the lobby again.

"Ally, I think we should take a walk down to the apartment building, see what's going on," Gramps said with a gleam in his eye. "Maybe we'll learn something."

"And maybe Noah will kick us out," she countered. "Gramps, there's no way we're going to get close enough to the crime scene to learn anything. Besides, I need to tell you about Hilda Green."

He leaned forward, his expression full of anticipation. "What about her?"

Ally explained how she had met the woman while walking Domino and Hilda had apologized for her behavior in the hospital emergency department.

Gramps grunted. "So she should."

"Yes, well, that wasn't the most important thing. She was wearing a red-and-navy-blue paisley scarf around her neck—you know, tied in a bow?"

"So?" After a couple of seconds, Gramps's eyes widened. "A scarf like the one you saw around Pricilla's neck?"

"Exactly." Ally propped her elbows on the counter. "Don't you think that's a strange coincidence? I mean, think about it. The last time we saw Pricilla, she was wearing a cropped blue-and-white-striped top, bright-green skintight short shorts, and three-inch red-and-white polka-dot heels. No sign of a paisley scarf." Until it was wrapped around her neck while she was lying beneath the weeping willow.

Gramps folded his arms across his chest. "So Hilda killed her daughter and Jake."

She sighed. "Didn't you just say Colin did it? And why would Hilda kill them both? Sure, she might have lost her temper with Pricilla, but to kill her? And then kill Jake?" Ally shook her head. "It just doesn't make sense."

"Only because we don't know all the facts." Gramps narrowed his gaze. "That detective of yours needs to fill us in on what he's found."

And that is about as likely as little green men beaming down from Mars, Ally thought. "Speaking of facts, Wendy Granger stopped in with Bandit. She apparently called the police to report Jake Hammond for puppy abuse because he didn't pick up Bandit as promised."

Gramps blinked. "That doesn't make any sense."

"Yeah, well, that's Wendy for you. But anyway, I assumed Wendy's nuisance call caused the police to head over to the apartment building."

"Not sure why they'd bother," Gramps muttered.

"Too bad we don't know what time Colin came home to find Jake's body." Ally looked at Gramps. "We saw Jake last at Pricilla's funeral. But Wendy mentioned that Jake hadn't returned her calls yesterday either."

"That supports my theory that Colin might have been staying elsewhere," Gramps said with a nod.

"Maybe." She had to admit it was possible Colin had stayed somewhere else overnight, coming home early in the morning to get ready to work at Electronics and More.

And to find his roommate dead.

"What do you think about having lunch at the Lakeview Café?" Gramps asked. "We might learn something there."

Ally hesitated; it was barely eleven o'clock. Then again, she didn't have any appointments scheduled, so why not? "Okay. Let me take the dogs out first."

"Too bad Domino can't join us," Gramps said, eyeing the poodle. "Maybe he'd find something with his nose."

"Speaking of which, he didn't seem to recognize Hilda Green's scent. So maybe she's off the hook."

"Maybe, but the scarf is a pretty big link to Pricilla's murder."

"Too obvious, though." Ally took Roxy out first, knowing Gramps wasn't about to cross anyone off his suspect list. After she finished with Domino and kenneled both dogs, the bell over her door rang.

Noah entered the clinic, his expression grim. "Ally, do you have a minute to talk?"

She glanced at Gramps, then nodded. "If we're going to stay here, I'd like to bring the dogs out. No sense in keeping them locked up."

"Fine, but this won't take long." The shuttered expression on his face wasn't reassuring.

Ally quickly released both dogs, who immediately ran around the clinic lobby. Used to their antics, she ignored them.

"I'm sorry to hear about Jake." Ally joined Noah near the front desk.

Noah's gaze narrowed. "How did you hear about that?" He glanced at Gramps. "Never mind, I can guess."

"I heard it from Rosie, who heard it secondhand from Susie, who saw his dead body," Gramps confirmed. Ally winced at the smug smile on Gramps's face. "What can I say? I have a lot of friends in this town."

"I'm well aware of your infinite communication network," Noah said dryly.

"Was he strangled too?" Gramps asked.

Noah's gaze narrowed in warning. No eye twitch yet, but Ally sensed he was on the verge. "I need to know when the last time was either of you saw Jake Hammond."

"At Pricilla's funeral," Ally answered quickly. "Right, Gramps? We saw Jake talking to Marlie Crown."

"That's correct," Gramps agreed. "Marlie told Jake to leave the funeral so Hilda Green wouldn't be upset."

Noah frowned. "That was when he left, right?"

"Yep." Gramps didn't say anything more.

"Jake said it wasn't his fault that Pricilla's mother kicked her out," Ally added. "He said something along the lines of Marlie knowing him better than anyone, so she'd know he didn't hurt Pricilla."

"Their conversation was tense at first," Gramps finally added, in spite of himself. "But then it grew more cordial. They hugged each other at the end."

"Marlie seemed to infer Hilda Green suspected Jake of killing her daughter and that seeing him at the funeral would be distressing."

Noah's expression didn't change as they provided details of the conversation. "So you both last saw Jake yesterday morning at roughly what time?"

"Ten twenty-five?" Ally glanced at Gramps for confirmation.

Gramps nodded. "Why? Are you trying to estimate the time of his death? Isn't that what the ME's office does?"

The tiny muscle at the corner of Noah's left eye began to twitch. "Thanks for the information," he said in a professional tone.

"You know Wendy Granger was looking for Jake on Monday afternoon too," Ally offered. "She claims Jake was coming to take Bandit but never showed and didn't answer his phone. She said Jake came to see Bandit on Saturday. Maybe she can help with your timeline."

"Okay, thanks." Noah seemed slightly less tense. Thankfully, his left eye stopped twitching. Although it was usually Gramps who caused the malady. "Anything else?"

"Well, I did leave you the message about Hilda Green's paisley scarf," Ally reminded. "It was very similar to the one I saw around Pricilla's neck."

And the eye twitch was back. "Thanks for that information. I have to go." Noah spun on his heel and left the clinic.

"Well, that was rude," Gramps muttered darkly. "He didn't give us a single clue."

Ally didn't point out that Noah's job was to solve the murders, not provide them with clues. "I'm sure he's stressed out at the moment. Two murders in town is a big deal."

"Which tells me he oughta be looking to us for help rather than keeping everything to himself," Gramps said tartly.

Ally sighed and tried not to take Noah's abrupt departure personally. She could understand his feeling under pressure with a second murder so close to the first one. Especially if the chief of police was still getting pressure from Mayor Martha Cromlin and Hilda Green.

But the way he'd come in all professional and left just as quickly made it seem as if the brief kiss they'd shared had never happened.

At the rate things were going, it wasn't likely they'd have their first real date anytime soon.

*　*　*

Ten minutes after Noah left, her door opened again. Ally's heart sank when she saw ten-year-old Amanda Cartwright standing there cradling another kitten to her chest. Not the lost cat from a few months ago, but a small black kitten.

Where in the world does this kid find these animals? If Ally didn't know better, she'd think the girl sneaked them out of Jeri Smith's animal shelter.

"Dr. Winter? Midnight is injured. Will you please look at him?"

At least Ally knew better than to expect payment for her services. Last time the girl brought Pepper AKA Spot in for care, Ally had assumed the animal belonged to her. "Amanda, what did I tell you about bringing in stray animals?" Then she frowned. "And why aren't you in school?"

"I'm sick." Amanda sniffled loudly and forced a cough. Ally rolled her eyes. "Principal O'Malley sent me home yesterday because I had a fever. But I'm better now. And I found Midnight hiding in the bushes a few houses down from me."

"And how do you know Midnight doesn't belong to the owners of that house? Some people like having outside cats." Ally wanted to scold the little girl but didn't have the heart. She knew how badly Amanda wanted a pet of her own. And how firmly her mother refused to allow it.

"He doesn't have a collar."

"He might have a chip," Ally explained.

"I don't think so. I don't feel anything."

Ally suppressed a sigh. The girl had helped Ally with Roxy on occasion, soaking up information about veterinary medicine like a sponge. That Amanda had even checked for a microchip was impressive.

At least this time Amanda had brought a kitten and not a dead baby bunny or an injured robin. Small things to be grateful for.

"Bring him into the exam room." Ally didn't see what choice she had but to take a look. If the kitten was fine, she'd call Jeri and turn the animal over. No more taking in strays.

Seemed as if she needed the lecture as much as Amanda did.

"What seems to be the trouble?" Ally asked as she drew on exam gloves.

"He has a deep scratch, see?" Amanda gently parted the black fur to reveal a jagged two-inch-long cut.

"Hmm." Ally couldn't tell if the wound was from a coyote bite or had been made by something sharp, like the edge of a fence or a thorn. "First thing we have to do is wash it."

"Okay." Amanda stared up at her with adoring eyes. Ally hoped that by the time Amanda was old enough to be a vet tech, which seemed to be her goal in life, Ally would be able to afford to hire her.

Amanda held the kitten firmly, unlike a previous time where she'd let go as Ally was injecting asthma medication into another of her rescue projects. When the wound had been cleaned, Ally considered her options.

Normally, she didn't glue or suture wounds unless she knew they weren't more than twenty-four hours old. This one appeared recent, but it was hard to tell. Closing an old wound could cause infection, but not closing it could too.

A dilemma, since the cat didn't have a collar or a chip.

Yep, there was no doubt about it. She'd have to close the wound and keep the kitten there to watch for infection.

"I'll glue the wound closed, but I'll need to keep the kitten here for a few days. I'll give him antibiotics and watch him closely for any signs of an infection."

"I can help," Amanda offered. Then hastily added, "After school is out."

"That's fine, but you could also help me by finding out who Midnight belongs to. I don't want him to end up in the shelter."

"I know." Amanda's gaze clouded. "I don't want that either."

"Pepper's owner came to find her when I put up some flyers. Maybe you could put some up for Midnight?" Ally brought out the tools she'd need to repair the cat's laceration.

"I can do that," Amanda agreed.

"Good. Now again, I'll need you to help hold him still." Ally worked quickly to repair the cat's injury, then injected him with an antibiotic. The animal also looked a little dehydrated and underfed, so when that was finished, she gave him a small fluid bolus. "I'll need to take him into the back to put him in a kennel and give him some food, okay?"

"Okay." Amanda watched wistfully as Ally picked up the cat. "Can I come by after school tomorrow to help take care of him?"

"Yes, that would be great. Now don't forget the flyers," Ally reminded her.

"I won't. Thanks, Dr. Ally!" The girl certainly didn't look sick as she skipped out of the exam room.

Ally gave the cat some wet cat food and left him in a large kennel complete with a litter box.

When she returned to the lobby, Gramps glanced up. "You're giving away your services for free again, aren't you?"

She shrugged. "I can't turn that girl away."

Gramps grinned. "You're a softy. Ready to go eat?"

"Sure." After she kenneled the dogs, Ally and Gramps walked down Main Street to the Lakeview Café. As they approached, there was a small group of people talking together. Before Ally could say a word, Gramps hurried over to join them.

Battling a wave of trepidation, Ally joined them.

"I'm telling you, it was the most awful thing I've seen in my entire life!" A short, plump woman who looked to be about Ally's age placed a dramatic hand over her heart. "A dead body, lying right there on the floor!"

"Did you notice anything in particular?" Gramps asked. "Blood from a wound, or something tied around his neck?"

Ally subtly tugged on Gramps arm, but he shrugged her off.

The plump woman, who Ally deduced was Susie James, turned to face Gramps. "Well yes, I saw something around Jake's neck. But I was too far away to see what it was."

"Maybe a flowery or paisley-patterned scarf?" Gramps prompted.

Ally winced, instinctively knowing Noah wouldn't like his witness spouting off like this or getting information fed to her by Gramps. She tugged on his arm again. "Gramps, I'm hungry. Don't you think it's time to eat?"

"It could have been a scarf," Susie agreed, a slight frown wrinkling her brow. "Although I'm not really supposed to talk about it."

A little late, don't you think? Ally glanced around surreptitiously, hoping Noah wasn't anywhere nearby. When she saw him striding toward the group, her heart sank.

"Gramps, lunch. Now." She tugged harder on his arm, and he must have caught sight of Noah as well, because he came along with her. Based on the scowl on Noah's face, he was giving Susie James a lecture.

Tailing Trouble

At least this time, Gramps wasn't the one caught in Noah's cross hairs.

Ally took a seat across from Gramps, wondering if Susie was right about a scarf possibly being used as the murder weapon.

And if so, why on earth would Hilda Green continue to wear them out in public?

Chapter Eighteen

"I think you're onto something with Hilda Green and the paisley scarf." Gramps glanced over his shoulder. "Your detective doesn't look happy."

"He has a right to be upset. Susie James should know better than to blab to everyone within earshot about the crime scene." Ally set the menu aside, since she already had it memorized. "And the more I think about it, the scarf seems too obvious. I mean, why would Hilda wear one around her neck if she'd used one just like it to kill her daughter and her daughter's boyfriend?"

"Good point." Gramps drummed his fingers on the table, and she could practically see the wheels in his mind, spinning round and round. "Someone who wanted to frame her for murder might use it, though."

Ally sat back in her chair, her heart thumping in her chest. The possibility hadn't occurred to her, but now that Gramps said it, she could see he might have something there. "Wow, Gramps, that's creepy."

"Crazy kills," Gramps said with a nod.

She winced. "Not the motto we want Willow Bluff to be known for, remember?" He'd used the same phrase this past June. Although she hated to admit it, it kinda fit.

Gramps shrugged. "Can't help it if it's true."

Their server, Darla, came to take their order. Ally remembered how Darla and Marlie had been in deep conversation. "I'm sorry for your loss," Ally said.

Darla frowned. "My loss?"

"I saw you and Marlie talking. You seemed upset." Ally offered a sad smile. "I'm sure it was hard losing Pricilla. She worked here with you, didn't she?"

"Um, yeah, she did." Darla quickly changed the subject. "What can I get you?"

She and Gramps placed their order. When Darla left, Ally glanced over to where Noah and Susie James had been talking, but they were gone.

Her gaze caught on a tall man with salt-and-pepper hair sitting two tables over. She frowned, then remembered he was the guy who'd come up to put his arm around Hilda Green at Pricilla's funeral.

"Gramps, do you know who that guy is?" Ally subtly gestured to the man at the table.

Gramps spun in his seat to look.

"Don't be so obvious," Ally hissed.

"He looks familiar." Gramps turned back. "Why?"

"He was very supportive of Hilda Green at the funeral, put his arm around her." Ally thought the guy was pretty good-looking for a man in his mid to late forties. "You think maybe he and Hilda Green have something going on?"

"Why? You think it has something to do with Pricilla's murder?"

"Well, it might be another reason why Hilda kicked her daughter out of the house." Ally shrugged and sipped her water. She'd cut back on the lemonade in an attempt to avoid sugar. Not that it stopped her from eating Harriet's wonderful desserts. "You know, the old saying about how two is company and three is a crowd?"

"Hmm." Gramps's keen blue gaze went back to the man. He was sitting alone but glanced at his watch as if waiting for someone.

Just as Darla brought their meals, Hilda Green walked over to kiss Salt and Pepper's cheek. She dropped into the chair across from him, a tired smile on her face. Ally noticed she was still wearing the paisley scarf around her neck.

She felt certain Noah must not have told her that a similar scarf had been used to kill her daughter, or she wouldn't be wearing it.

"Gramps, look." Ally nudged him beneath the table.

"Well, well, well." Gramps nodded in satisfaction. "I guess you were right about them seeing each other."

"They could just be good friends," she felt compelled to point out.

"Not the way they're making googly eyes at each other." Gramps waggled his eyebrows, making her laugh.

"I'd like to know his name," Ally mused. She took a bite of her salad.

"We'll stop over there on our way out," Gramps said. "She'll have to introduce us."

"You think so?" Ally wasn't convinced, but she didn't have a better idea.

"I wonder if Noah has already asked her about the scarf." Gramps frowned. "Surely he would have investigated where the scarf came from. At the very least, it should be tested for DNA evidence."

Ally pointed her fork at him. "I'm sure they've sent it for testing. You know from this past June that DNA evidence takes a long time."

"I wonder if the scarf was actually taken from Hilda's closet or purchased to look just like the ones she likes to wear."

Gramps was talking to himself more than to her, but she nodded. "I was curious about that too. I'm sure Hilda would know if a scarf was missing from her wardrobe."

"Or two scarves," Gramps corrected. "If Susie James is right about Jake having been murdered with one too."

Ally considered that. One missing scarf could go unnoticed, but two? She found that hard to believe. "Who would have the opportunity to take them from Hilda's bedroom? I assume she doesn't keep them lying around in the living room or kitchen."

"Good question." Gramps chomped on a bite of his salad, an unusual choice for him. "Makes it more likely they were purchased from a store."

Ally tended to agree. When she'd finished eating, she waved Darla back in order to pay the bill. Gramps reached for his wallet, but she shook her head. "No, Gramps. My treat."

"Business doing better?" Gramps asked.

"Yes." It wasn't as good as she'd like, but it had picked up a bit. Besides, she wasn't about to mooch off her grandfather. Bad enough that she ate dinner at the Legacy House far more than she should.

And there was always the possibility Amanda would find Midnight's owner, someone who would love to have him back and pay for the treatment and meds.

"Let's go find out who Hilda's mystery man is." Gramps struggled to his feet.

Ally highly doubted his plan would work but gamely followed his lead. He headed in the general direction of Hilda's table, then looked at her as if surprised to see her.

"Ms. Green?" Gramps offered his most charming smile.

"Oh hello, Mr. Winter." Hilda's gaze fell on Ally. "Dr. Winter. It's nice to see you both."

"We just wanted to offer our condolences once again," Gramps said earnestly. He looked pointedly at the man with salt-and-pepper hair. "I'm sorry, I don't think we've met. I'm Oscar Winter."

"Darrel Steinbach." He smiled and shook Gramps's hand. "Nice to meet you."

"Are you new to Willow Bluff?" Gramps asked. He pointed to his cane. "I don't get out as much as I used to, but I don't remember seeing you around."

Hilda spoke up. "Actually, Darrel is just visiting. He lives in the Madison area."

"This town is a wonderful place to visit," Ally said. "Thanks to all the work of Ms. Green, our city executive, and Martha Cromlin, our mayor, we've seen an increase in our tourism over the past two years." Ally fudged the numbers a bit but figured no one would notice.

"Hilda is an incredible woman," Darrel said, his gaze warm as he looked at the woman seated across from him. "I can see she's done an amazing job here."

Yep, definitely more than friends, Ally thought as the couple gazed into each other's eyes for a long moment.

"Are you interested in the Thompson property?" Gramps asked.

The blunt question clearly caught Darrel and Hilda off guard. Ally knew her grandfather was right when a flash of guilt flickered across Hilda's eyes.

"What makes you think that?" Hilda demanded with a dark scowl.

Gramps shrugged, apparently deciding the time to ooze charm was over. "I heard Trevor Thompson wanted to develop the property but needed financial backing. Seems logical to assume Mr. Steinbach here might be interested."

"Well, that's really not any of your business," Hilda said stiffly. Ally hid a smile. The city executive couldn't have been more obvious in her response. "Now if you'll excuse us? We haven't ordered yet."

Gramps waited a beat, making Hilda look uncomfortable. Finally, he nodded. "Of course. Have a good day."

Ally fell into step beside him and waited until they were on the sidewalk to say in a low voice, "I can't believe you put them on the spot like that."

"What have I got to lose?" Gramps asked with a satisfied expression on his face. "Figured they'd either confirm the allegation or deny it."

"Or avoid answering altogether, which pretty much indicates you were right." Ally glanced back to see Hilda and Darrel having an intense discussion. "Although I'm not sure it matters. It doesn't seem like the land deal is related to the murders."

"Unless Jake and Pricilla found out that Hilda was cutting some sort of side deal with Darrel Steinbach that she didn't want anyone to know about," Gramps countered.

"Gramps." Ally sighed. There he went again, pulling theories out of thin air. It made her want to scream. "I thought we already decided the scarves were being used to frame Hilda. That she would never be so stupid as to use a paisley scarf to kill two people, then wear one out in public."

Gramps tapped his temple. "Gotta keep an open mind, Ally. Anything is possible."

He was probably right about keeping an open mind, but she still didn't see any correlation between the land deal and the murders.

She steered him toward the clinic, knowing she needed to check on Midnight. Gramps might have gone overboard on his theories, but one thing was certain: Hilda Green was proving to be more complex than Ally had given the woman credit for.

And she wasn't entirely convinced that was a good thing.

* * *

Ally took both dogs out for a bathroom break, letting them have the run of the clinic, then checked on Midnight. The cat had eaten all his food and had used the litter box. Two great steps in the right direction. She called Jeri Smith.

"Hi, Dr. Winter, what's new?" Jeri asked.

"Amanda Cartwright found another stray cat, a young black male, roughly a year old. He had a laceration that I took care of, but I'd really like to find his owner."

"No chip or collar, I assume?"

"No." Ally sighed. "I'm telling you, that girl is a stray animal magnet."

"Maybe she wouldn't be out looking for strays if her mother allowed her to have a pet," Jeri said dryly.

"Yeah, but I wouldn't want to cross Ellen Cartwright. Frankly, that woman scares me. Listen, does the cat sound familiar?"

"I had a couple of black kittens maybe six months back that I adopted out. Let me check my records and get back to you," Jeri offered. "I'd like to know if someone I gave a pet to mistreated it."

"I can't say for sure the laceration was done by a person," Ally hastened to assure her. "I think it's more likely a thorn or maybe a coyote or a dog."

"Still, I don't like it." Jeri sounded upset. "I try so hard to give these animals a good home. I hate the idea someone might have abandoned it."

"Or the cat escaped from a house in the neighborhood and Amanda found it before the owners did." Ally knew Jeri Smith had a soft spot for animals the same way she did. Which was why she performed free veterinary services for the shelter. In turn, Jeri recommended the Furry Friends clinic to all adoptive animal parents.

"I'll call you back," Jeri repeated.

Ally hung up the phone and checked on the dogs, who were actually behaving themselves. When she glanced at Gramps, she frowned. He was using his two index fingers again to peck at the computer keyboard.

"What are you doing?" She leaned on the counter, trying to see the screen.

"I'm searching for information on Darrel Steinbach." Gramps didn't look up from his task.

Ally wanted to pound her forehead against the counter top. "Gramps, you already know he's interested in the Thompson farmhouse. What more do you think you're going to find online?"

"Won't know until I search." *Peck. Peck. Peck.*

She couldn't stand it and came around to the other side of the front desk. She elbowed him aside, taking control of the keyboard. "Here, let me."

Gramps moved over, and she did a quick search using the keywords: *Darrel Steinbach Property Developer.*

Instantly Darrel's picture showed up on the screen. He looked younger in the photograph, not as much salt mixed in with the pepper. Still, it was clear the guy owned property over in Madison.

"Wonder why he's interested in Willow Bluff," Gramps said.

"Hey, it's a great town," Ally pointed out. "And maybe he's getting the farmland for a good deal."

"Type in Trevor Thompson's name."

Ally did, but the results were overwhelming. "Thompson is too common."

"Try again, adding 'Property Developer,' " Gramps encouraged.

She did, but still nothing. It was odd but didn't mean much.

The sound of toenails on the floor had her glancing over. The dogs had begun their playful romp. Maybe she should consider having the lobby chairs bolted to the floor?

"Maybe we should try . . ."

"Look," Ally interrupted, losing patience. "We already know Darrel is interested in the farmland. We're not going to find any dark secrets about the land deal on the internet."

"Maybe it's time you take me to the party house. I've never seen it." He scowled. "Because you went there without me."

"Not happening." She glanced at her watch, wondering when Kayla Benton was going to pick up Domino. She'd sounded pretty sick, so it was possible the woman wasn't going to come until tomorrow. "It's getting late. Why don't I take you back to the Legacy House?"

"It's only one forty-five," Gramps protested. "We need to keep working the case."

"It's not *our* case." Ally pushed away from the computer. "And you already learned what Susie James saw at the crime scene of Jake's murder. What more do you want?"

Gramps sat silently for a moment, then reached for his cane. "I have an idea."

Uh-oh. She was suspicious of Gramps and his ideas. "Now what?"

"We should have thought of this before. Let's take a walk down Main Street. Check out the stores, see where they might be selling paisley scarves."

Ally inwardly groaned. "I'm sure Noah or one of the Willow Bluff police officers has already done that."

"No reason we can't do the same." Gramps looked excited at the prospect. "Let's go."

Ally didn't move. She lifted a hand. "On one condition."

Gramps frowned. "What?"

"That afterwards you go back to the Legacy House without complaining."

"I can do that."

Ally doubted it, but whatever. Stopping Gramps when he was hot on the trail of something was impossible. He'd just go by himself, which wasn't an option.

The break-in at the Legacy House seemed like eons ago rather than just two days. And Noah was no closer to finding the person responsible.

She made a mental note to call Kayla when they were finished shopping. She needed Domino to go home so she could sleep on the widows' sofa with Roxy.

Doubtful Noah would do it a third night in a row. Especially now that he had a second murder to investigate.

"I have to take care of the dogs first." She took Domino out first, then Roxy. After peeking in on Midnight, she grabbed her keys. "Let's get this over with."

"Hey, we might find a clue that detective of yours missed," Gramps said. "You know people tend to open up to me."

By people, he meant women. For his age, Gramps sure rivaled Noah Jorgenson for being Willow Bluff's most eligible bachelor.

Ally locked the clinic, then followed Gramps as he crossed the street. There were a couple of smaller boutiques located a few doors down from the sandwich shop.

The first one was already showing a large Thanksgiving display. "It's still September, isn't it?" Gramps asked as he glanced around.

"Yep. Be thankful it's not full of Christmas decorations." Ally moved through the store, eyeing the merchandise. "I don't see any clothing items."

"Nah, just a bunch of that knickknack stuff some women like." Gramps moved toward the door.

The next store was full of different kinds of art, everything from oil paintings to watercolors to sculptures. Ally caught a glimpse at one of the price tags and nearly choked.

"This is all way out of my price range," she whispered to Gramps. He nodded and once again headed for the door.

The third shop was called Nancy's Nook and had a display of women's clothing in the window. "Bingo," Gramps said with a satisfied grin.

Ally held the door for him. The place was small and cramped, but there were lots of different articles of clothing available for sale.

Including silk scarves.

Gramps made a beeline toward them. "This is paisley, isn't it?" he asked in a loud whisper.

"Yes." Ally was impressed he knew what paisley was. "Looks very much like the one Hilda was wearing."

And the one that had been wrapped around Pricilla's neck.

"May I help you?" A woman in her midsixties smiled broadly. "Are you looking for a gift for your wife?"

Like a switch, Gramps turned on the charm. "Is this your shop? It's incredible and something my wife would have loved, if she were still here." His expression turned sorrowful. "Amelia passed away two years ago."

"Oh, I'm so sorry to hear that," the woman said. "My name is Nancy Graham, and yes, this is my store." Nancy beamed. "Your daughter might like one of these scarves."

Daughter? Ally almost choked again.

"You flatter me," Gramps said with a wide smile. "My name is Oscar Winter, and this is my granddaughter, Dr. Ally Winter. She owns the Furry Friends Veterinary Clinic across the street."

"Oh yes, of course. Nice to meet you." Nancy smiled at Gramps again. "What can I help you with?"

"These scarves are very pretty. I noticed Hilda Green wearing one just today. Tell me, do you sell a lot of them?" Gramps asked.

Nancy's smile faltered. "Yes, these are very popular. Which color do you like the best?"

"Well, I'm partial to blue, you know, to match my eyes." Gramps winked. "Do you remember if you sold any scarves like this in the past week or two to anyone in particular?"

Now Nancy's eyes narrowed suspiciously. Ally knew the jig was up. "Why do you ask?"

"Did you know a scarf like this was used to kill Pricilla Green?" Again Gramps's blunt statement caught her off guard.

"Like I told that detective, it's not my fault if someone steals something from my store and uses it for something terrible."

"Steals it? You're saying a shoplifter took the scarf?" Ally asked.

"Yes. Now, if you'll excuse me." With that, Nancy Graham turned and stalked off.

Leaving Ally to wonder if Nancy was being truthful. Or perhaps knew more than she was letting on?

Chapter Nineteen

"What do you think?" Gramps asked as they walked back to the clinic. "Were the paisley scarves used to kill Pricilla, and maybe Jake, really stollen?"

"I don't know, Gramps." Ally glanced at him. "Why would she lie? Especially since Noah can likely get a warrant for her sales records?"

"The killer could have paid in cash." Gramps leaned heavily on his cane. Ally could tell he was growing fatigued, not that he'd ever admit it to her.

"Wait here, Gramps. I'm going to bring the car around. It's time to take you back to the Legacy House."

"Bah." Gramps looked grumpy but didn't argue, which told her his hip was bothering him.

Stubborn old man. Ally shook her head as she ran around the building to get her car. She hadn't wanted to go through the clinic past the dogs, because then they'd want to go out.

Which reminded her about Domino. It was going on two thirty in the afternoon, and she still hadn't heard from Kayla Benton. She was growing concerned. Was she still so sick? Or had the family decided their life was chaotic enough without adding the dog? Would they abandon poor Domino? Her stomach clenched, and she decided to call Kayla after dropping Gramps off at the Legacy House.

The trip didn't take long. Ally helped Gramps inside, where the widows flocked around him.

"Oscar, can I get you anything to eat?" Harriet asked.

"No, thanks." Gramps waved a hand. "I can wait for dinner."

"We haven't played any poker lately," Tillie piped up.

"What about your cast?" Lydia asked. "You can't play poker with just one hand."

"Can too." Tillie scowled. "I have a plastic card holder thingy my daughter gave me."

"Oscar, you look tired. Maybe we should just sit in the living room and rest a bit?" Lydia turned her back on Tillie. "You can play a card game later."

"Playing cards isn't taxing," Gramps said testily. "And Tillie's right, we haven't played poker in a couple of weeks now."

"I'll find the poker chips." Tillie eagerly headed to the hallway closet.

"If you're all set, Gramps, I'm going to head back to the clinic." Ally put her arm around his shoulders. "Try not to beat Tillie too badly, okay?"

"Why don't you come back for dinner?" Gramps suggested.

Ally hesitated but shook her head. "No, but I'm hoping to be able to sleep here on the sofa tonight."

"What about Noah?" Harriet demanded. "I thought he was staying here until the burglar was caught."

"He might be too busy with the new murder," Gramps said.

"I still need to make sure Kayla Benton is coming to pick up Domino too," Ally added. "I thought I'd have heard from her by now."

"Call the police!" Tillie shouted from the hallway.

Ally shot over to her side. "What's wrong? Are you hurt?"

"No, but my poker caddy is missing!" Tillie shouted as if this was the crime of the century.

"Are you sure you didn't misplace it?" Ally asked in a calming tone.

"I'm sure. I always keep it in the hallway closet." Tillie waved her noncasted hand. "The burglar stole it!"

Ally frowned. It didn't make sense that the burglar would break in to steal poker chips. Especially since she had to assume that the police doing routine checks at the farmhouse had put an end to any gambling. "When did you last play?"

"I know we played a few weeks ago, remember, Oscar?" Tillie said.

"It could have been taken prior to the break-in," Ally pointed out. "Right?"

"I guess." Tillie scowled. "I bet Pricilla stole it. That girl was always up to no good."

"Now, Tillie, don't speak ill of the dead," Harriet cautioned.

Ally stared at the empty space in the back of the hall closet. Had Pricilla taken the poker chips? Had she partied with the other kids at the farmhouse? Why hadn't any of the widows noticed the poker chip caddy was missing before now? Although, as far as she knew, only Gramps and Tillie played poker and cribbage.

Likely Domino's discovery of Pricilla's diary had sidetracked them.

The fact that Pricilla's diary had been in the closet at all made it likely that Tillie was right about Pricilla being the thief. If she had taken the poker chips, had the dead girl also found out about the marked deck of playing cards?

It would be interesting to know who had organized the games and who had provided the marked deck. Ally could see how stealing from Electronics and More could be related to the gambling, maybe in an effort to pay off debts.

But how on earth did all of this factor into the two murders?

"Aren't you going to call your detective?" Gramps asked.

Ally swallowed a sigh, thinking Noah would be far too busy with Jake's murder to worry about missing poker chips. Although the poker caddy was likely connected to the parties going on in the old Thompson farmhouse.

"I'll leave him a message." Ally reluctantly pulled out her phone. "But don't expect him to rush over to talk to you. We don't even know when these went missing."

"I already told you, it vanished in the past couple of weeks," Tillie insisted, closing the closet door with a loud *thunk*.

Ally dialed Noah's number, fully expecting her call to go to his voice mail. Hearing his husky voice in her ear was distracting.

"Yes, Ally, I'll stay at the Legacy House again tonight," he said by way of greeting.

"Ah, okay. I thought you might be too busy." Ally could feel her cheeks flush and hoped the WBWs didn't notice.

"I may be there later than planned, but I can make it work." Noah sounded exhausted. No doubt he'd been going nonstop since the discovery of Jake Hammond's body.

"If the Bentons pick up Domino tonight, I can stay. But that's not the reason I called."

"Oh?" She sensed a hint of suspicion, as if she were going to pry into his investigation.

"I'm at the Legacy House now, and Tillie just noticed their poker chip caddy is missing."

There was a moment of silence. "And that's a police matter why?"

"Look, you know Tillie and Gramps play poker. She says they haven't played in the past couple of weeks. Remember the marked ace of spades I found at the Thompson farmhouse? Don't you think it's possible Pricilla took the poker chips so she and the others could play with a marked deck?"

She couldn't see him, but in the prolonged silence, she could easily imagine Noah's left eye twitching. "Okay, it's possible, but not sure that it helps my case."

"I understand, but still thought you should know."

"Thanks, Ally. I'll head out there later to check it out. Where did Tillie keep it? In her room?"

"No, in the same hallway closet where we found Pricilla's diary."

"And they just noticed it was gone now?" Noah asked. "They should have said something after the intruder broken in."

"Yes, I know, but they didn't. What can I say? They're elderly and didn't notice because it's not exactly a high-value item. I appreciate you checking into it. Thanks, Noah."

"See you later, Ally."

She slid her phone into her pocket and turned to see all the widowers staring at her expectantly. "Um, Noah will be here later to follow up with you."

"Ally, you should have invited him for dinner," Harriet scolded. "That poor man probably hasn't eaten all day."

"And we need a chance to talk to him too," Gramps added.

Ally threw up her hands. "I have to go take care of the dogs and my new stray cat. If you want Noah to come to dinner, Gramps, you can call him. I'll check in on you later."

As she left to return to the clinic, she couldn't help smiling to herself at the thought of Gramps shouting into Noah's ear while using his cell phone.

Better Noah than her.

*　*　*

Ally took both dogs outside and checked on Midnight before calling Kayla Benton. The young mom didn't answer, forcing Ally to leave a message.

Perched on a waiting room chair, she looked at both dogs sitting in front of her. "If I'm stuck with Domino, I'll find a way to make it work," she promised.

Domino licked her hand. She buried her fingers into his soft, dark curly hair, so similar to her own. "The curls look better on you, Domino."

Not to be left out, Roxy rested her chin on Ally's knee. She stroked Roxy's fur, giving her some attention as well. When her phone rang, she pulled it out, expecting the caller to be Kayla. But it wasn't.

"This is Dr. Winter. How may I help you?"

"I think my dog had a seizure," a concerned male voice said. "Do you have time to look at him?"

"Of course. What's your name?" Ally gently pushed the dogs away so she could go over to her front desk to get a paper and pencil.

"Pete Rollins, and my dog is a beagle named Lucky."

She didn't remember ever treating a beagle named Lucky but would search Hanson's files. "Okay, I'm here, so bring him in as soon as you can," Ally advised. "Oh, and if you can bring in a recent stool sample, that would be great too."

"On my way."

Ally quickly kenneled Domino and Roxy, then went over to power up her computer. Searching her client list, she found Lucky the beagle. She hadn't cared for him yet, as it seemed he'd gotten his immunizations a month before she'd taken over the clinic. The dog was eight years old, which was a common age for some dog breeds to come down with a seizure disorder.

There were other possible factors too, but she couldn't begin to guess what the cause might be without seeing the animal.

True to his word, Pete Rollins arrived ten minutes later, cradling his beagle in his arms. He also had a small stool sample in a baggie.

"Bring him into the first exam room." Ally led the way. She took a moment to don gloves, took the stool sample, and then began to examine the dog.

Lucky was showing signs of being postictal from a seizure. He was listless and seemed to be looking around as if confused. To Pete's credit, the guy kept up a soothing commentary as she examined the dog.

Listening to Lucky's heart, she thought he might be a bit dehydrated. "I'm going to give him a fluid bolus, see if that doesn't help perk him up a bit."

"Okay."

Ally took the stool sample back on her way to get the IV supplies. Once she'd given the dog a 500 cc fluid bolus, she began to ask some questions.

"Is this the first time you've noticed Lucky having a seizure?"

"Yes."

"Describe what happened."

"His whole body was shaking, and his eyes were closed. He peed on the floor, too, which he never does." Pete's gaze was full of concern. "Does this mean something serious is wrong with him?"

"There are many possible reasons for a dog to have a seizure. What about his diet? Do you give him a lot of table scraps or stick with dog food?"

Pete grimaced. "He's a hound; he's always finding a way to snatch table scraps. But yes, he recently got into a bag of potato chips."

"Well, high salt levels can lead to seizures, and people food is often very high in salt. Especially potato chips. I would recommend you keep him on a strict diet from now on." Ally stroked the beagle's fur. "I'll take some blood from him, see what else might be going on. If changing his diet doesn't work, we can get a scan of his brain, see if he has a tumor."

"Can you do brain scans here?" Pete asked.

She shook her head. "I can do X-rays and some simple blood work, but anything more, you'll need to go into Sheboygan, Madison, or Milwaukee."

"Do you think he has a tumor?"

"I can't say for certain, but I think you should try the diet change first and let me check his blood levels. If those don't work, then go for the more expensive diagnostics. But if he's eating a lot of table food, I suspect that may be the problem."

"I did this to him?" Pete looked devastated by the news. He lowered his head to rest his forehead on the dog. "I'm so sorry, buddy. I'm so sorry."

"Mr. Rollings, you need to understand, some breeds are more prone to seizures than others." Ally did her best to console him. "Beagles are one of those breeds, especially because, as you say, they'll eat anything. And I know it's difficult to not give your dog food from your plate. But if you stick to dog food and dog treats, Lucky will be better off."

"I will." Pete's voice was muffled.

"Okay, give me a minute to take a blood sample." Those supplies she kept in the room. Lucky flinched but didn't bark when she poked him. "I can do some testing here but have to send out the blood to check for infection or other parasites. I'll call you when I get those results, okay?"

"That would be good, thanks." Pete still looked upset but seemed determined to take better care of his dog. "No more table food for you, buddy."

"Good." Ally took the blood into the back and performed the initial testing. As she suspected, his sodium levels were high. Thankfully, his glucose level was normal.

She returned to the clinic, where she stripped off her gloves and washed her hands. "His sodium levels are high, so I really think fixing his diet should help."

"I understand." Pete lifted Lucky into his arms.

Ally led them through the lobby to the front desk. Pete rested the animal on the surface to reach for his wallet.

It took a minute for her to prepare the invoice, including the supplies she'd used and the blood she'd taken and tested. She added the stool sample processing too and hoped Pete wouldn't faint at the amount of the bill.

Thankfully, Pete didn't hesitate to pay the fee.

"Would you like me to email the receipt?"

"Yes, please." He still had the dog in his arms. He rattled off his email address, which she added to the client list. "Thanks, Dr. Winter."

"You're welcome." She smiled encouragingly. "Keep an eye on Lucky and call me back if he has another seizure. I'll call you as soon as I have the rest of the lab work finished."

"Thanks again."

After Pete and Lucky left, she sat at the computer to add detailed notes about the treatment she'd provided, including the initial test results. Then she went back and took care of dropping the labs in the mail. As much as she hated it when pets became sick, she couldn't deny feeling good about the fact that she'd had another paying customer.

Her stomach rumbled with hunger. Glancing at her watch, she realized she'd spent a good portion of the afternoon with Pete and Lucky, more so than she'd realized. It was going on five o'clock in the afternoon.

And still no response from Kayla Benton.

Looked like she wouldn't be able to spend the night at the Legacy House after all.

Another check on Midnight proved he was doing well, no signs of infection. She took both dogs out of the kennels, taking turns with them outside, Roxy first, then Domino. As she walked Domino down Main Street, it took her a few minutes to realize that he was staying right at her side, even without being bribed with a treat.

"You finally learned how to heel, huh, Domino?" She grinned like a fool. "Maybe I should charge Kayla extra for training you so well."

Actually, she was very much afraid she wouldn't be charging Kayla anything at all, even his boarding fees. The thought was depressing. She reminded herself that the woman was sick, not dumping her dog for good. But no call back was concerning.

"I don't know, Domino." She shook her head and sighed. "I'm worried your family has forgotten all about you."

Domino looked up at her, then lowered his nose to the ground.

Her cell phone rang, and she grimaced when she recognized Gramps's number. "Hey, Gramps."

"ALLY! WE REALLY WANT YOU TO COME TO DINNER."

"I don't know, Gramps, I haven't heard from Kayla Benton yet." Although that possibility was looking less and less likely anyway.

"NOAH IS COMING."

Her heart gave an extra thump. Maybe sharing dinners at the Legacy House would be the closest they'd have to an actual dinner date.

"AND HARRIET IS MAKING SPAGHETTI AND MEATBALLS."

Darn it! How was she supposed to resist Noah and spaghetti and meatballs? Impossible.

"Okay, I'll be there soon. I'm walking Domino."

"GREAT! HARRIET WILL BE THRILLED."

"Bye, Gramps." As she tucked her phone into her pocket, she sensed movement behind her. She turned in time to see a car coming down Main Street at a speed well above the posted limit.

Ally instinctively shortened Domino's leash, not trusting the animal not to lunge forward.

Suddenly the car appeared to veer off the road, coming up and over the curb, heading straight toward her.

"Hey!" With herculean strength, she yanked Domino's leash so that the dog was behind her as she jumped back out of the way.

The bumper of the vehicle brushed her leg, causing her to stumble against the side of the building, squashing Domino too. The driver straightened the car and drove off.

Ally gathered her bearings and tried to catch the license plate, but she was too late.

Shaking in the aftermath of the near miss, she dropped to her knees and pulled Domino close. "Are you okay, boy? You aren't hurt, are you?"

She ran her hands up and down his legs and along his torso. There was no sign of injury, thankfully. She'd been grazed by the reckless driver but wasn't hurt either.

She stared down Main Street, trying to remember anything specific about the vehicle. A sedan, maybe a dark color? She couldn't be sure. It had all happened so fast.

A reckless teenager, texting and driving?

Or had someone targeted her on purpose?

Chapter Twenty

On shaky legs, her mind whirling, Ally returned to the clinic to put Domino in his crate. She wanted to call Noah but decided it would be easier to explain what had happened face-to-face.

She locked up the clinic and headed outside. When she slid behind the wheel, she realized her hands were still trembling. Taking several deep breaths, she attempted to calm her racing heart.

Surely the car hadn't tried to hit her and Domino on purpose. Why would she be a target?

Some of the tension eased in Ally's shoulders when she pulled up to park beside Noah's SUV. Harriet answered her knock and ushered her in.

"Dinner is ready, so sit down, Ally." Harriet bustled over to the stove.

The enticing scent of oregano and tomato sauce made her stomach rumble. Dropping into her seemingly assigned seat between Gramps and Noah, she lightly squeezed her grandfather's hand. "Gee, Gramps, long time no see," she joked.

Gramps chuckled. "You should just come for dinner every night. Would be easier."

Easier, maybe, but a detriment to her waistline. She glanced at Noah. "How are you doing?"

"It's been a long day." Noah's green gaze clung to hers. He frowned a bit. "Looks like for both of us."

"Yes." She thought it would be better to discuss the near miss after dinner so as not to worry the WBWs.

Harriet began passing plates of food around the table. Ally did her best to take only small portions, although it wasn't easy. Comfort food and being with family were a balm to her frayed nerves.

"How are you doing with chasing down suspects?" Gramps asked.

"No talk of murder at the dinner table," Harriet said firmly, pinning Gramps with a narrow look. "I worked hard on this meal, and I don't want anyone to suffer a ruined appetite."

"It's delicious, Harriet," Ally said with a smile. "Spaghetti and meatballs is one of my favorites."

"Really? I'll have to remember that," Harriet said with a knowing smile. "Oh, and I have a homemade blueberry streusel for dessert."

No dessert! Ally told herself the spaghetti, meatballs, and garlic bread were more than enough.

"How's your arm, Tillie?" Ally asked.

"Itches like mad," the older woman confessed. "I can hardly stand it."

"That's a sign of healing." Ally realized it had been a week since Tillie had fractured it. "Try to hang in there, and whatever you do, don't stick anything between your arm and the cast."

"She's already tried that." Harriet scowled at her sister. "I had to get rid of all the wire hangers in our closet."

"Tillie." Ally sighed. "You'll only hurt yourself worse by shoving things down there."

"It itches so much I can't stand it," Tillie insisted.

"Try taking an antihistamine before bed. That should help." Ally realized she probably shouldn't be giving medical advice, since her job was to take care of animals, not people. "Or better yet, call your doctor and find out what he thinks you should do."

"See? I told you to try Benadryl." Harriet looked irritated. "But oh no, why listen to me?"

Ally caught Noah's smile. She had to give him credit for tolerating the widows. He was a really great guy when he wasn't annoyed with her and Gramps.

Which was more often than not.

"Bandit is still looking for a home, Noah." She lifted a brow. "I think you should consider taking the little guy. I will say one thing for Wendy Granger, she's been very diligent about house-training the puppies."

Noah frowned. "My schedule is unpredictable."

"I know, but present concerns aside, it's not like Willow Bluff is a hotbed of crime. In those busy times you can't be there for him, I'd be happy to keep him at the clinic with me."

"Oh yeah?" Noah eyed her over his meatball. "Why don't you just take him yourself, then?"

She sighed. "I might be stuck with Domino. I'm not sure I can handle a third dog full-time."

"The Bentons haven't picked him up yet?" Gramps asked. "What is wrong with them?"

"They've had the flu." Ally wasn't sure why she was defending them. Hadn't she wondered herself if they'd given up taking care of the poodle?

"I'm sure it's not easy for Kayla to take care of the twins and a dog," Noah said in a soothing tone.

"I left a message with her but haven't heard back." She turned to Noah. "If you could stay here one more night, I'd appreciate it."

"Just one more night? Or until the burglar is caught?" Noah asked with a wry smile. "I'm not going to lie, getting paid in home-cooked meals is pretty nice. Especially when Harriet is cooking." He winked at the widow, who blushed like a teenager with a crush.

"I wish I knew," Ally admitted. "I like Kayla. It's hard to believe she'd just give up on Domino."

"Give her the benefit of the doubt," Noah advised. "Having the entire family down with the flu can't be easy."

"You're probably right." She took a bite of crunchy garlic bread and tried not to moan. It was so good.

"We went to Nancy's Nook earlier today," Gramps said, drawing the conversation back to the murders. "Saw several paisley scarfs she has for sale."

"Oscar." Noah's tone held a strong note of warning. "Stay out of it."

"Do you really think they were stollen?" Gramps asked, as if Noah hadn't spoken. "I have my suspicions about that."

"Gramps." Ally put a hand on his arm. "We agreed not to discuss the case at the dinner table, remember?"

"I didn't agree to any such thing," Gramps muttered.

Ally quickly glanced at Noah, relieved that there was no sign of the eye twitch. "You really should consider taking Bandit home."

Noah sighed. "I'll think about it."

"You will?" She wanted to throw her arms around him but managed to refrain. "Bandit will be a great dog, and maybe you could take him for K-9 training."

"He's not a purebred," Noah pointed out.

"Mixed breeds are often used as police dogs. Depending on the breeds. Labs have a great sense of smell and can be trained to identify a particular scent, while Great Danes have highly protective instincts. If you ask me, that's a perfect combination for a K-9 cop."

"Maybe," Noah said cautiously. "But I only agreed to think about it, Ally. Right now, I have bigger problems on my plate."

"Like finding Pricilla's and Jake's murderers," Gramps interjected.

"Is anyone ready for blueberry streusel?" Harriet stood and crossed over to the counter. "It's still warm."

Ally could feel her resolve to skip dessert melting away. "I'll have a very small piece."

"I'll have a big one," Gramps said.

It wasn't fair that Gramps was as lean as always while her jeans pinched at the waist. She glanced at Noah, who was also eyeing the strudel.

"I'd love some too, Harriet." Noah grinned. "The same size as Oscar's."

"Men," Ally muttered. She took a small bite of her streusel, the crumbly cake and tart blueberry melting in her mouth.

She took very small bites but still finished before everyone else. In an attempt to refrain from having seconds, Ally began clearing the table.

Her cell phone rang. Recognizing Kayla Benton's number, she quickly answered, moving into the living room. "This is Dr. Winter."

"I'm so sorry I haven't been able to get over there to pick up Domino," Kayla said wearily. "Mark got sick, and then Brooke started throwing up all over again. I had to take her to the emergency room for IV fluids. It's been so awful." Kayla sounded as if she was about to cry. "I just can't believe our wonderful four days away ended like this."

"Hey, it's okay, don't worry about Domino." Ally hated to admit Noah had been right about the young mom's struggles. "Really, it's no problem. He and Roxy have actually learned how to get along." *Most of the time.*

"Thank you." Kayla sniffled loudly. "One more night should do it."

"I don't mind keeping Domino," Ally said reassuringly. "But I'm sure he misses you and the kids."

"I know. The twins keep asking about him." Kayla sniffled again. "We love him, but it's been a long couple of days. I just now got back from the hospital."

No wonder Kayla hadn't responded earlier. "I'm sorry to hear about the hospital visit, but don't worry about Domino. He and Roxy will enjoy having more playtime."

"Thank you, Dr. Winter. You're a lifesaver."

"Not at all. Take your time. You can pick him up when things have calmed down and you're ready, even if that means keeping him with me another day or two."

"Okay, that's such a relief. Thanks again." Kayla disconnected the call.

"Everything okay?" Noah came up behind her.

"Huh?" She turned to face him. "Oh, yes. You were right. That was Kayla Benton. One of the kids had to go to the emergency room to be treated with IV fluids, and her husband Mark has also come down with the bug. I'll have Domino at least until later tomorrow, maybe even Thursday."

"Sorry to hear that, but I knew it must be something important to keep her from picking up the dog."

"Yeah." Realizing they were alone, she tugged Noah's arm and drew him further into the living room. "Listen, I need to tell you what happened."

"When?"

"Just before I came here." She drew in a deep breath. "I have to take the dogs out separately; it's hard enough to get Domino to walk alongside me without adding Roxy to the mix."

"Makes sense," Noah agreed.

"I was walking Domino down Main Street—you know, I've avoided the lakefront ever since finding Pricilla's body beneath the weeping willow. We were on our way back to the clinic when a car came speeding toward us."

"Speeding?" Noah echoed.

"Way faster than the posted limit. Then at the last moment, it veered up and over the curb of the sidewalk straight toward me and Domino. I jumped out of the way while managing to protect Domino." It occurred to her that she probably should tell Kayla Benton about the near miss.

"Did the car hit you?" Noah asked in concern.

"Just brushed me, but you know how clumsy I am; I fell against the side of the building and squished Domino too."

"You're not clumsy if a car tries to run you down." Noah's tone held repressed anger. "Did you get the license plate number?"

"No." She grimaced. "I tried, but the whole thing happened so fast. By the time I turned to look, the car was too far away to see the license plate clearly enough."

"Can you give me a description of the car?"

Again, she felt like a complete failure. "I can tell you it was a sedan, dark in color, but that's it. I wouldn't have noticed it at all except that the driver was going so fast. Remember when poor

Amos the golden retriever got hit on Main Street last June? I didn't want another animal to suffer like that."

"Or any people to be hurt either," Noah added with a wry smile. He reached up to tuck a stray curl behind her ear. "Are you sure you're okay? Why didn't you say something right away?"

"I didn't want to worry anyone." She hoped Noah didn't notice her blush. She couldn't seem to control her response to his slightest touch.

"I'm hurt you didn't tell me about nearly being run down by a car, Ally," Gramps's tone was full of reproach.

She hadn't heard Gramps enter the room because he was using his walker, which was quieter than his cane.

"Like I said, Gramps, I'm fine. And so is Domino." She glanced at Noah. "To be honest, I can't say for sure the car came at me on purpose or if the driver was simply texting while driving and lost control of the vehicle."

"It's a crime either way," Gramps said. "Right, Detective?"

"Sort of," Noah agreed. "Texting while driving is only a traffic violation."

"And it doesn't matter anyway, since I can't identify the make or model of the car."

Gramps surprised her by setting aside his walker to give her a hug. "I don't like the idea of you being in danger."

"Me either." Ally hugged him, then eased back. "I'm sure it's nothing."

"I'm not convinced." Gramps pinned Noah with a narrow glare. "You need to solve these murders as soon as possible."

"Gramps." Ally put a hand on his arm. "Noah is doing his best."

"I am," Noah agreed, his expression grim. "But I understand your concern, Oscar. I don't like Ally being in danger either. I plan to assume the attempt to run Ally over was deliberate until I can prove otherwise."

Ally was touched by his concern. "Thanks, Noah. I wish I could be more help."

"Do you remember anything about the shape of the car? The lights, anything?"

"It wasn't anything fancy, just a plain sedan." She thought about her Honda. "Maybe similar to my car, but not as low to the ground."

"That's good," Noah said encouragingly. "Anything else?"

"Dark in color. I wish I could tell you more." She frowned. "I guess my observation skills aren't as good as Gramps's."

"You're doing fine," Noah assured her. "Most people don't pay much attention to cars on the street. It's one of those things you expect to notice, until something unusual like this happens."

"I guess." Ally glanced at her watch. "I better get going. I have a stray cat to take care of, and the dogs need to go out again."

"Maybe you shouldn't take the dogs out alone." Gramps frowned. "What if the idiot driver tries to flatten you again?"

"I can take the dogs out the back. There's less traffic there." Although now that Gramps mentioned it, she couldn't suppress a shiver. "Besides, I'm sure the near crash was nothing but an accident."

"I'll come with you," Noah offered. He looked at her grandfather. "If you think you'll be okay here alone for a while with the widows?"

"We'll be fine." Gramps waved a hand. "I'd rather you go with Ally."

She scowled. "But I'd rather Noah stay here with you. There was nothing accidental in the way the intruder broke into the house."

"We weren't hurt," Gramps shot back. "You were almost killed."

"No need to be so dramatic," Ally insisted. "I'm fine, and so is Domino." Which had truthfully been her greater concern at the moment the car jumped the curb. She hated the idea of anything happening to the dog.

"I'll follow you home, Ally, and make sure you're okay walking the dogs." Noah's firm tone ended the argument. "Then I'll come back here to spend the night. Deal?"

Ally looked at Gramps, who nodded. "Deal."

"Give me a few minutes to help clean up the kitchen," Ally said to Noah.

"I'm sure Harriet has everything under control," Gramps pointed out. "She sees the kitchen as her domain, and everyone else should stay out."

No lie, but Ally intended to offer anyway, to be polite. She skirted Noah and saw that the table had already been cleared. "Need help, Harriet?"

"No, thanks, dear." Harriet smiled broadly. "I don't mind doing the dishes."

"There can be something calming about that chore at times," Ally agreed. "But I don't mind helping."

"No need. I like things done in a particular way." Harriet shrugged. "Go on now, enjoy some time with your handsome detective."

"He's not my detective . . ." The denial came out automatically, but of course Noah had chosen that moment to come find her.

"Not for lack of trying," he said with a wink.

Flustered, she couldn't think of a snappy response. "I guess Harriet doesn't need help, so I should get home to the dogs."

"Right behind you," Noah said.

Ally was far too conscious of Noah's SUV following her all the way back to the Furry Friends clinic. Using her key, she entered through the back door and checked on Midnight before focusing on the dogs.

"I'm here, don't worry, I'll take you outside." Talking to the dogs as if they could understand might be considered foolish by some, but she did it all the time.

"Hey, why don't I take one of the dogs while you handle the other?" Noah offered. "That way we could walk them at the same time."

It wasn't a bad idea. With two adults, they should be able to keep them from getting too crazy. "Okay, but I'd better take Domino. He doesn't always listen very well." Although the dog had responded better to Noah. And recently, to her too.

Progress.

"Now if Bandit was more like Roxy, maybe I'd consider taking him," Noah said as he clipped Roxy's leash to her collar. "She's amazing."

"Puppies can be a handful the first year, but after that they calm down to become just like Roxy. You just have to give a puppy some time and attention."

"Two things I don't have a lot of," Noah responded dryly.

She led the way outside, keeping Domino on a short leash. "Walk with Roxy on your left and I'll keep Domino on my right."

"Got it." Noah fell into step beside her. "I'm really glad you're okay, Ally."

The hour wasn't that late, so she angled her head down to hide her blush. "Thanks, but I'm fine."

Domino tugged hard at the leash in a way he hadn't for the past two days. "Heel, Domino."

He strained again and then growled low in his throat. Ally frowned. This was new. Domino rarely growled.

"What's bothering him?" Noah asked.

"I don't know." She glanced around the area. At seven o'clock the sun had already begun its descent, but it was light enough to see there was no one suspicious hanging around. There were a couple of young kids tossing a baseball and another kid riding a bicycle.

Domino lunged hard against the leash again, still growling. She couldn't imagine what had caught his attention, but then she saw it.

A paisley scarf partially hidden beneath a bush.

Chapter
Twenty-One

"Noah? Do you see it?" Ally whispered. She wasn't sure why she was whispering, but under the circumstances it seemed appropriate.

"Yeah. Here, take Roxy for a moment." He handed her the leash and reached into his pocket. In a minute, he had scooped the scarf into an evidence bag.

"Is it blue and red?" Ally asked, thinking of the one she'd seen Hilda wearing earlier.

"No, it's green and aqua blue," Noah said, showing her the scarf. "Why?"

"Hilda had a red-and-blue paisley scarf on earlier today. I thought maybe she dropped it."

"Someone sure did." Noah glanced around again.

"You mean the murderer?" Ally knew she'd never look at a paisley scarf the same way ever again. "That must be why Domino was growling."

"Ally . . ." Noah sighed and took Roxy's leash from her hand, his warm fingers brushing hers. "Domino isn't a police dog."

"Neither was Roxy, but she helped bring down a murderer this past summer." The back of Ally's neck tingled, as if they were being watched. "Domino might be able to do the same."

"Doubtful." Noah tucked the evidence bag into the pocket of his dress slacks. "Come on, let's finish up with the dogs and take them back inside."

She wasn't about to argue. There were several houses nearby but no sign of anyone watching from a window. Still, it was nerve-racking to have found a paisley scarf on the ground so close to the clinic.

"Do you think the killer dropped it recently?" Ally asked as they paused to let both dogs take care of business. "Or earlier today?"

"We don't know for sure it was the killer who dropped it." Noah's expression was noncommittal. "And it's hard to say when it was dropped."

Her temper slipped. "Come on, Noah. Are you seriously going to stand there and tell me that finding a paisley scarf exactly like the murder weapon used on both Pricilla and Jake is a coincidence?"

"I didn't say Jake was killed with a paisley scarf," Noah protested.

"Susie indicated she saw something that could have been a scarf," Ally repeated. "I may not watch as much *Dateline* as Gramps, but I've learned enough over the past few months to know killers often use the same MO on their victims. It's not like I was interfering with your case when we stumbled across the scarf."

Noah glanced away, then sighed. "Okay, fine. I personally think the killer dropped it. You're right that Jake was also strangled with a paisley scarf. And from what I can tell, the scarf we found wasn't lying outside for long. It's not very dirty, just snagged a bit from the bush."

"I wonder if the killer saw us coming outside the clinic and took off, dropping it along the way?" Ally could easily envision the scenario. "Only Domino caught the killer's scent and led us straight to it."

Noah glanced at Domino, who'd stopped growling and was squatting to go number two. "You really think he's that smart?"

"Poorly trained doesn't mean he's not smart," Ally said defensively. She pulled out a baggie to take care of Domino's stool. "And if you have a better explanation for why Domino acted the way he did, I'm all ears."

"I don't." Noah swept a gaze around the area. "And I didn't see anyone, did you?"

"No." She didn't feel guilty for not being perceptive this time, since Noah was a cop and hadn't noticed anything unusual either. "The killer must have left the instant he or she saw us." She couldn't help but wonder if the killer had taken off because Ally hadn't been alone.

Had Noah scared the killer off? Probably.

"Went where?" Noah was still looking over the area. "Into one of the houses?"

"That or disappeared between two houses to the street that runs parallel to this one."

"Let's get back to the clinic." Noah turned his attention back to the dogs. "I, uh, missed whether or not Roxy is finished out here."

It was cute the way Noah didn't like talking about the dog's elimination habits. "She isn't, so let's walk a little more." Ally felt safe with two dogs and Noah at her side. But what about once Noah left to head back to the Legacy House? Should she risk keeping both dogs up in her apartment?

Just the thought of the two dogs playing rough and damaging her furniture made her wince. Then again, better destroyed furniture than someone sneaking inside.

She couldn't forget about Midnight, too. No way could she handle all three of them in her apartment.

Another block up and Roxy did her thing. Ally took care of that too, and they turned around to head back to the clinic.

She put Domino in his kennel. Having Roxy upstairs was enough protection. Besides, Domino would bark and growl the way he did before if anyone tried to break in.

"Are you sure you'll be okay here alone?" Noah asked as they stood near the doorway.

Why, are you volunteering to stay? Ally managed to hold back the comment, offering a smile instead. "Positive. I have Domino and Roxy guarding me."

Noah gazed down at her for a long moment. She hoped he'd kiss her, and he did, but only on her cheek in the general area of her scratches that were finally beginning to heal. "Okay, be safe. I don't want anything to happen to you."

"Thanks again for agreeing to watch Gramps and the WBWs," Ally said breathlessly. The man had only kissed her cheek, and she still felt light-headed. His woodsy aftershave should be declared a lethal weapon. At least against females.

"Lock the door behind me," Noah murmured before leaving.

She shot the dead bolt home, then leaned weakly against the door. All in all, this had been a very long day, starting with the news of Jake Hammond's murder. But the way it had ended, with Noah's chaste kiss, had made it all worthwhile.

Even after nearly being run over by a car.

Yep, she had it bad for Noah. The man turned her to mush without much effort at all.

Not good for her sense of well-being. She didn't do well in relationships. Tim and Trina taking off together was proof of that.

"Come on, Roxy. I need to take care of giving Midnight his next antibiotic before we head upstairs."

Despite her exhaustion, and partially because of the various aches and pains from the near collision with the dark car, Ally had trouble sleeping. And when she finally succumbed, she dreamed that dozens of paisley scarves were hanging around her clinic, taunting her.

The following morning, Ally staggered to the kitchen, peering through bleary eyes at the coffeepot. She filled the machine, then took Roxy outside.

In the bright light of day, her nightmare seemed foolish. Still, she didn't take Roxy very far and switched her with Domino as soon as possible.

Only when the dogs had both been fed and she'd checked Midnight's wound and given him another dose of antibiotic did Ally have time to drink her coffee and make her customary oatmeal. She carried both the coffee cup and the bowl of oatmeal downstairs, where she let both dogs roam the clinic.

Double-checking her schedule, she noted that she had a cat immunization scheduled for ten o'clock, a Siamese cat known as Frankie. In honor of famous old blue eyes, Frank Sinatra? Maybe. Ally didn't have any notes on the animal, as Hanson hadn't made a practice of that, but she verified what the cat was due for so she could have the medication ready to go by the time Frankie's owner brought him in.

It was depressing to have only one appointment for the entire day. Better than having zero appointments, but not by much.

At this rate, she'd never make enough to pay a vet tech.

Ally finished her oatmeal, then set about cleaning the exam rooms and getting Frankie's immunizations ready to go.

Her cell phone rang, and she inwardly groaned when she saw Gramps's name come up on the screen. She belatedly realized it was Wednesday, his normal day to come in to work at the clinic and head to the library over lunch.

"ALLY, DID YOU FORGET TO COME GET ME?"

"I don't really need you this morning, Gramps. How about I take you to the library later?"

"BUT TODAY'S MY DAY TO WORK THE CLINIC."

"Yes, but you've been here the past two days, right?" She rubbed her temple. "Seriously, Gramps, I'll take you to the library after lunch, okay?"

"BEFORE LUNCH," he shouted. "WE NEED TO WORK THE CASE."

Talking in person would be way easier than this one-way yell fest. "I'll fill you in on the paisley scarf we found later."

"YOU FOUND A PAISLEY SCARF?" She hadn't thought it was possible for him to get any louder, but he did.

"Please stop yelling. I have an appointment coming in soon. I'll come pick you up afterwards, before lunch." It was easier to give in than to keep going back and forth.

"OKAY, I'LL BE WAITING."

"See you soon." She hung up as the dogs crashed into one of the lobby chairs. Again. This was her life, she thought with a sigh. And while it might not be glamorous by any stretch of the imagination, she was beginning to feel as if she belonged here in Willow Bluff.

*　*　*

Frankie was indeed named after Frank Sinatra, as indicated by his owner, a lovely woman by the name of Maria Gomez.

"I still listen to all those old songs," Maria confessed with a dreamy sigh. "Sometimes I wonder if I've been reincarnated from the 1950s, I love that era so much. My kids think I'm crazy."

"Oh, well." Ally had no idea what to say to that. "I grew up reading classics because of my parents and grandparents, which is kind of the same thing."

Maria Gomez's eyes widened. "Do you think you were reincarnated too?"

"Um, who knows, right?" Ally glanced at the Siamese cat. "Do you have any concerns about Frankie? Is he eating okay? Any trouble with his bowel habits?"

"Oh, no, Frankie is fine. Sammy's the picky eater."

"Sammy?" Ally hadn't seen a notation in Frankie's records about a second cat in the home.

"Named after Sammy Davis Junior, of course," Maria said with a sigh. "Oh, I love that big-band era."

Ally gave Frankie his immunization, causing him to howl, but thankfully he didn't try to bite her. When that was finished, she disposed of the needle. "Is Sammy another Siamese? Is he due for his shots too?"

"No, he's all black, from head to toe." Maria's face crumpled. "Unfortunately, he ran away."

A runaway black cat? Was it possible Midnight was really Sammy Davis Junior?

"Maria, a young girl named Amanda found a stray black cat. Would you like to take a look to see if he's your Sammy?"

"Oh, yes!" Maria looked excited at the possibility.

"He has a cut on his side that I treated," Ally said to prepare the woman. "Wait here, and I'll bring him out."

Ally ducked into the back and found Midnight batting at the small furry mouse toy she'd given him. It was the first sign of him playing that she'd seen and a good indication that he was on the mend. "Hey, are you Sammy? Or Midnight?" She gently removed the feline from the kennel and carried him into the exam room.

"Sammy!" Maria's eyes welled with tears. "Oh, Sammy! You naughty boy, you shouldn't have run away like that." She pulled the black cat into her arms and nuzzled him. The cat purred in her arms.

"Well, he's fine, but you really should get collars for both cats," Ally said with a smile. "That way, you might have gotten him back sooner."

"I looked all over for him, then waited for him to come home when he got hungry." Maria swiped at her eyes. "Thank you so much."

"You're welcome. You'll need to give Midnight—I mean, Sammy—antibiotics twice a day for the next six days, okay? And keep an eye on his wound to make sure it doesn't get infected. If it changes in any way, give me a call."

"Okay." Maria looked from one cat to the other. "I'll take them into my car separately."

"Good idea, but I'll need you to pay the bill first." Ally couldn't believe she'd found Midnight's owner. This was definitely her lucky day.

She prepared the invoice, including treatments for both cats. She expected Maria to complain, but the woman didn't bat an eye. This was what she loved about pet people.

Well, most pet people. Some complained about every dime they had to spend caring for their pets. As if they hadn't anticipated such an expense.

"Oh, and here's a pamphlet on getting personalized collar tags," Ally added, handing it to Maria. "Please consider getting one for each cat."

"I will. Thanks again, Dr. Winter."

When the two cats were gone and both the exam room and kennel had been cleaned, Ally called Jeri Smith at the Clark County animal shelter. "Hey, I found Midnight's owner. Maria Gomez."

"Yes, that was one of the two who'd adopted my black kittens," Jeri agreed. "I was going to call each of them first before contacting you. Sorry for the delay."

"It's no problem. I just couldn't believe it when Maria brought her Siamese cat, Frankie, in, then mentioned her black cat Sammy who ran away."

"I know Maria; she's a sweetheart. No way did she abuse that cat," Jeri said firmly.

"No, I don't think so either. But she should have them identified with a collar or a chip."

"I always recommend that." Jeri's tone was defensive.

"I know you do," Ally assured her. "I think she'll follow through this time, though."

"I'm glad you found the kitten's owner. I'm hearing I may end up with one of Patsy's Labradane puppies too."

Ally sighed. "I'm trying to find a home for Bandit but so far coming up blank. I really think Noah would be great with the puppy, but he's kinda busy with the two murders at the moment."

"I've told Wendy to hang on to the puppy a little longer," Jeri said. "Hopefully someone will step up."

Ally felt herself caving under the pressure. "I'm not sure I can handle adding Bandit to my home, especially when I have pets boarding."

"Keep working on Noah," Jeri advised. "Listen, I have to go; I have someone coming in to look at one of my cats."

"Good luck." Ally set her phone aside and went back to the kennels. She took both dogs outside, one at a time, then let them run loose.

It took her a moment to remember she needed to head out to pick up Gramps. In her mind, there was no rush. He'd been worn out by the end of the day yesterday. The longer he stayed home to rest, the better.

She worked a bit with Domino, teaching him to sit and stay using treats. The poodle had come a long way in the past week. She hoped Kayla and Mark could keep working with him once they'd taken him home. As difficult as it would be for them to manage with the twins, she knew having a well-trained dog was worth the effort.

"Right, boy?" She threaded her fingers through his curls. Roxy came over and nudged her for attention too.

She put both dogs in their respective kennels and locked up the clinic. Grabbing her keys, she headed out the back to her Honda.

When she arrived at the Legacy House, Gramps was inside finishing up a game of cribbage with Tillie, who did have a plastic device that held her cards, allowing her to play one-handed. "Ready to go, Gramps?"

"Yep. Gotta get my book." He struggled to his feet.

Ally helped lever him up and handed him his walker. "Where is it?"

"Right here." Gramps leaned over to grab the library book off the end table.

"*The Billionaire Murders*." Ally read the title out loud. "Was it good?"

"Very interesting," Gramps said with a nod.

Probably better than some of the books he's chosen, Ally thought as she tucked the book beneath her arm.

She decided to drive straight to the library rather than have Gramps walk down Main Street with his cane. She drove through the parking lot outside the municipal building, searching for a close parking spot.

As she pulled in, the sound of sirens split the air.

"What do you think is going on?" Gramps asked, leaning forward eagerly. "Another murder? Maybe Colin this time? Or Marlie?"

"I hope not," Ally muttered. She frowned when she saw an ambulance and a police car pull right up to the front of the municipal building.

"Come on, Ally, we need to get closer." Gramps was doing his best to jump up and out of the passenger seat of her car.

"Gramps, it's not like there's a crime going on. I'm sure someone needs medical attention."

"Yeah, but who?" Gramps grabbed his cane and began thumping toward the ambulance.

Ally grabbed the library book, locked her car, and quickly followed him. The EMTs and an empty gurney disappeared inside the main doorway.

"Wonder who the patient is." Gramps stood near the entrance, looking as if he were settling in to watch a movie.

"It doesn't matter, Gramps. Come on, let's go inside."

"No, let's just wait a minute." If he'd had a bucket of popcorn, he'd be chewing on it, his avid gaze taking in the scene.

Ally was grateful there was no sign of Noah. All the more reason to believe this was nothing more than some poor person suffering a medical malady.

Certainly none of their business.

"Come on, Gramps." Ally lightly tugged on his arm. "How would you feel if you were the one on a gurney and people were standing here gawking at you?"

"If I happened to be unconscious, I wouldn't care, would I?"

"Gramps . . ." Her voice trailed off as the EMTs returned with a patient strapped on the gurney.

"Hilda Green," Gramps hissed in a low voice.

He was right. The patient was indeed Hilda Green. "Okay, now that you know, let's go."

Before they could move aside, Noah strode out of the building, following in the wake of the gurney. When he saw them standing there, his gaze narrowed.

"Come on, Gramps." Ally tried to nudge her grandfather along.

The man didn't budge. "Well, well. I wonder if Noah tried to arrest Hilda for the murders, causing her to faint?"

Ally hated to admit that Gramps's wild theory was a distinct possibility.

Or Noah had confronted Hilda about the paisley scarf used to strangle her daughter and Jake.

Either scenario might have been too much for the woman to handle.

Chapter
Twenty-Two

"Call your detective," Gramps said for the third time as they headed into the library. "We need to find out what happened."

"He's not going to fill us in on his investigation, Gramps." Ally was regretting bringing Gramps into town. "Now do you want another library book or not?"

"Yes." He looked crabby as he approached the desk.

"Hi, Oscar." Rosie smiled. "Thanks again for lunch the other day. Are you ready for your next book?"

"Absolutely." He pushed *The Billionaire Murders* across the counter. "This was a good one, Rosie. Thanks."

"You're welcome." Rosie took the book, scanned it, and set it aside to be reshelved. "The one I found for you next is called *Love Lies: A True Story of Marriage and Murder in the Suburbs.*"

"Sounds great," Gramps said with enthusiasm.

Ally suppressed a shudder. No way would she read something like that. Give her a nice romance any day of the week. Since Gramps had become obsessed with true crime, she'd even found it difficult to get through her romantic suspense books.

Why couldn't Gramps have picked a better hobby? She still thought the croquet league was a good idea. It looked like fun.

Too bad Gramps wasn't interested. Maybe Erica would like to join?

"Here you go, Oscar." Rosie handed him the book. Because Gramps had his cane in one hand, Ally gently took it for him.

"Rosie, have you heard what happened next door?" Gramps asked.

"I haven't heard a word, why?" Rosie's brown eyes were wide with interest.

"Looks like Hilda Green was taken out on a stretcher after getting bad news."

Ally winced. "Gramps, you don't know for sure she received bad news."

"Why else would she need medical care?" Gramps demanded. "It's just like how she had heart trouble when she learned of Pricilla's murder."

That Noah had been there tipped the odds in Gramps's favor. "But we shouldn't spread rumors."

"We know Hilda was taken out by ambulance," Gramps said firmly. "And that your detective was there with her."

His stubborn attitude was giving her a headache. "Are you ready to go?"

Gramps glanced back at Rosie. "If you hear more about what went down, let me know."

"Of course, Oscar," Rosie agreed. "I'm sure I'll hear something soon."

Ally knew Rosie was the hub of the town's gossip. Many people came to the library to chat, use the computer, have their kids pick out books to read, or get books for themselves. Rosie was one of those women who people tended to confide in. And Gramps sure knew how to ply her for information.

"I'm hungry," Gramps announced. "Let's eat at the Lakeview Café."

"Fine." Ally had already assumed he'd want to eat there. The weather was still nice enough to sit outside, but fall was in the air, and soon it would be too cold.

Note to self: Once winter arrives in full force, I'll need to make sure Gramps doesn't slip and fall again.

They were seated near the front of the restaurant, probably because Ally didn't have Roxy along. Their server was an older woman, who looked harried. Her name tag didn't have a name but identified her as the manager.

"Where's Darla?" Gramps asked as the manager filled their water glasses.

"Darla doesn't work here anymore. Can I get you something else to drink?"

"Water is fine for me," Ally said, thinking about how she'd stuffed herself with spaghetti, meatballs, and blueberry streusel.

"I'll have lemonade," Gramps said. "What happened to Darla? She quit?"

"I'll get your lemonade." The manager turned and hurried inside the café.

"Interesting," Gramps mused, resting his elbows on the table.

"Only you would think a woman quitting her job at a café is interesting, Gramps," Ally said dryly. "Don't make a mystery out of nothing. Maybe she ended up getting a job at Electronics and More. It seems to be the popular place for the younger crowd to work."

"If Darla had quit for a new job, why wouldn't that manager woman say so?" Gramps countered. "She can't tell us if Darla was fired; that breaks human resources privacy laws. But an employee who quits shouldn't be a secret."

Ally barely refrained from banging her head on the table. "I'm taking you home right after lunch, Gramps."

"You still need to fill me in on the paisley scarf you found," Gramps reminded her.

Ally was surprised he'd waited this long to ask. She told him about how she and Noah had taken Roxy and Domino out for walks together and how Domino had growled before she spotted the paisley scarf.

"The same one Hilda had been wearing?" Gramps asked.

"No, different colors." Although for all she knew, the woman had a closet full of them. "Noah took it in as evidence."

"Where were you?" Gramps asked.

She was about to respond, then thought better of it. "Behind the clinic, but I can't remember exactly where the scarf was."

Gramps's clear blue gaze drilled into her. "I find that hard to believe."

"Doesn't matter." Ally waved a hand, glad to see the manager returning with Gramps's lemonade. "We're not going to walk the area."

"Are you ready to order?" The manager woman didn't look at all happy to be relegated to a lowly server position.

"I'll stick with my Cobb salad," Ally said. "Gramps?"

"I'll have a Cobb salad too." Gramps eyed the manager as she noted their order. "Was Darla stealing from you?"

The woman was so startled by Gramps's question that she dropped her notepad. "Who told you that?"

"Did she?" Gramps pressed.

The manager bent to pick up her pad. "I can't talk about it. I'll get your order placed." She hurried away.

"Bet you a dollar Darla did steal from them," Gramps said with a satisfied smile. "I bet it's connected to the big-box store robberies too."

Ally couldn't help being secretly impressed by the way her grandfather's convoluted mind worked. "You don't know that for a fact, Gramps."

He leaned forward. "You saw her reaction. Clearly I hit a nerve. And the robberies are likely related to the poker games that were being held at the Thompson farmhouse. I wonder if Darla found out Jake Hammond was cheating."

"Again, you don't know Jake was the one who brought the marked deck," Ally insisted. "Could have been Pricilla or even Jake's roommate, Colin Felton."

"Possibly," Gramps conceded. "But Jake and Pricilla are the ones who ended up dead."

Ally tried to steer the conversation away from murder and mayhem. "Remember the black cat Amanda brought in? Found her owner today, *and* she paid for the services I provided to the kitten."

"That's great news." Gramps smiled broadly. "And you'll get paid for boarding Domino today or tomorrow too, right?"

"Yes." At least, that was the plan. "With the couple emergency cases that came in, things are looking up."

"You're going to do fine," Gramps said with a nod.

The manager brought their salads, then left without asking if they needed anything more.

"She doesn't make a very good server," Gramps grumbled.

Ally kept her thoughts to herself. The Cobb salad was as good as always, and when they finished eating, she insisted on paying.

"But it was my idea to come here," Gramps protested.

"Doesn't matter." Ally slipped some cash into the bill folder and stood. She picked up Gramps's library book. "Ready to go?"

"Maybe you can drive by the spot where you found the scarf," Gramps suggested as they walked back to her Honda. "Just so I can picture it in my mind."

"You're killing me, Gramps."

"It's practically on the way!" Gramps looked put out. "I'm not asking for much."

"Fine." She opened the passenger door and helped him in. After handing over the cane and the library book, she went around to the driver's side. "One quick drive-by, that's all."

"Fine."

Suppressing a sigh, she pulled out of the parking lot and turned down the street she and Noah had taken the night before. When she came across the spot where they'd found the paisley scarf, she slowed down. "See that bush? The scarf must have snagged on it and fallen to the ground."

"Or the killer was hiding behind the bush," Gramps murmured, mostly to himself. "Do you know who lives in either of those houses?"

The bush appeared to be near the property line between two homes. "No, and it doesn't matter, because there's no evidence that the homeowners are involved." She glanced at him. "You're looking at a bunch of kids, remember?"

"Or Hilda Green," Gramps pointed out.

She thought about the poor woman being carted out of the municipal building on a gurney. What had happened? She couldn't imagine Noah would have confronted the woman right there in her office when the police station was located in the same building.

Each had their own entrance, though, and Hilda had been brought out through the municipal building doorway.

Maybe Noah had intended to arrest her. And if so, the danger was likely over.

Which would be a welcome relief. She was more than ready for life in Willow Bluff to return to normal.

*   *   *

Despite Gramps's objections, Ally drove him back to the Legacy House.

"It's still my turn to help answer phones," he muttered once she had him seated in the living room.

"Things have been relatively quiet, Gramps. We can reassess on Friday."

"I can take Tillie's turn on Friday," Lydia offered.

She hesitated. Between the break-in and the near miss with the car, she wanted the WBWs to be safe. Yet with Hilda being taken away, it was possible the danger was over. "Okay, that should be fine, thanks."

"Looking forward to it, dear." Lydia beamed.

Ally made a mental note to wear the blue sweater on Friday. According to the weather app on her phone, there was a cold front moving in from the northeast over Lake Michigan.

"Bah," Gramps grumbled. "I should be doing the work until we know for sure Noah has the murderer behind bars."

"I'll call Noah to check in later," Ally promised. Noah had agreed to let her know if and when he found the person responsible for the break-in. "Take care, Gramps."

He waved her off, still looking disgruntled. Ally decided not to take his bad mood personally. If there was one thing Gramps hated, it was being left out of the action.

Thankfully, the action was over. Or so she hoped.

Ally headed back to the clinic, determined to spend more time with Roxy and Domino. Of course, she'd rather have more appointments, but so far they were few and far between.

As the dogs played, knocking over her plastic lobby chairs for what seemed the tenth time, she went through her list of immunization reminders. There were three more clients to bother, so she quickly made those calls, leaving voice mail messages for all of them.

So far, her grooming updates on her website hadn't garnered any new business, and that was a bummer. Those first few months her income had been bolstered by offering grooming services. She remembered with a smile that her clients had included Domino.

Now her grooming suite was practically gathering dust.

Wait a minute. She straightened in her chair and brought up a search engine. What if someone else had started offering grooming services too?

A quick search brought up Gail's Grooming, newly opened on September 1. Ally sat back in her chair, scowling at the website. It wasn't nearly as nice as hers, but at least this explained the lack of customers.

She tapped her fingers, trying to think of a way to recoup some of her lost business. Maybe a package deal? Get your immunizations and a grooming at half price?

Couldn't hurt. She went to work updating her website and social media, adding the new information. Ally decided to add email addresses to her client list so she could send notifications that way rather than leaving messages.

The dogs wore themselves out playing and stretched out on the floor beside each other. Ally grinned and took a picture with her phone. Looking at the photo gave her another idea.

A pet board!

Ally leaped to her feet and scanned the lobby. The wall right between the first and second exam rooms would work perfectly.

After measuring the space, she found a bulletin board online and ordered it.

She was so excited about the idea that she called Erica.

"Hi, Ally, how are you?" Erica greeted her warmly.

"Good, except I didn't realize someone named Gail opened up a grooming salon."

"Gail Winston. She's not that good, Ally. She's been offering rock-bottom prices, but I doubt she'll be able to compete with you."

Erica's loyalty warmed her heart. "Thanks, but I'm going to offer some specials of my own, so I'll get some of those customers back." And if that meant Gail's Grooming had to close down, so be it. She'd had her grooming services open first. "I called because I need a picture of Tink for my new pet board."

"Ooooh, that's a great idea. Shh, Tommy, I'm on the phone." Ally could hear Erica's toddler babbling in the background. "I'll get one for you right away. I have dozens on my phone; just need to print one out."

"Great, thanks. Oh, and spread the word. The board is on order, but I'd like to get several pictures posted as soon as possible."

"I will. Just a minute, Tommy." Erica sighed. "He just woke up from his nap, so he's a bit clingy, but I wanted to ask how things are going with Noah."

"Oh, well, nothing really new there." Ally lightly touched the scratches he'd kissed last night. "But now that his murder case is wrapping up, I'm hoping we'll finally have our dinner date."

"The murder case is wrapping up?" Erica sounded surprised. "That's wonderful."

"Oh, well, I guess I don't know that for sure, but I think so." Ally raked her hand through her curls. "I'm hoping to learn more about that soon."

"Two more murders in Willow Bluff," Erica said in a wry tone. "Who would have thought there'd be so much excitement in one small town?"

"Right?" Ally totally agreed with her friend's sentiment. "I'll let you go take care of Tommy; just try to get me a pet picture as soon as you can. Or better yet, just text it to me and I'll print it here."

"Will do. Bye, Ally."

Minutes later, her phone dinged with an incoming text message. Tink looked adorable with a bow in her silver-gray hair. Ally sent it to her email so she could print it out.

The pet board seemed like a good idea, but Ally realized that most people don't print photos from their phone. Rummaging through the cabinets behind the desk, she found a small stack of old photo paper.

Good enough. She started by printing the picture of Tink, then quickly took some of Roxy and Domino so she could print those as well. No reason she couldn't print photos of people's pets as they came in to see her. Maybe it would be a conversation piece and spur grooming services as people compared their pets to others'.

She wasn't above a little competition.

Her phone rang, and she nearly tripped over her own feet in her haste to answer it. "Furry Friends Veterinary Clinic. This is Dr. Winter."

"You left me a message about my dog's immunizations?" a woman's voice asked.

"Yes, what was your name?" Ally glanced down at her notes. There were two pets with female owners.

"My name is Willow Kramer, and Poe is my Yorkshire terrier."

"As in Edger Allan Poe?" Ally was always amazed at how people chose their pets' names.

"Of course," Willow said with a laugh.

"When would you like to bring Poe in?" Ally asked. "Oh, and I'm running a special if you're interested; all pets getting immunizations can have a grooming at half price."

"Really? That's wonderful. I'd love to have Poe groomed. How about tomorrow morning?"

"Nine thirty?" Ally made a quick note to book extra time for the grooming.

"Perfect. See you then."

Ally did a little jig, excited to have another appointment. She forgot to mention the pet board, but she could do that in the morning. Yorkies were adorable, and if she gave Poe a bow or a kerchief, the picture would be a great addition to her pet board.

Her phone rang again, and this time her heart raced because the caller was Noah. "Hi, Noah."

"Hey, Ally. How are things at the clinic? Do you have appointments scheduled yet for this afternoon?"

"No, but there's always a chance for an urgent or emergency visit." She glanced over at the dogs. "Tell me you have good news."

"Not exactly, but I'd rather discuss it in person." He paused, then added, "Is your grandfather there?"

"No, he's at the Legacy House." There was something in Noah's tone that didn't sound good. "Why? Is there a problem?"

"No problem. I'll see you in a bit."

"Okay." Noah disconnected so quickly that she stared down at her phone in confusion.

She made a quick dash upstairs to draw a wide-toothed comb through her wild curls and freshen her makeup. The scratches were almost healed now, but there were still tiny marks on her face.

"My luck, I'll probably be scarred for life," she muttered at her reflection.

Thankfully, Noah hadn't seemed to mind. She thought again about Bandit and almost called Wendy Granger to invite Bandit over for a playdate.

Maybe after Domino went home. Adding a third dog, and a new puppy at that, might be pushing it.

She returned to the clinic just as Noah walked in. His expression was grave, and she felt a jolt of fear.

"What's wrong?"

"I just wanted to let you know that Hilda Green is not a suspect in the murders."

She blinked. "Okay, but why are you telling me this? Is it because you've arrested someone else?"

"Not yet, but I'm working on it." Noah's tone was testy. "I've already heard people saying Hilda was arrested and charged for the murders. I'm here to set the record straight. She has not been charged with any murder."

"I never said that," she protested. But on the heels of that thought, she remembered Gramps alluding to that very thing outside the municipal building, and at the library, and again at lunch.

Noah scowled. "Stay out of it, Ally. And tell your grandfather to do the same." He turned and walked out, the door shutting loudly behind him.

Well. So much for fixing her hair and makeup. She hadn't noticed Noah's eye twitching, but it was clear he wasn't happy with her. Or Gramps.

And since they were pretty much a package deal, she suspected there might not be any romantic dinners with Noah in her future.

Chapter
Twenty-Three

Ally needed to talk to Gramps but shied away from using the cell phone. Glancing at her watch, she hesitated. If she headed over to the Legacy House now, she'd likely end up staying for dinner.

She put Domino in his crate. She decided to take Roxy upstairs to her apartment. She still wasn't sure yet if Kayla would come pick up Domino tonight or wait until tomorrow. But if she did come in tonight, it was better to have the two dogs separated. She could imagine Roxy whining when it was time for her boyfriend to go.

At least one of us has a love life, Ally thought as she gave Roxy one last rub. "See you later, girl."

Feeling dejected, Ally drove to the Legacy House. Was it her fault that Gramps had shot off his mouth? No, but she'd defend her grandfather's right to say whatever he wanted. The fact that the library and the Lakefront Café were gossip hubs wasn't her problem.

Well, it sorta was now, but still. It wasn't as if she'd personally spread any rumors.

Ally parked in the small lot, noticing that Noah's SUV wasn't there the way it had been the past two days. She gave herself a mental shake and walked up to the front door.

"Ally, how are you?" Harriet beamed as if Ally hadn't visited in a month. "It's great to see you."

"Thanks, Harriet." She gave the widow a quick hug. "Something smells good."

"Oh, you must stay for dinner," Harriet said, bustling back to the stove. "Nothing too fancy, as Tillie had an appointment this morning, but I'm sure you'll enjoy my potato-kielbasa skillet."

The scent was tantalizing. "I'm sure I will. I didn't realize Tillie had an appointment. Why didn't you call me? I would have taken her."

"The nice doctor's office arranged for a ride." Harriet glanced at her. "And he says her wrist is healing well. Still needs the cast, which didn't make her happy."

Ally had never broken a bone but could imagine how annoying it might be. "I'm happy to hear she's on the mend."

"Yes, she is." Harriet's tone was matter-of-fact, but Ally could see a hint of relief in the widow's eyes. The two sisters argued like crazy, but she knew they cared for each other deeply.

Moments like this, Ally wished she wasn't an only child.

"Ally? What brings you here?" Using his walker, Gramps entered the kitchen.

"Hey, Gramps." She went over to give him a hug and kiss. "Noah stopped by the clinic to provide a brief update on the case."

"He did?" Gramps's blue eyes widened. "I'm surprised he decided to tell you, since he's always so closemouthed about everything."

"Yeah, well, he wasn't very happy to hear the rumors going around town that Hilda Green had been arrested for Pricilla's and Jake's murders."

Gramps shrugged. "Can't stop people from speculating."

She grimaced. "He thinks those rumors started with us, Gramps. You and me." *Mostly you.*

"Bah." Gramps waved an impatient hand. "Plenty of people saw Hilda being wheeled out of the municipal building with that detective of yours right behind her. Anyone could have started them rumors. And who could blame them? It looked exactly as if she'd been told she was under arrest and passed out as a result."

Ally suppressed a sigh and strove to remain patient. "Well, the bottom line is that Hilda Green is not a murder suspect. Noah specifically told me he wanted to set the record straight."

"Then who is?" Gramps demanded.

Ally could feel a tension headache starting in her temples. "I don't know. Noah didn't say anything about that. But you have to admit it's nice to have one suspect in the clear."

Gramps waved a finger. "I told you someone is using those paisley scarves to frame Hilda, didn't I? To make it look as if she'd killed them."

Yes, that had been *one* of his *many* theories.

"It's one of those kids who worked at the store, or played poker up at the Thompson farmhouse." Gramps gave a nod of satisfaction. "And if your detective hasn't figured it out yet, he's not very good at his job."

"He's not my detective, Gramps." Especially not now. "And for all we know, he's building a case against one of them as we speak."

"Hrmph." Gramps so did not look convinced. "He'd better get on with it then, before something else happens."

"Dinner's ready," Harriet said loudly. "Ally, is your detective joining us again?"

Smiling had never been so difficult. "No, Harriet. It'll just be me tonight."

"Well, I'm sure he's working hard. Such a nice man." Harriet used the hem of her apron to pull something out of the oven. "I made a lemon tart for dessert as well."

Ally didn't even bother trying to tell herself to stay away from dessert. "Everything smells delicious, Harriet, as always."

"Go on now." Harriet attempted to sound modest, but her wide smile was full of pride. "Oscar, let Tillie and Lydia know to come in for dinner."

"I'll get them," Ally offered. She ducked into the living room to let the widows know dinner was ready, then assisted Gramps to his seat.

The empty spot where Noah had been the past two days made her feel sad. Not only would she miss him, but now the widows wouldn't be seeing him anymore either.

Harriet passed the platter, and Ally managed to stick with a single helping, although it was so good she could easily have eaten more.

She didn't feel guilty sampling Harriet's lemon tart either. When dinner was over, she rose to clear the table.

"Sit, Ally, and relax," Harriet scolded.

"You should be the one relaxing, since you did all the cooking," Ally pointed out. "And I'll have to get back to the clinic soon to take care of the dogs."

"Want company?" Gramps offered.

It was a tempting offer, but she shook her head. "No, thanks. I'll be fine. The dogs will keep me busy."

Gramps eyed her thoughtfully for a moment. "Sorry if I made that detective of yours mad at you."

"Aw, Gramps. You didn't." She gave him another hug. "Take care of yourself. I'm sure things will calm down around town by tomorrow."

Gramps followed her to the door. "You really think he has a suspect in mind?"

Honestly, she had no idea, but she figured if Gramps thought Noah did, he'd leave the case alone. "I did get that impression from him. Especially the way he insisted Hilda Green wasn't under arrest."

"Hmm." Gramps seemed to be thinking that through. "I'm going with Colin Felton, then. I believe Jake killed Pricilla, using a scarf to make it look like Hilda did the deed. Colin found out and was so upset over losing Pricilla that he did the same to Jake."

"Using a similar scarf?" Ally asked.

Gramps shrugged. "Maybe Colin found one in the apartment and figured out Jake's plan. They probably fought over the rigged poker games too. Colin accused Jake of killing Pricilla, then used the scarf to kill him too."

"Gramps." Ally shook her head wearily. "You have to stop doing this."

"What? Solving crime? Not going to happen."

Yeah, that was pretty much what she was afraid of.

"Good night, Gramps." Ally opened the door and left the Legacy House.

"Bye, Ally," Gramps called out after her.

Ally's phone rang on the trip back to the clinic. The call was an unfamiliar number, so she quickly pulled off to the side of the road and answered with her professional title. "This is Dr. Winter of Furry Friends Veterinary Clinic. May I help you?"

"This is Karen Shephard. My cat, Daisy, is acting weird. Do you have time to see her?"

"Of course," Ally assured her. "What sort of symptoms is Daisy having?"

"She's been peeing in small drops on the carpet, which isn't like her. And she seems to be in pain." Karen's tone was distressed.

"Sounds like she might have a bladder blockage. Bring her to the Furry Friends clinic. I'm on my way there now."

"Okay, thank you." Karen disconnected from the line.

Ally put the Honda in gear and returned to the clinic. She headed in through the back door, walking through to unlock the front door before taking Domino out for a quick bathroom break.

As she was returning him to his kennel, she heard the bell ringing. "Dr. Winter?"

"I'm here," Ally called out. Shrugging into her lab coat, she hurried out to greet her client. Karen was a woman about her mother's age, holding a cat carrier.

"Let's go into exam room number two, okay?" Ally led the way inside. Ally waited as Karen took Daisy out of the carrier, the cat meowing loudly in protest.

Ally watched as a few drops of cat urine hit the stainless-steel table. She'd treated cats with feline urinary tract disease before, and this was a classic symptom.

Still, she examined Daisy carefully. When she finished, she looked up at Karen. "The good news is that the cat's urethra isn't blocked, so I'm glad you brought her in right away. I think she has an infection which is causing an irritation in the bladder. I'm going to get a urine sample from her and take a blood sample too but then treat her with fluids and antibiotics."

"Okay." Karen looked scared. "Does Daisy need to stay here?"

"I don't think so, as she's not blocked. The antibiotics and fluids should do the trick." As a rule, Ally generally preferred to try noninvasive treatments first. Veterinary bills could be expensive enough; no reason to add to them unnecessarily. If there hadn't been any urine coming out, that would absolutely have been cause for alarm. "Hold Daisy for a few moments while I get some supplies."

"Okay, thank you." Karen looked calmer now that they had a plan.

Ally ducked into the back to get the testing supplies. As she gathered the items, she belatedly remembered she hadn't gotten the results back yet from Lucky the beagle's blood and stool sample either.

How could she have forgotten them?

Worrying about Gramps and the murders was having a negative impact on her veterinary business. Normally she would have called to check on a delayed test result. But she'd been too distracted to make the call earlier today.

No more, she silently vowed. She needed to stay focused on what was important from this point on. No more investigating crimes with Gramps.

Not that she'd ever intended to be his codetective. It had just worked out that way, mostly to keep Gramps out of trouble.

Domino gave two short barks, but she ignored him. He'd already gone outside; he could wait until she'd finished with Daisy to go out again.

When Roxy barked from the upstairs apartment in response, Ally rolled her eyes. They were doing a great imitation of the barking network from the movie *101 Dalmatians.*

When Ally returned to the exam room, she found Karen cuddling Daisy close. "Poor thing is really shaking."

"Sorry about that, but animals often have that reaction when coming to the vet."

Ally attached the small pouch device designed to collect urine to Daisy, no easy feat. Then she poked the animal to obtain the necessary bloodwork.

Thankfully, it didn't take long for Daisy to provide enough urine for a sample. "Okay, now that we have blood and urine samples, I'll give her a small fluid bolus and an antibiotic injection."

"Another poke?" Karen echoed with a frown. "She's already been through so much."

"Two more pokes and I promise she'll start feeling much better," Ally promised. "Give me a minute to get the antibiotic injection prepared."

"Okay."

Domino barked again as Ally went over to her locked medicine cabinet. She shot him a narrow look. "Behave. I'll get to you soon."

Carrying the antibiotic and the IV supplies into the room, she got ready. Daisy appeared most comfortable in Karen's arms, so Ally did her best to give the small fluid bolus into the scruff of the cat's fur while she was being held. Then Ally grabbed the antibiotic and injected that into the cat's flank too.

Meow! Daisy's high-pitched cry made it clear she did not like that one bit.

"Is there anything else I can do for her?" Karen asked. "Did I cause this problem somehow?"

"No, I'm sure you didn't cause it. But we can try a prescription diet that is made specifically for cats who tend to have bladder issues." Ally lifted a brow. "Has Daisy had other problems with her bladder?"

"No, but I've only had her for about eighteen months." Karen cuddled the cat close. "Poor thing, I don't want her to go through all this again."

"Me either," Ally assured her. She stripped off her gloves and washed her hands. "Stay with Daisy a while longer. I'm going to prepare your invoice, okay?"

"Okay." Karen summoned a smile. "Thanks for seeing us on such short notice."

"It's not a problem. As I said, it's good you brought her in right away. Once a cat's urethra is blocked completely, emergency surgery and several days in the hospital are the only option. And honestly, that can turn out to be fatal."

"Fatal! As if surgery isn't bad enough." Karen cuddled Daisy closer. "How awful."

"Again, you did the right thing bringing her in. I'm sure she'll be fine." Ally left the exam room and went to the computer to create Daisy's invoice. First, though, she logged on to find Daisy's record. As expected, there was nothing there other than the vaccinations the animal had received.

She typed in several notes about the cat's bladder issues and the blood and urine samples she'd send out for testing. When that was finished, she turned her attention to the invoice.

Although it was almost seven thirty in the evening, she decided not to add the extra emergency services fee. Especially since the bill would be high enough just for the treatments she'd provided.

Considering her lack of scheduled appointments, this was turning out to be a good week for business. Granted, she'd rather have more routine care mixed in to help keep a nice and steady influx of cash, but beggars couldn't be choosers.

And she'd gladly take any and all business that came her way.
No job too small.

Ally printed the invoice and carried it back into the exam room. "Here you go."

"Thanks." Karen didn't wince or give any indication she might not be able to pay, which was an added bonus.

"Ready to put Daisy back in her carrier?" Ally asked.

"Sure." Karen set the cat down on the stainless-steel table. The cat squatted and peed, a larger amount than she'd given in the urine sample.

"Oh, Daisy, no!" Karen scolded.

"It's okay," Ally reassured her, reaching for some thick paper towels. This was what happened when you gave a fluid bolus. And thankfully, the animal hadn't peed on Ally's lab coat. "Looks as if she's already doing better."

"I'm so glad," Karen murmured.

The cat didn't like going into the carrier, but eventually they managed. Ally ended up with fresh scratches on her hand, but they weren't deep.

Karen hauled the carrier into the lobby, set it down, and then opened her purse.

Ally smiled when the credit card worked without a hitch. "Sign here, please."

Karen signed, and Ally printed a second copy as a receipt. "What about the prescription food?" Karen asked.

"Thanks for reminding me. I have some in back." Ally went to her supply cabinet, frowning when Domino let out two barks again. "What is with you tonight? Calm down; you're getting Roxy all riled up too. Don't worry, I'll take you out very soon."

On cue, Roxy let out another couple of short, staccato barks. Ally shook her head wryly and carried two sample cans of low-protein food into the main lobby.

"Here you go. Give this a try, see how Daisy likes it. I'll let you know as soon as I get her lab results back," Ally added.

"Okay. Thanks again." Karen tucked the cans in her purse, then picked up the cat carrier.

As the woman left, Ally stood at the doorway for a moment, realizing that these types of emergencies could happen at any time. Like in the middle of a dinner date.

Would Noah become upset at this type of interruption? Or would he take it in stride?

She'd probably never know.

With a sigh, Ally closed and locked the front door, thinking it was probably better in the long run that she and Noah remained friendly acquaintances.

No sense in getting her heart broken for a second time in her thirty-one years. Tim Mathai had already hurt her, and she saw no reason to go down that road again.

Domino barked again, louder this time. "Hang on, I'm coming."

Ally crossed the clinic lobby, debating whether she should clean the exam room with bleach before taking the noisy dogs outside, when the clinic lights went out.

Ally froze, her heart pounding as she listened intently for any sounds indicating that an unexpected storm had blown in and taken out the power.

But there was nothing. Until Domino began to bark once again, in a frenzied tone.

In that moment, Ally knew she and Domino weren't alone.

Someone was in the clinic.

Chapter
Twenty-Four

Ally crept through the lobby, using the ambient light from the front window to avoid the plastic lobby chairs. A lack of windows in the back of the clinic meant the darkness there would be far more absolute. She reached in her pocket for her phone, then remembered she had left it on the front desk. Still, she didn't change her course. She needed to get to Domino before something happened to him.

Mentally kicking herself for leaving the back door unlocked in the first place, she went through the first exam room, hoping to catch the intruder unawares by showing up in the hallway running along the back. She paused just long enough to pick up a small scalpel, the only item she could think of to use as a weapon.

She hoped and prayed she wouldn't need it.

Easing the rear door of the exam room open, she slipped out. Domino's barking grew louder and louder. A metallic sound caught her attention, but it took another couple of seconds to figure it out.

The intruder was opening Domino's kennel!

It didn't make sense; the dog could easily bite the intruder. But Ally wasn't going to wait for that.

"Stop!" she shouted at the top of her lungs, rushing forward toward Domino's crate.

A yelping sound almost brought her to tears.

"No! Domino!"

"Ouch!" The voice was female, and for an awful second, Ally thought Hilda Green was the intruder. But when she stumbled over a figure lying on the floor and landed on top of the person, she realized it was someone much younger.

Having dropped the scalpel, Ally used her weight to hold the person down. "What did you do to Domino?"

"He's biting me," the girl whined. "Make him stop!"

"Because you hurt him!" Ally yelled. "Didn't you? I heard him yelp in pain."

"Get him away from me," the girl pleaded.

Ally didn't move, especially upon hearing police sirens. Help was on the way! Less than a minute later, the back door flew open and Noah came in with a gun and a flashlight.

"Marlie Crown, you're under arrest for the murder of Pricilla Green and Jake Hammond," Noah said. "You have the right to remain silent. Anything you say can and will be used against you in a court of law. You have the right to an attorney; if you cannot afford an attorney, one will be appointed to you free of charge. Do you understand?"

Marlie? Ally shielded her eyes from Noah's flashlight, stunned at the revelation. She looked around for Domino. The dog had his mouth locked around Marlie's right wrist, where she still held a knife. Despite the way Domino had yelped in pain, the shiny blade wasn't marred with blood.

Ally scrambled up and off Marlie and went over to kneel beside the poodle.

"Are you hurt, boy? You can drop her wrist now, Domino. Drop it," she repeated sternly. Surprisingly, the dog released Marlie's wrist as if understanding the command. His dark coat made it difficult for her to assess him for an injury. She glanced up at Noah. "I need your flashlight for a minute."

Noah snapped metal handcuffs around Marlie's wrists, then handed it over. Pulling an evidence bag from his pocket, he gingerly picked up the knife.

Ally barely noticed. She played the light over the dog and let out a sigh of relief when she didn't find any blood. "Are you okay, boy? What did she do to hurt you?"

Domino didn't answer but licked her face.

Maybe Marlie had stepped on his foot. Or hit him in the abdomen. Ally tried not to overreact, but she couldn't help herself. She glared at the girl. "You were going to cut him!"

Marlie didn't respond, and it was all Ally could do not to throw the flashlight at her. Instead, she gave it to Noah. "I need the lights restored in the clinic so I can examine Domino more closely, make sure he isn't hurt." Examining a dog by flashlight wasn't optimal.

"Timmons? Find the lights," Noah called out.

Ally recognized the name Timmons as one of the Willow Bluff police officers who'd come to the crime scene at the lakefront when she'd found Pricilla's body.

Looking at Marlie, who had a paisley scarf dangling from her pocket, made Ally realize that she and Domino had both been targets.

"Why?" she asked, staring Marlie down. "Why would you do this?"

"You have the right to remain silent," Noah repeated to Marlie, scowling at Ally. "And the right to an attorney."

"Yeah, fine," Ally muttered. "I'm more worried about Domino than her anyway." She turned her attention to the dog. He was so big, she wasn't sure she could carry him. "Can you get up, boy? Can you?"

She was glad when Domino stood and was able to walk under his own power. Maybe he wasn't hurt very badly at all.

"You ruined everything!" Marlie abruptly shouted. "I wish I'd hit you with my car."

"Me?" Ally rounded on her. "How?"

"You found Pricilla, asked nosy questions, used that dog to try to track me down. You even found Cilla's diary! I was so close to getting it, but you found it!"

"Are you saying you cheated on your best friend with Jake Hammond?" Ally asked incredulously. Not just that, but it was clear Marlie had broken into the Legacy House too.

"That part didn't matter." She waved an impatient hand. "Colin had a crush on Cilla anyway. They would have gotten together."

Ally realized Gramps had been right about Colin's feelings for Pricilla. But Marlie's lack of empathy for her friend was appalling. "What part *did* matter? The poker games?" Suddenly Ally knew. "*You* were the one cheating! I heard you tell Steve he owed you, and I saw you talking to Darla too. They both owed you money, didn't they? You were the big winner, and they needed to pay up. That's why Darla stole from the café. And that's why someone broke into my clinic."

"That was Steve, the idiot. He left work claiming he was sick and came here to steal from you. The stuff he stole from the store is probably still hidden in his attic. He was waiting for the hubbub to die down before finding buyers for the computers and phones he'd taken."

Ally remembered how Steve had paid cash for the heartworm meds. She should have realized he'd known about her petty cash drawer. But the worst part of this was Marlie's callousness about her crimes. "Why did you cheat?"

"I grew up with nothing after my mother died; my grandparents barely had enough to get by. It's only right that I get what I need now. And Pricilla should have just kept her mouth shut about the marked cards." There was a weird gleam in Marlie's eyes. "Don't you see? She was going to ruin everything. She had to be silenced. And when Jake found one of the scarves I'd stolen, he accused me of killing Pricilla. He threatened to go to the police, so I had to silence him too."

Ally shook her head in disgust. "You killed two people, tried to kill me and to hurt Domino. You're rotten to the core, Marlie."

"Enough, Ally," Noah said sternly. "Come on, Marlie, I strongly suggest you invoke your right to remain silent and your right to an attorney." Noah pushed the young girl toward the back door.

Marlie began to cry, but Ally couldn't garner much sympathy for the girl. Especially not after she'd tried to hurt Domino.

"Come on, boy. This way," Ally led him into the exam room. She stared down at him for a moment. He weighed roughly seventy-five pounds. Instead of lifting him by herself, she knelt beside him, trying to examine him while he was on the floor.

"Need help?" Noah asked.

She glanced up in surprise. "Yes, please." She took his offered hand and let him help her up. "We need to get him onto the table. I heard him yelp. I need to make sure Marlie didn't hurt him in some way."

Noah did most of the heavy lifting, and soon Domino was on the exam table. Ally took her stethoscope and listened intently to

Domino's heart and lungs. Then she gently palpated his abdomen to make sure he didn't have any signs of bruising or internal bleeding.

"Is he going to be okay?" Noah asked with concern.

"I think so." Ally looped her stethoscope around her neck. "Where's Marlie?"

"I handed her over to Officer Timmons." Noah glanced at Domino. "I'm glad he's not injured."

"Me too. But she shouldn't have gotten to him at all." She blinked tears from her eyes and stroked Domino's curly fur. "This is my fault, Noah. I was dealing with an emergency case involving a cat with a bladder infection and totally forgot to lock the back door. That wretched girl just walked right in."

"This is Willow Bluff, Ally. Half the town doesn't lock their doors." Noah offered a reassuring smile as he also stroked the dog. "The fault rests with Marlie, not you."

"I didn't help any," Ally insisted. "I can't believe a young girl her age actually killed two people." It was truly mind-boggling. Then she frowned. "How did you get here so fast? I left my phone in the clinic so hadn't even called 911."

"I was driving down Main Street when I saw your clinic lights go off," Noah explained. "I parked and called for backup when I heard the dog barking. He sounded distressed."

"He was," Ally agreed.

"Your front door was locked, so I ran around back and saw the door hanging ajar." He caught her gaze. "From there, it was easy, because you and Domino had everything under control."

Ally weakly smiled. "She tried to hurt Domino, which made me mad."

"I know, I'm sorry about that. But he did a good job grabbing Marlie's hand," Noah pointed out.

"He's a better police dog than you gave him credit for," Ally said with a smile.

"Yeah. And I'm sorry he almost got hurt because of it."

"Me too. I'm just glad you arrived in time." She stared down at her trembling fingers for a moment, then drew in a deep breath. "But to be fair, I didn't do anything heroic. The hallway was so dark, I tripped and fell on top of Marlie, I even dropped the scalpel I was going to use as a weapon. You know how clumsy I am."

"Ally, you're not clumsy. And regardless of how it happened, you kept her in place long enough for us to get there. Which is all that matters, right?"

"Yeah, but mostly because Domino had her wrist in his jaw." She wanted to throw herself into Noah's arms but stayed focused on Domino. He seemed to be his normal self, which was a relief. "Help me get him back down on the floor."

"Sure." Without waiting for her to help, Noah lifted Domino in his arms and gently set him down. Ally led the dog back toward the kennel, glad when he didn't balk at going inside.

"You're a good boy, Domino." She gave him a treat before closing and latching the door.

"Ally." Noah instantly pulled her into his arms, hugging her tight. "I'm so glad you weren't hurt. I hate knowing you were in danger."

She had a fleeting thought that it was worth it if the reward was being held by Noah. "It's not like I was trying to investigate the case or anything. I was just taking care of my clients."

"I know." Noah pressed a kiss to her temple. "Marlie was a prime suspect, but I didn't have any proof. I should have been following her more closely. If I had, I could have intercepted her before she got inside."

She smiled at the way he was taking the blame, even though he'd just told her that the fault rested with Marlie. Noah's woodsy scent filled her senses, and Ally wished she could stay here with him forever. She reluctantly pulled back to look up at him. "I'm sure Marlie wasn't your only suspect, Noah."

"No, I had Darla Turner, Steve Norris, and Colin Felton on the list as well. Colin had an alibi for the night of Jake's murder; he went to stay with his parents. I know Steve Norris fixed the security video so that the robberies went unnoticed; he was the mastermind behind that. I figured he was sitting on the loot, which Marlie confirmed. I have to admit, I didn't suspect Steve of being the one who broke into your clinic; I suspected Marlie of doing that too." He gazed into her eyes. "I'm just glad you're okay."

Ally smiled. "Me too."

Noah chuckled, then as if reading her mind, tipped her chin upward with his index finger and covered her mouth in a deep kiss.

*   *   *

"I need to get back to the station," Noah murmured when they'd taken a moment to breathe. "And I'll need your formal statement."

Ally wasn't surprised by his request; she'd been down this road before. Her heart was still racing from the impact of his kiss, making it impossible to resist.

"Okay," she readily agreed. Then she added, "Oh, but I need to get Gramps."

Noah sighed but nodded. "Yeah, okay. Go pick up your grandfather. May as well include him now; otherwise he'll just find a way to grill me about the details later."

"Thanks, Noah." She went up on her tiptoes to give him another kiss.

"See you soon." Noah left the clinic through the back door.

Ally took Roxy outside, soothing the animal, who'd been barking upstairs while all the commotion was going on below. Then she put Roxy in the kennel right next to Domino so the poodle would have company. She had to laugh as the two dogs nosed each other through the mesh of the crate.

"I'll be back as quickly as possible," she promised the dogs before going through to retrieve her phone. She called Gramps's cell.

"HI, ALLY."

"Gramps? Marlie Crown has been arrested for murder, and I have to give a statement. I'm on my way to pick you up, okay?"

"MARLIE CROWN? I KNEW IT! I'LL BE WAITING."

Ally shook her head as she pocketed her cell phone. Trust Gramps to take credit for solving the murder. When she pulled up in front of the Legacy House, Gramps was standing outside with his cane.

"What happened?" Gramps asked, after she'd helped him into the passenger seat. "Why do you have to give a statement?"

Ally filled him in on how Marlie had come into the clinic with a knife and attempted to hurt Domino. "Domino had her wrist in his mouth, and I pretty much fell on her, which together helped Noah arrest her."

"Noah believes she killed Jake and Pricilla, huh?" Gramps mused.

"Yes, and she was the one who broke into the Legacy House and the one who tried to run me and Domino down. All related to the gambling debts the others owed her because she cheated at poker. Oh, I forgot to mention the paisley scarf she had in her pocket," Ally added. "I think she was planning to kill me and Domino."

"Ally." Gramps clutched her arm with a tight grip. "I hate knowing you were in danger like that."

"It was partially my own fault, Gramps." Ally smiled reassuringly. "And thankfully, Noah arrived just in time."

"So that detective of yours solved another one." Gramps actually sounded disappointed. "And the paisley scarf means she was trying once again to frame Hilda."

"Yes, but that was a stupid move on her part, since Hilda had been taken to the hospital earlier that day," Ally said thoughtfully. "I mean, talk about having the perfect alibi."

"How do you know Hilda wasn't treated and released like last time?" Gramps pointed out. "You should have asked Noah about that."

Ally pulled into the parking lot behind the municipal building. "Gramps, I'm here to give my statement, not to grill Noah over the details of the case."

Gramps shrugged. "You don't get answers without asking questions. There are still several aspects of this case that don't make sense."

"Don't make me regret bringing you along," Ally warned. "Noah didn't have to let me pick you up. It's only because he likes you that he's allowing you to participate."

"Bah." Gramps released her arm to push open his car door. "I've been helping him solve these cases, whether he admits it or not."

Ally inwardly sighed as she escorted her grandfather into the police station. She'd been there several times before, but she still found the place intimidating. Up until this past June, she'd never been inside a police station.

"Ally, Oscar," Noah came out from the back to greet them. "We'll head over to interview A."

"My favorite interview room," Gramps joked.

Ally rolled her eyes. Gramps was enjoying this far more than he should.

"Maybe you should have been a cop rather than running your own construction company," Ally said dryly.

"Maybe I should have," Gramps agreed. "But Amelia and I had a great life together, so no complaints. Besides, I'm helping solve crimes now, which only proves that it's never too late to change your career."

Noah coughed loudly. "Oscar, keep in mind you are not a police officer. You're here to support Ally, nothing more."

"Sure, sure." Gramps waved a hand. "Go ahead, Ally."

"Gee, thanks, Gramps."

Noah hid a smile. "Ally, for the record, I just need to hear exactly what happened. I'm going to audiotape this; okay with you? I'll have your statement typed and printed for you to sign later."

"Um, yes. That's fine." She rubbed her damp palms on her jeans. There was no reason to be nervous; she was a victim in this mess.

And Domino had nearly become one of Marlie's victims too.

Ally repeated the backstory of her clinic appointment. "I was standing in the middle of the clinic when the lights went out." Ally felt Gramps take her hand and smiled at him. "When Domino's barking changed, I knew I wasn't alone. That someone was in the back. I was scared, but I didn't have my cell phone. It was on the front desk."

"Oh, Ally." Gramps sighed.

"I know." She glanced at Gramps and shrugged. "I was more focused on the animals than my phone."

"Then what happened?" Noah asked.

"As you know, my exam rooms have two doors, one going in from the front and one leading out to the back. I heard the sound of the kennel door opening, so I snuck through exam room number one, grabbing a scalpel along the way, hoping to get to Domino in time. When I heard him yelp, I rushed forward, but ended up tripping over Marlie's body and dropping the scalpel. Domino managed to fight back. When you arrived, Noah, Domino had Marlie's wrist in his mouth. She was still holding the knife she was planning to use against him."

Noah's green gaze was sympathetic. "Anything else?"

Ally thought back over the recent events. "I noticed a paisley scarf hanging partially out of her pocket. I have to think her intent was to kill Domino first, then me."

"Thanks, Ally." Noah reached over to shut off the tape recorder.

"So Marlie was trying to frame Hilda for the murders?" Gramps asked. "I can't think of another reason she'd use the paisley scarves."

"That's one theory," Noah agreed. "But we haven't completed all our interviews yet."

"Ah, so you're going to try to get more information about those poker games from Colin Felton, Steve Norris, and Darla, huh?" Gramps leaned forward eagerly.

"I can't discuss an ongoing investigation," Noah said firmly. Ally had to give him credit for keeping his temper. No sign of the eye twitch.

"Come on, Gramps. I'll take you home."

Gramps shook off her hand. "Why can't we hear the rest of the story?"

"Because I don't have all the answers yet." Noah rose to his feet and looked at Ally. "Thanks for coming in to provide your statement. I'll let you know if I have any additional questions."

"Sounds good. Come on, Gramps." Ally helped her grandfather to his feet.

As Noah left, she remembered their kiss and tried not to be disappointed that he hadn't mentioned going out for dinner or anything else that resembled a date.

Even though the case was obviously about to be wrapped up once and for all.

Chapter
Twenty-Five

Ally waited until the following morning to let Kayla Benton know about the near miss with Domino. Thankfully, the dog hadn't been hurt, but Ally wanted Kayla to hear about it from her rather than through local gossip. The young mom was surprised and promised to come in as soon as possible to pick up the dog.

"I guess I should have come last night." Kayla wrapped her arms around Domino's neck. "Mark was feeling better and so were the twins, and I thought it might be nice to have one good night's sleep."

"I'm so sorry," Ally apologized. "I never considered Domino a target."

"It's not your fault, Dr. Winter," Kayla assured her. "It's mine for dragging out his boarding for this long." She sighed and shook her head. "You just don't know how awful these past few days have been. Both kids throwing up, then me, then Mark, then taking Brooke to the hospital . . ."

"I can't even imagine." Ally was sympathetic to Kayla's plight. "I'm so sorry Domino was in danger, but you should know he saved the day. If he hadn't grabbed Marlie's wrist, she might have hurt him and me too."

"Such a brave boy," Kayla said, stroking Domino's fur. "Yes, you're a very brave boy."

"You don't have to pay for boarding," Ally began, but Kayla quickly interrupted.

"Yes, I do. I truly appreciate you keeping Domino longer than planned." Kayla rose to her feet and gazed down at Domino. "If I had picked him up sooner, he wouldn't have been in danger."

"You don't know that," Ally protested. "Plus, he helped save my life, so I'm grateful things worked out the way they did."

Kayla pulled out her credit card and handed it to Ally. "Please let me pay for boarding." The corner of her mouth tipped up in a lopsided smile. "We really had a great four-day weekend alone until the flu wiped us out."

"Okay." Ally gratefully printed the invoice and showed it to Kayla. When she nodded, Ally ran the card through the machine. "Oh, I almost forgot."

"What?" Kayla asked.

"I've been working on training Domino." She gave Kayla her card back and reached into her pocket for a treat. "Watch this." Ally took Domino's leash. "Heel."

Domino came to her side. She rewarded him, then began walking around the clinic. When Domino began sniffing and tugging on the leash, she told him to heel, and he obediently returned to her side.

"Wow," Kayla said in awe. "Normally he yanks at the leash when I try to walk him."

"I know." Ally instinctively rubbed her sore shoulder. "But you need to keep working with him, force him to listen and heel. Trust me, it will be time well spent."

"Okay, I will." Kayla took the leash from Ally's outstretched hand. "Domino, heel."

Domino came over to stand at her side, looking up as if waiting for a reward.

"Don't necessarily give him a treat every time, but enough to keep him obeying you." Ally handed her a treat. "Walk around and make him do it again before rewarding him."

Kayla did as suggested, and when Domino began to stray, she called for him to heel, then gave him a treat. "Well, look at that. You might not be as hopeless as we thought."

Ally managed not to point out that training a dog was the owner's responsibility, not the animal's. After Kayla and Domino left, Ally's phone rang. She sighed when she saw Gramps's name on the screen.

"What's up, Gramps?"

"COME AND GET ME!"

Ally held the phone from her ear. "Why? What's going on?"

"I NEED TO STOP AT THE LIBRARY."

She hesitated, sensing he wasn't being entirely truthful. Then again, she didn't have any appointments until later that afternoon. "Give me a few minutes."

"OKAY!" Thankfully, Gramps hung up.

Ally went upstairs to grab Roxy from her apartment. Downstairs in the clinic, the boxer seemed to realize Domino was gone and looked up at Ally with wide brown eyes that seemed to ask why she had sent her boyfriend away.

"I'm sorry, girl." Ally stroked the boxer's fur. "I'll arrange a play-date, okay?"

Roxy sniffed along the floor of the clinic, tracking Domino's scent. Ally led Roxy out through the back door to her Honda.

Gramps was once again waiting outside the Legacy House for her when she arrived. Ally jumped out to help him into the car.

It wasn't until they'd parked in the lot behind the municipal building that Ally realized he hadn't brought his library book.

"Where's your book?"

"We're not going to the library," Gramps confirmed after he struggled to get out of the car. "I want to check something out in city hall."

"Check what?" Ally didn't like the sound of this. She let Roxy out of the back hatch, then tucked a hand beneath Gramps's elbow. "Noah said to stay out of the investigation."

"I want to know if that guy—what was his name?" Gramps frowned. "Darrin Stanley?"

"Darrel Steinbach," Ally corrected.

"Yeah, him. I heard that he finalized a deal with Trevor Thompson for developing the property."

"Okay, but why?" Ally dug in her heels, refusing to move.

"I'm curious," Gramps admitted. "Humor me, okay?"

Didn't she spend most of her time humoring him? Ally sighed and walked with Gramps and Roxy, taking care to keep Roxy out of Gramps's way. "It doesn't matter if Steinbach has the property or not. That wasn't the motive for murder."

"No, but I think it played an important role," Gramps said stubbornly. "And I think that's what Noah confronted Hilda about yesterday when she ended up being taken to the hospital."

"If Noah knows the truth, why are we here?" Ally asked impatiently.

Gramps didn't answer but stopped abruptly when he saw Hilda standing outside the entrance to the building.

The woman looked as if she'd aged about twenty years in the past few days. She wore a black business suit, without any accent color, and definitely no paisley scarf. Hilda turned to look at them with dull eyes.

"Ms. Green? Is everything okay?" Ally frowned in concern, wondering if the woman should have been kept in the hospital for observation rather than being released.

"He's gone. That's what you're here for, right?"

Ally had no clue what the woman was talking about. "Ms. Green, maybe you should sit down."

Hilda let out a harsh laugh. "I was so stupid. So naïve. And to think, part of the reason I kicked my daughter out of the house was so I could spend more time with him, and now she's dead . . ." Her voice broke, and she abruptly buried her face in her hands.

"It's not your fault, Hilda," Gramps said, moving forward to put his arm around the woman's shaking shoulders.

Ally still didn't quite get what was going on. "He who?"

Gramps shot her an exasperated glance. "Darrel Steinbach."

"Ohhh." Realization dawned. "He dated Hilda just to get the land."

"Yes." Hilda sniffled loudly and raised her head, her gaze full of self-contempt. "I'm the stupid woman who fell for his charms."

"Now, now," Gramps soothed. "How could you know what Darrel had planned? He's the one who exploited the situation, not you."

"But now Pricilla is gone, and it's all my fault . . ." Her eyes filled with fresh tears.

"Marlie Crown did this, not you," Gramps said firmly. "And worse, she pretended to be supportive when all the while she was setting you up to take the blame."

Ally came up on Hilda's other side. Even Roxy nudged the woman, as if to offer comfort. "Let's sit down, okay? You've been through a lot."

"I heard you were almost killed, Dr. Winter." Hilda sank down on a bench in front of the building. "And that the poor giant black poodle was almost injured too."

"Yes, but Domino is fine, and I wasn't hurt either," Ally assured her. She glanced at Gramps, then added softly, "I know you feel guilty, but this isn't your fault, Ms. Green. It was all Marlie."

"And it started with cheating at poker," Gramps said, plopping down beside Hilda on the bench. "We know Pricilla discovered the fixed poker games and confronted Marlie about them. And if that wasn't bad enough, Marlie was also stealing Jake Hammond away from Pricilla too."

Ally could easily imagine how things had played out. "Marlie admitted Jake found out she killed Pricilla and confronted her, so she had to kill him to prevent him from talking."

"But if I hadn't kicked Pricilla out, she wouldn't have been living with Marlie in the first place, and none of this would have happened!" Hilda's tone rose in anguish.

"She still would have wound up dead," Gramps interrupted. "We believe Pricilla was involved in the poker games while she was still living with you. Don't you see? This wasn't about you tossing Pricilla out of the house. It was about your daughter standing up for what was right. You should take comfort in the fact that Pricilla tried to do what was right."

Ally caught movement and the hint of woodsy aftershave a few seconds before Noah drawled, "Is there any part of this case you haven't figured out yet, Oscar?"

Gramps eyed Noah speculatively. "Not that I'm aware of. Why? Are you here to tell me I'm wrong?"

Noah sighed. "You're not wrong. In fact, I came here to let Hilda know that Marlie confessed to everything."

"Everything?" Ally echoed.

"Yep. She admitted Pricilla stole the poker chips from the Legacy house. Marlie used a marked deck to steal from her friends and then put pressure on them to pay up, which in turn resulted in their stealing from others. The only thing she wasn't directly involved in was the robberies from Electronics and More. We arrested Steve for tampering with the security video and taking the electronics so he could sell them for cash. We found them in Colin's closet; the kid tried to set up Colin to take the fall. Poor Colin wanted nothing more than to move back home to get away from it all, which made it easy for Marlie to kill Jake while he was gone. Steve apparently owed Marlie a lot of money. The cash he took from your clinic was barely a down payment on what he owed her."

Ally shook her head. "Darla stole from the café and Steve from me and the store, all because Marlie cheated at cards, as a way to make up for growing up poor."

"Yes," Noah confirmed, a look of resignation in his gaze.

"How did Pricilla end up under the weeping willow?" Ally asked.

Hilda winced, and Ally realized she should have kept her big mouth shut.

"Marlie took her for a drive after work," Noah said. "Allegedly to convince Pricilla to keep her mouth shut about the robberies and the poker games."

"I knew it," Gramps said. He glanced at Hilda. "I told you Pricilla tried to do the right thing."

Noah offered a wry smile. "I should have known you'd put the pieces of the puzzle together eventually, Oscar."

Gramps beamed. "I'm not dead and buried yet, Detective." He wagged his index finger at Noah. "You'd do well to remember that."

"How can I forget, with you constantly reminding me?" Noah shot back. His gaze rested on Hilda. "Are you okay, Ms. Green?"

"Not really." Hilda waved a limp hand. "I'm on my way in to resign my position."

"What? Why?" Ally frowned. "Just because Darrel Steinbach acted as if he cared for you doesn't mean the old Thompson property shouldn't get developed into something useful." She glanced questioningly at Noah. "Right?"

"But I only gave him that permit because we were . . ." She didn't finish.

Noah nodded slowly. "I understand, but as far as I know, you didn't break any laws by giving him the zoning permit that he requested. Wouldn't you have given him the permit if you weren't dating him?"

"I don't know." Hilda sighed. "Probably. But I still feel like a foolish old woman. Maybe it's time for me to start over, doing something different."

"Ms. Green, you have done a lot of great things for Willow Bluff," Ally said softly. "Don't throw it all away over a slimy guy. He's not worth it."

"But Pricilla . . ." Her voice broke. "I can't imagine living without her."

"I know." Ally truly felt bad for the woman. Especially since Marlie, the girl who'd claimed to love Pricilla like a sister, had been the one to kill her. "But quitting your job won't bring her back. Maybe you can work on a way to honor your daughter's memory."

"You think so?" Hilda perked up at this idea. "Like a statue or something?"

"Maybe an engraved bench at the lakefront, or planting a tree in her memory," Ally said, trying not to imagine a statue of Pricilla Green in her high-heeled red-and-white polka-dotted shoes in the center of town.

She'd prefer a statute of Domino, who'd bravely caught Marlie, saving Ally's life.

"I can do that." Hilda brushed at her tears, smearing her makeup. She stood, looking better than she had when they'd first arrived. A woman with a new mission. "Yes, I can definitely do that."

"Good." Ally glanced at Gramps. "Ready to go?"

"I'll walk with you," Noah offered.

"We're parked right down here," Ally said. "It's not far."

"I know." Noah fell into step beside her.

"Ally? Yoo-hoo, Dr. Winter?" A female voice floated across the parking lot.

Ally eyed Wendy Granger warily as she hustled over, holding Bandit in her arms. "Have you found someone to take care of my sweet Bandit yet?"

Ally shook her head. "I'm afraid not, Wendy."

The woman's face fell. "But—what am I supposed to do? He's so adorable, and the woman at the shelter said she's full and can't take in any more animals."

Jeri Smith normally made room for animals in need, and Ally suspected this was Jeri's way of forcing Wendy Granger to keep Bandit. "I'm sorry, but you may have to hold on to him for a while longer."

The black puppy strained toward Noah, his entire body wiggling with excitement. His tongue lapped at Noah's hand.

"Oh, Detective, look how much Bandit loves you," Wendy said in a cajoling tone.

"He is a cutie," Noah admitted, reaching out to pet the dog. "But my schedule would make having a dog nearly impossible."

"Unless you had help," Ally interjected. "From someone like me."

"You're really serious about helping with the puppy?" Noah asked.

"Yes, and I won't even charge you for it. I'm all yours."

"Really," Noah echoed, a smile tugging at the corner of his mouth. "You're all mine, huh?"

Her cheeks flushed as she realized what she'd said. Flustered, she waved a hand at the dog. "Look at him, Noah. Bandit needs a home, and if you ask me, you're a natural with dogs. You were amazing with Domino last night. I know you'll be great with Bandit too."

Sensing Noah was on the brink, Wendy thrust the puppy into Noah's arms. Bandit licked Noah's chin, making him laugh, then snuggled close, draping his head over Noah's shoulder as if he were a baby being carried by his father.

Ally grinned as she watched Noah's heart melt, his broad hand coming up to stroke the animal. "You're a good boy, aren't you, Bandit?" He stroked the puppy's dark fur as the dog clung to him.

"Thank you so much for taking him," Wendy gushed. "I have a little care package for you. I'll drop it by the veterinary clinic, okay?"

There was only the barest hint of indecision before Noah acquiesced. "Okay. Thanks, Ms. Granger."

Wendy hurried off, as if unwilling to give Noah the opportunity to change his mind.

"Furry parenthood looks good on you, Noah," Ally teased.

"Why do I have the feeling I'm going to regret this?" Noah asked dryly.

"You won't. You'll love him." She couldn't seem to wipe the silly grin off her features.

Roxy sniffed Bandit with interest, her stubby tail wagging.

"You know what this means, don't you?" Noah asked, pinning her with an intense stare.

"I said I'd help you, Noah," Ally assured him.

"Not that, although I will need your help on days I have to work late. I'm talking about the two of us having dinner."

"Dinner?" she echoed, surprised he'd brought it up.

"Alfonzo's, the two of us, tomorrow night." Noah gently set the puppy down on his feet. The pup immediately jumped up to playfully nip at Roxy. Ally could swear the boxer eyed her through sad eyes, as if to ask why she was being punished. "I'll pick you up."

"I'd like that, Noah. Very much," Ally agreed.

Noah bent to haul the puppy up and into his arms again, much to Roxy's relief. The boxer hugged Ally's legs, as if anxious to stay far from Bandit. "Meet you back at the clinic? I'll need you to make a list of what I'll need to take care of this little guy."

"Of course." Ally watched as Noah and Bandit walked away, resting her palm on Roxy's broad head. "Sorry, girl, but you're going to have to get used to having Bandit around."

Roxy made a huffing noise that sounded suspiciously like a sigh.

"Well, well, well," Gramps drawled. "Looks as if he's your detective after all."

Ally didn't have the strength to argue with him. Because she kinda thought Gramps was right.

It appeared as if Noah and Bandit would be a part of her life in the foreseeable future.

A smile bloomed. She could hardly wait.

Acknowledgments

A s always, a book needs tender loving care from an amazing team of people. Thanks to Pamela Hopkins for believing in my idea for this Furry Friends series. Also, a special thanks to the team at Crooked Lane Books especially my editor Faith Black Ross, her editorial and production associate Melissa Rechter, production and editorial assistant Rebecca Nelson and marketing associate Madeline Rathle. You've all helped make this book the best possible!

For veterinary medicine insights, I've used a variety of sources, including Dr. Elaine Binor of Wauwatosa Veterinary Services. I appreciate all your help and insight.

A quick shout out to my critique group: Lori Handeland, Olivia Rae and Pam Ford. I enjoy our wine and pizza brainstorming sessions very much.

Lastly, I'd like to thank my husband Scott for his unwavering support as I live my dream!